ONE FELL SOUP

Or,
I'm Just a Bug
on the Windshield of Life

ROY BLOUNT, JR.

PENGUIN BOOKS

Penguin Books Ltd, Harmondsworth, Middlesex, England
Penguin Books, 40 West 23rd Street, New York, New York 10010, U.S.A.
Penguin Books Australia Ltd, Ringwood, Victoria, Australia
Penguin Books Canada Limited, 2801 John Street, Markham, Ontario, Canada L3R 1B4
Penguin Books (N.Z.) Ltd, 182–190 Wairau Road, Auckland 10, New Zealand

First published in the United States of America by
Little, Brown and Company, Inc., in association with
the Atlantic Monthly Press 1982
First published in Canada by
Little, Brown & Company (Canada) Limited 1982
Published in Penguin Books by arrangement with
Little, Brown and Company, Inc., in association with
the Atlantic Monthly Press 1984
Reprinted 1984

LIBRARY OF CONGRESS CATALOGING IN PUBLICATION DATA
Blount, Roy.
One fell soup, or, I'm just a bug on the windshield of life.
I. Title. II. Title: One fell soup.
PN6162.B6 1984   814'.54   83-13454
ISBN 0 14 00.6892 9

Printed in the United States of America by
R.R. Donnelley & Sons Company, Harrisonburg, Pennsylvania

Many of these pieces have previously appeared in the following publica-
tions: *Atlanta Journal-Constitution*, *The Atlantic*, *Boston University Journal*,
Columbia Journalism Review ("The In-House Effect," September/October
1980; "Weekly News Quiz," September/October 1979), *Cosmopolitan*,
Country Journal, *Eastern Airlines Pastimes*, *Esquire*, *Harvard Magazine*,
Inside Sports, *More*, *New Satirist*, *New West*, *The New Yorker* ("Whose
Who?," "That Dog Isn't Fifteen," "Notes from the Edge Conference,"
"For the Record"), *Organic Gardening*, *Oui*, *Playboy*, *Soho News*, *Sports
Illustrated*. "One Pig Jumped" and "Merely Shot in the Head" copyright ©
The New York Times Company, 1978, 1980; reprinted by permission.

Excerpt from *The True Confession of George Barker* reprinted by permission
of New American Library; copyright © George Barker, 1964. "The Bourgeois Blues," words and music by Huddie Ledbetter, edited with new material by Alan Lomax, reprinted by permission; TRO copyright © Folkways
Music Publishers, Inc., 1959.

CONTENTS

USED WORDS

LOVE AND OTHER INDELICACIES

SPORTS AFIELD

WIRED INTO NOW

To Susan and Lou

ACKNOWLEDGMENTS

Right, right. Acknowledgments. *"What do I care?"* cries the poor scuffling soul who paid for the book. Or badgered the town librarian into ordering it; or may even have hijacked a light plane and flown over the metropolitan area towing a banner saying "Buy [for instance] *ONE FELL SOUP*, so I can borrow it." Imagine, going to the trouble of an aerial banner, that long, *with italics*.

And does this general reader ever get "acknowledged"? No, it is always the same old editors, wives, and (not in this case) foundations. And the reader is supposed to *read* this? There aren't enough demands on his or her time? Hey, the reader could be out *boating*.

I would like, even so, to list a great many people who have made everything, except breathing under water, possible; but they would probably start fighting among themselves, as at a wedding reception. You know, you always want to assemble your polymorphous friends from all over. Then when you do manage to pull some of them together, they stand around wondering, "What are *they* doing here?"

I will say this: If it weren't for Ann Lewis I would probably be an astrophysicist or some damned thing. Part of "Chickens" comes from a theme I wrote for her in the tenth grade.

And here, more or less chronologically, are the editorial folk who have enhanced, boosted, harbored, commissioned, or stood still for, on an actual hands-on or hands-off basis, the particular stuff in this book (just *this book,* otherwise I would have to mention . . . never mind):

Jack Spalding, Reese Cleghorn, Barbara LaFontaine, Pat Ryan, Ruth Rogin, Liz Darhansoff, Peter Davison, Dick Pollak, Geoffrey Norman, Lee Eisenberg, Roger Angell, Paul Kurt Ackermann, James Seay, Pauline Kael, Jon Swan, St. Nemeg del Wonkca, Gordon Lish, John Walsh, Kerry Slagle, Jon Carroll, Esther Newberg, Rob Fleder, Jim Morgan, Rust Hills, Bruce Weber, Bill Whitworth, Garrison Keillor, Tracy Young, Dominique Browning, Natalie Greenberg, Mike "Sey Hay" Brandon, and Peter Davison again. And Joan Ackermann-Blount, in a capacity that resists definition.

Could I quickly mention, also, Joel McCrea? I just thought he was a hell of an actor. *And Julie Christie is the most attractive woman in the movies.* There. I've said it.

Other key names abound in the text.

INTRODUCTION

I then tendered an explanation spontaneous and unsolicited concerning my own work, affording an insight as to its aesthetic, its daemon, its argument, its sorrow and its joy, its darkness, its sun-twinkle clearness.

— Flann O'Brien

ON MISCELLANEITY;
JUICE-SWAPPING

I wrote all these pieces myself. They are all, like life and Albert Einstein, short. And if you take one letter, or sometimes two, from each piece and arrange them all in a certain order, they spell out THE PROPER STUDY OF MANKIND IS PROBABLY SOMETHING THAT IF IT EVER HIT YOU, YOU WOULD BE AT A LOSS FOR WORDS.

And yet no single *title* seems to cover the whole shebang. *All of a Piece? Fifty-nine Easy Pieces? President Franklin Piece?* How about *Umbrella Organization?* It may be that I am just not good at titling books.

No, no, I mean it. I can title *songs*. (Though I may, see p. 13, be singing-impaired.) "You're Nothing But a Hickey on My Heart" is mine, and "Styrofoam Woman," and "I-40, You Jane" (an interstate highway song). "We Did Everything Right (And Now There's Nothing Left)." "We Pool Our Incomes Together (But Go Out and Get Sloshed All Alone)." And "I'm Just a Bug on the Windshield of Life" — which brings together such concerns of this book as animals (the bug), sex (but then I live in a remote area), the media, and disintegration.

Take my first book, though: *About Three Bricks Shy of a Load.*

People today call it things like *Two Bucks Short of a Lot*. They get the *of a* right.

How about *More Fool I?* (To be followed by *More Fool II*.) *"The Iliad" Hasn't Been Used in a While?*

Friends of mine produce great titles: *I Lost It at the Movies, Semi-Tough, Pumping Iron, Crazy Salad, Caged Heat, Long Gone, Acting Out, Fighting Back, Happy to Be Here, Kiss Kiss Bang Bang, Soft, Babe, Embryo, Wrinkles, Blessed McGill* (now, I realize, I'm going to have to put in a title by every god damn person I know), *Blood Will Tell, The City Game, The Hog Book, The Best Little Whorehouse in Texas, The Last Day the Dogbushes Bloomed, Whiskey Man, Annie, North Dallas Forty* (well, I'm leaving out several people, mostly kings and glamorous actresses), *Let Not Your Hart, A Door to the Forest, Calling Collect, Robert Lowell: Nihilist as Hero*. What this book is, you know, is a collection.

Okay! Okay! Every movie you see anymore, it's people hollering "Asshole!" in ways meant to be ingratiating. And yet you hear the word *collection* and you flinch. My second book *wasn't* a collection. I swear. But many reviewers alleged that it was, because a few parts of it had surfaced earlier, between covers that were . . . less then hard. One called it a "shameless" collection.

I reject that point of view. Some of my favorite things are collections. The Bible. How about the Bible? And the United States. I thought of changing my first or last name, so this book could be called either *E Pluribus Eunice* or *E Pluribus Noonan*.

Crackers was my second book's title. I wanted something fancier, like *Pollyanna Cracker* or *Jimmy Cracker Corn and I Don't Care*. But I figured, keep it simple. And yet the book itself was classified, in various stores and on various lists, as Current Affairs, Sociology, Humor, Fiction, Politics, Essays,

Southern Studies and Belles Lettres. There it was, in the (dwindling) Belles Lettres section of the Fifth Avenue Doubleday's, the one up around Fifty-sixth. That's when you wish you had a camera.

Essay Have No Bananas. Available in Stores. A Load of This. A Can of Words. League of Notions. Used Frontiers.

The Book of Love. Answering the question, raised by the Monotones in 1958, "I wonder wonder wonder who . . . m'ba-doo-oo *who,* who wrote the Book of Love?"

Selected Shorts. Ties in with the Jim Palmer piece (p. 204). The cover could show people standing around in different kinds of underwear.

I Love Your Hair. To attract the woman book-buyer. (Just kidding, women! Oh, Jesus.) For a while, recently, one set of women was urging me to take as my title *The Family Jewels* (see p. 139), and another set of women was saying, No, Never, and the first set on hearing the response of the second was clearly wondering whether I was a person or a mouse. The irony of this situation — as opposed to the situation itself — did not escape me.

A title that appeals to me thematically is *Wanton Soup.* I always wanted a title that derived, at least partly, from either Shakespeare or a folk song. The only folk-song line left is "Her feet all over the floor," but there is this from Shakespeare:

Lear: Oh me, my heart, my rising heart! but, down!

Fool: Cry to it, nuncle, as the cockney did to the eels when she put 'em i' the paste alive; she knapped 'em o' the coxcombs with a stick, and cried "Down, wantons, down!"

For are we not all eels thrashing about in paste, or soup, or casseroles, alive? This quotation not only shows that I have read at least part of *King Lear*. It also evokes several specific concerns of this book: eels, batting, food, people's entanglements with media, and, excuse me, male sexuality. Male sexuality, I realize, is not something that men are to be trusted with, at least in mixed company, but still. Sometimes I *feel* it. I can't help what I feel!

And I love collections! I even love to read the page, up front, that tells where the various pieces first appeared (see up front). I got a whole level further into a person once because of how eagerly she crouched by the anthology shelf at the Gotham Book Mart. What kind of fool am I? Miscellaneous.

But mixed-breed dogs are best. And name three great Americans who weren't mixed blessings. Just my luck to be writing in a time of (at best) one-track-mindedness. A time of Shiites, Moral Majoritarians and Ronald (see p. 22) Reagan.

There the President stands, in jodhpurs, pointing toward an off-camera horse. The horse, at least, has a job. And Evolution is back in the courts. And the conscience of the Senate is a man who once caused a college professor to be fired for teaching "To His Coy Mistress." Hey, I hold some reactionary views: that sports heroes should not pose in their briefs, that the Edge is not all it is cracked up to be, that if there were a Revolution we wouldn't like it either. I even considered calling this book *In With the Neo-Old Era.* However, it is not an era that I feel in with. To me, anyone who would cause a college professor to be fired for teaching "To His Coy Mistress" should be kept in a box with tiny airholes, and Ronald Reagan is a pod person.

Okra (see p. 59) is something like eels. I like to think that the vivacity-in-paste of vegetables and meat comes through in my food songs. *Wild Giblets? Scrambled Edge?* "When you got to the table," complained Huckleberry Finn, "you had to wait for the widow to tuck down her head and grumble a little over the victuals, though there warn't really anything the matter with them. That is, nothing only everything was cooked by itself. In a barrel of odds and ends it is different; things get mixed up, and the juice kind of swaps around, and the things go better."

Until now, these pieces have never had a chance to join gravies. Most of them have been served before, but in twenty-one almost pathologically disparate publications. If the truth be known, I have also written for thirty-two periodicals *not* represented here — and have long wanted to appear in *Hood and Trunk,* but I don't know anything about cars and in any case *Hood and Trunk* is a magazine my friend Paul Hanes made up, and claimed to be the editor of, one night in an Atlanta hotel at a stock-car reception. That was the night we went over to the Waste Management banquet in the next ballroom and got up on the dais and announced that the banquet was over, everybody should hustle on out and take their silverware to the kitchen, and a Waste Management League official tried to hit me with a plaque.

These pieces include reviews, diatribes, investigations, meditations and worse; fiction, nonfiction, semi-nonfiction, and even, there is no getting around it, verse:

> There was an old person of Lee
> Who had an affair with a bee.
>   She said,"I can't say
>   Just exactly what way
> It hit me, but he is for me."

Some of these pieces are gamier than others. (For a partial explanation, see "The *Times:* No Sh*t.") Some of them any fool could read, and some of them I myself view, in retrospect, with consternation. One item is more or less about ballet, which I don't know anything about, and one is roughly about bowling, which I don't know anything about.

Occasionally you will find a reference to "this column." Well? I have had a regular column somewhere, off and on, since I was fifteen. ("Roy's Noise," *Decatur High Scribbler* — no examples here.) Sometimes in conversation with family and friends, or even just out in the woods nude, glowing eerily, late at night alone, I will refer to myself as "this column." But it doesn't make me feel monolithic.

It makes me feel like writing about teeth, hyphens, cryptorchidism, TV and chickens. Genius, nude grandmothers, cricket-fighting, pigs, wigs, dogs, lentils, a man willing to dye himself green to wrestle, grits, nuclear holocaust, Eugène Delacroix, black holes, socks, pork bellies and flesh wounds.

Maybe you think I should have written something heftier and more unified. A novel. Preferably a great novel. At least a novel entailing wave after wave upon wave of top-of-the-line orgasms (see p. 133), or vast sweeps of historical pageantry, or serious miniseries (rhymes with *miseries*) possibilities. Or one of those massive novels about what goes on inside the massive novel industry. Well, I started to call this book *You're Entitled (But Not This Book)*. Personally, I see novelism as a snare. It traps people who think they will at last feel whole if they can get a novel written, and also people who feel called upon to *keep on* writing novels. A couple of these pieces started out to be novels, but they wound up shorter. Hey, a lot of novels never wind up.

Legs in the Air: A Series of Leaps and Bounds. Or *Leaps and Bounds: A Series of Legs in the Air.* Well. I guess whatever I end up with won't be as good as *Wise Blood,* or as bad as *We Must March, My Darlings.*

At one point I nearly yielded to the suggestion — put forward by a blue-ribbon panel of title experts including Phyllis George, Martin Chuzzlewit, Winton Blount, Mel Blount, Y. A. Tittle and the Duchess of Windsor — that this book be called *Blountly Speaking*. In the tradition of *Said and Donne, Putting It Wildely* and *Poe-Mouthin'*. Such a title would have helped to redress an outrageous thing that happened when James M. Cain's novel *The Butterfly* was filmed: the character Wash Blount, who winds up with the sexpot, was changed to Wash Gillespie.

But not all of these pieces are in the same person. (My friend Lee Smith once assigned her class to write something in the third person and got back a paper that began: "When I entered the room, Mack and Irene were there.") In some of these pieces, it's as close as I can come (in all good conscience) to me speaking; but in others, it is God knows whom. (In some pieces I scoff at people's grammar, in others my own grammar is spotless, and when it isn't — don't ever forget this — I am just screwing around.)

Oliver Reed is working on Vol. II of his life story. So far he has written down only a great title, "Sit Down Before I Knock You Down."

— Liz Smith

One-trackism. Of course you can err on the side of too many tracks, too. Jimmy Carter did that. And you see it in the recording industry: "Now We Are Taping on Thirty-two Tracks (But Which One of Them Is for Heart?)."

Mack! How's it going, boy? And Irene! Irene . . . .

ISSUES
AND ANSWERS

Home of the brave, land of the free —
I don't want to be mistreated by no bourgeoisie.

— "Bourgeois Blues," a song
by Huddie Ledbetter

THE SINGING-IMPAIRED

A WORD about the singing-impaired. The singing-impaired are those who like to sing, who are frequently moved to sing, but who do not sing — according to others — well.

When the singing-impaired begin to sing, others do not join in. When others are singing, and the singing-impaired join in . . .

There is nothing quite so vulnerable as a person caught up in a lyric impulse. The singing-impaired are forever being brought up short in one. When the singing-impaired chime in, they may notice a sudden strained silence. Or just a sudden loss of afflatus in the music about them. (The singing-impaired can tell.)

No national foundation exists for the singing-impaired. Nor does any branch of medical science offer hope. No one provides little ramps to get the singing-impaired up onto certain notes. There are, to be sure, affinity groups. One of these has a theme song. I wish you could watch a group of the singing-impaired sing it together, it would touch your heart:

Don't be scared

If you're singing-impaired.
Sing out, sing free;
Just not audibly.

I, myself, was once singing-impaired.

Perhaps that surprises you. But people once looked at me as if I had no more sense of melody than a Finn has of cuisine.

I would lie awake nights wondering: "Is there no other soul in America who, while trying to stay on the tune of *'La donna è mobile,'* will lapse, now and again, into the tune of 'It's Howdy Doody Time'?"

I did not ask whether anyone *should* do it. I did not ask whether it argued a fine musical sense. All I asked was, did it not make some sense?

All the people I ever lived with said it didn't. They said "It's Howdy Doody Time" was nothing like *"La donna è mobile."* Categorically. Whatsoever.

"All right," I would say. "Not nearly so good, certainly. Not nearly so sophisticated. But surely . . ."

They never wanted to discuss it further. They would suck their breath in, just perceptibly, and change the subject.

For some years of my life, as long as I sang only in church, I was harmonious. At the evening service there was a man up front pumping his arms and urging everyone to "let the rafters ring." I could do that.

Then I went to grammar school, and had to be in the clinic. The clinic was conducted by our music teacher while the chorus was off to itself, running over the tones it had mastered. Many of the people in the clinic were there because they couldn't behave in the chorus. I was there because, the feeling was, I couldn't sing.

Everyone in the fourth grade had to appear in the assembly

program given by the chorus. But some of us were directed to stand there and move our lips silently, as the rest rendered "Mockin' Bird Hill," "The Aba Daba Honeymoon," and "The Thing."

Well, I was permitted to come in on "The Thing," which may be recalled as a Phil Harris recording of the late forties. The refrain ends, "You'll never get rid of that Boomp-boomp-boomp, no matter what you do." I came in on the "Boomp-boomp-boomp."

If it had been "Ave Maria," I wouldn't have minded so. But being deemed unfit to sing " 'Aba, daba, daba, daba, daba, daba, dab,' Said the Chimpie to the Monk" with other children . . .

In graduate school my roommate, besides having read all of Samuel Richardson, had perfect pitch. And perfect tempo, I suppose, because he would sit for hours by his FM radio, tuning it finer and finer and rolling his shoulders subtly to the classics and saying, "No, no, no, too fast." I could not hum where I lived without running the risk of shattering my roommate's ears like crystal. So I didn't hum.

It is only in recent months that I have taken hold of myself and said, "Listen. This is not American. This is not right." It is only in recent months that I have begun, whenever the chance arises, to say a few words about singing-impairment; about how my life was marked by it for so many years. I pause for a moment to let it all sink in. And then I sing.

And do you know what people say? After a pause? "You don't sing as badly as you think you do."

Which I have no doubt is true. And which I propose as a slogan for the nation's so-called singing-impaired. Another thing I have been doing is putting the finishing touches on a monograph that pretty well establishes that all known melodies can be boiled down to four or five basic tunes.

These are the four or five basic tunes I feel most comfortable with. "It's Howdy Doody Time," as it happens, is one.

LOSS: A GUIDE TO ECONOMICS

MANY humanists prefer to know as little about economics as they do about heavy-vehicle maintenance or how their parents really are. And yet economics is the watchdog of a free society. Thanks to the vigilance of large investors, who serve somewhat the same function here as the Academy does in France, the state of our economy is a key to our moral fiber. Say there is rioting and ill humor in the cities, or too many loud parties in the small towns. Or the President responds to press-conference questions with an eerie, toneless hum. Or infestations rage through a great part of the Midwest. Immediately, the nation's serious investors discern that the time is out of joint, and, to bring America back to itself, start moving their money to other countries. When the nation straightens out, when the editorials in *Forbes* have brought an adequate response and things at last seem "right," then the key investor, even if he has taken a shine to one of those pert Swiss tellers, will start to buy shares in our future again. And we will have a future. This is known as "positive reinforcement," and is only one of the ways in which economics lends clarity and order to our lives. (Unlike rock music.)

To understand how the whole great process of economics

works, we must begin at the beginning. Take a dollar bill from your pocket, smooth out the wrinkles, and forget it. There is no longer any use talking in terms of one dollar, since it will not buy you coffee and a grilled cheese. Save the one, and when you get twelve more to go with it you can buy a lurid novel. Take out a twenty and look at that.

Now. This piece of "legal tender" (a poignant phrase, since so many things that are tender are still not legal, and vice versa) is not in itself "worth" anything. It bears a nice enough engraving of President Jackson, but few people need one. To realize how *relative* cash is, try spending a twenty on — to take a fanciful (for now!) example — Neptune, where they have never heard of President Jackson. Or probably of anyone named Jackson, if you can imagine. At least we hope they haven't. If they have, our intelligence is lagging dangerously behind theirs. Far from knowing who was Neptune's president from 1829 to 1837, we are not even sure whether they have "hands" or "feet." Or, more crucial, whether they have something we want badly. If Neptune has something we want badly enough, such as a cheaper material for making in-flight pudding, then Neptune can say to us, "Ordinarily we knock this down at five dollars a barrel, but for you, since it means so much to you, we'll make it twelve." Thus your twenty comes to be worth $6.67, if you act now.

Economics teaches us that other things can happen to your twenty:

• *Inflation.* Picture your twenty shrinking, ominously, and Jackson beginning to look like King Farouk. People smile too readily in the street. Your twenty isn't worth as much anymore.

• *Recession.* Picture your twenty growing, ominously, and Jackson beginning to look like Elisha Cook, Jr. Hat sizes run smaller. Your twenty is worth more (that is to say, it is becoming less valuable at a slower rate), but you can't afford to use it.

• *Depression.* Oh, God.

• *Action on the street.* Someone bigger than you runs up to you on the street and snatches your twenty and says, "Do something about it." Jackson doesn't want to get involved.

• *Obsolescence.* Because of the way things are made at certain — or all — points on the economic continuum, all of the ink on your twenty, including Jackson, fades away.

• *Boom.* Picture Jackson robust and hickory-strong, able to whip the pound, for what that is worth, at the Battle of New Orleans. (With the aid of pirates.) People run around slapping each other on the back, often too hard. You slip a disk. Your twenty helps to pay for new and improved medical service and your doctor's new boat.

• *BOOM.* It is gratifying to be able to say *"Boom"* in a public-service article. Boomboom! *Boooommm.* But don't get any ideas.

• *Famine.* Happens abroad.

All right. How about now? At this point in history, we in the United States enjoy plenty — of both inflation and recession. Thus, money is becoming at once less worth striving for and harder to get. Under these conditions, investments should be made with great caution, as indicated below.

• *Common stocks.* Not a good bet at this time. See *preferred stocks.*

• *Preferred stocks.* Not a good bet at this time. See *commodities* (pork bellies, for instance, and don't let an economist see you smile; nothing puts off an economist like the simplistic assumption that pork bellies in themselves — or even wearing vests and posed around a long table as the Council of Economic Advisers — are funny).

• *Commodities.* Not a good bet at this time. (Porkbellypork-bellyporkbelly. Did you smile?) See *silver.*

• *Silver.* Not a good bet at this time. See *gold.*

• *Gold.* Too late.

Other factors to consider at all times are the wage-price spiral, the supply-and-demand seesaw, and the principle of compensation. These are sometimes known as "real (or speculative) boogers."

• *The wage-price spiral.* You demand a raise from your company, which bakes cakes, so that you can buy shoes. By the time you get to the shoe store the increase in cake prices occasioned by your raise has caused the shoe-store operator, who had to buy a cake earlier that morning, to raise the price of shoes to the point where you need another raise. Even without taking into account the high-speed cab rides back and forth, this can become extremely complex, especially when your boss's son or daughter is going out with the shoe-store-owner's daughter or son and needs more and more money from his or her father in order to convince his or her potential live-in mate that he or she can raise his or her standard of living.

(The need to improve the quality of one's life, of course, is something to be reckoned with at every point along the spiral. Thus, you ask for a raise that will enable you to buy shoes and will also make things a little more mellow for you all around. The shoe-store operator does the same in raising his prices, and anticipates that *you* will, and figures that into his equation. This is true of every economic unit except doctors and lawyers, who, being essential guardians against death and/or ruin, simply increase their prices as much as they want to. Life being a serious proposition, a consumer cannot expect to have an easy choice between legal fees and prison, or medical bills and encephalitis. Furthermore, doctors and lawyers must go to school for years and years, often with little sleep, and at great sacrifice to their first wives.)

• *The supply-and-demand seesaw.* When there is enough of something, people tend to say, "Who needs it?"

• *The principle of compensation.* There is something to be said for, if not necessarily during, every economic period; every cloud has, for what it is worth, a silver-certificate lining. In a depression, for instance, when nobody has any money (and people *eat* pork bellies), that very fact creates among people a common bond.

• *Common bonds.* See *common stocks.*

REAGAN, BEGIN, AND GOD

DON'T get me wrong, I think the world of God. But it seems to me that He is too much with us lately, *in a certain form*. Israel's Menachem Begin is wooing hardcore religionists for a coalition government. America's (oh, come on) Ronald Reagan is being praised for statesmanship because his first Supreme Court nominee doesn't quite please that luminous Christian, Jerry Falwell. (Strom Thurmond likes her, though. Great!) And both Begin and Reagan have been rather cavalier — *in my view* — about the risk of blowing things to perdition. I wonder — *I know, it's none of my business, I don't tithe* — whether the Judeo-Christian ethic is . . . in ideal hands.

With this thought in mind, and with apologies to Eugene Field, who anyway is dead, I have dashed off — which accounts for any infelicities — the following verses.

> *Reagan, Begin, and God one night*
> *Sailed a trilateral ship*
> *Way out past the farthest Right*
> *On a celestial trip.*
>
> *"Whither are you fellows hurled?"*
> *The moon asked, out of the blue.*

"Far away from the, quote, Third World,
As well as worlds One and Two.
No time to chat with you,"
    Said Reagan,
    Begin,
    And God.

The old moon sighed and took off, too —
He guessed what had gone down.
He told the stars,"If I were you,
I would not hang aroun'."
So moon and stars and Holy Three
Distanced themselves from the globe —
And the sun cried, "How about me?"
"Join the trip (this one's no probe)
If you're a good xenophobe,"
    Said Reagan,
    Begin,
    And God.

So close your eyes while Frankie sings:

Things are simpler today.
At any moment worrisome things
Will be nuclearized away.
And you'll get to heaven, at least you may,
    With Reagan,
    Begin,
    And God.

(**Note:** As is often the case in poetry, a certain amount of realism has been sacrificed here to exigencies of the verse form. And vice versa.) You are not going to tell me that Jerry Zipkin won't be on that ship, not after all he's put himself through;

and there is bound to be a berth for — but I can't bring myself to write the man's name, except just this once, for purposes of illustration — Edwin A. Meese III.

> *E-D-W!*
> *I-N-A!*
> *M-E-E-S-E!*
>
> *Edwin Meese! Edwin Meese!*
> *Forever let us hold his banner high!*

How can more than twelve or fourteen people in this entire nation have voted for a man who made no bones about having an aide named Edwin Meese? *III!*

Why is it that so grotesquely named a person's closeness to the Last Big Holocaust button does not inflame all those people who thought "Jimmih" and "Rose-a-lyn" and "Jerdan" were ludicrous names? *Meese.* The man's name is *Meese.* Edwin is bad enough. I have known some Edwins from Georgia, but never a Meese, by God!

Excuse me. I have gotten ethnic, after starting out so cosmic. But then, I ask you: what is less sublime than either religious bombing (*sorry, forget I said anything*) or politics that is deemed centrist because it is just to the left of a jackleg preacher?

99 PERCENT FOUNDATION

IT's not the money. Well, it is the money. But even if it weren't the money, it would be the principle. Not to mention the interest. (Is that an old joke?)

I want a goddamned genius grant.

It has been several weeks now since the MacArthur Foundation announced it was giving tens of thousands of dollars a year, tax free, no strings attached, to a number of Americans it deemed geniuses. I have waited long enough for the apologetic phone call: "Geez, it just hit us. Are we all sitting around here feeling red-faced! Casts the whole program into doubt. Forgot you *and* Jerry Lee Lewis. It's this new computer . . ."

"Let it go," say friends of mine. No. I am still frosted.

For I hold certain truths to be self-evident, among them that no American should be officially branded a nongenius.

Even if I get a grant next year, who wants to be a genius of the second rank?

I'm surprised the MacArthur Foundation didn't call me up and say, "Listen, we worked out a generalized assessment for everybody in the country as to how much of a genius each is, and you have to send Robert Penn Warren thirty-five dollars a month."

Don't get me wrong. I think the world of Robert Penn Warren. But what does he need to be designated a genius for? He's got a poem in every goddamned magazine you pick up. Every time you turn around he's being interviewed about how he reads Homer aloud to his wife every night up in Vermont. I believe the son of a bitch owns a couple of homes. He's won every goddamned prize in the nation. I think it's *tacky* to give him a bunch of money for being a genius.

And what do you think this does to my afflatus? Every time I feel a real flight coming on, I hear the critics: "Blount, though no genius . . ."

The only one of these certified geniuses I have met is Stephen Jay Gould. He and I taped the Cavett show on the same day. I taped first, as a matter of fact. Met him in the green-room on the way out. Seemed nice. Wrote a good book, I hear. About pandas, I think.

Pandas.

How much is that worth to the common weal? A genius on pandas.

Can I call him up and say, "Hey, Steve. My panda's got some kind of inflammation . . ."? Who's got a panda? Even rich people don't have pandas. The *President* doesn't have a panda. Give me $30,000 a year tax free, I could *buy* a panda; but what would I do with one?

Sure, I live in the country. I guess we could keep a panda. The dogs and the kids would probably enjoy it — at least until time came to feed it. But I don't *want* a panda. What I want is a little consideration.

What am I now? Just some kind of hack?

All right. I did a beer commercial once. *Is a man to be branded for life by one beer commercial?* "He doesn't need a grant, he's got all that beer money coming in." Come on, it was just a local Pittsburgh deal. I saw the last dollar and the free six-pack from it years ago. I didn't lie. I like Iron City beer. I was struggling; I needed the money. And I prefer to work for change from within.

Which is something I could do a lot more effectively with $30,000 a year, tax free, no strings. Are you trying to tell me that Stephen Jay Gould wouldn't do a beer commercial if somebody offered him one?

Now he wouldn't, no. Now he doesn't need it. But if you had offered him one six months ago, I bet ḥe'd be on your home screen right now. On a bar stool, surrounded by pandas. "When these little fellas and I work up a real thirst . . ." It would probably give everyone who saw it a lift. Some of those beer commercials are the best things on television.

I'll tell you what *will* offend me. If some of these grantees start popping up in commercials *now*. "Nobody feels like a genius first thing in the morning. Not even me — until I've had a cup of Maxwell House!"

I hope these guys are being ragged unmercifully in the streets. "Hey, Genius! How's your ineffable spark hanging!" I won't be surprised to start seeing, in the *Times* Science section, references to the new problem of Genius Block.

If you don't read *next* year that I got a genius grant, it may well be because I have refused it. On political grounds. It seems to me that the genius of the American system is that money is not linked to intrinsic worth, so that the best people don't make a whole lot of money. This means that the people who do make a lot of money get to make a lot of money. And the people who don't make a lot of money get to reflect that the best people probably don't make a lot of money.

I don't think it's healthy for people to have genius and money both. A genius, when his or her spouse comes running in yelling "They've come to repossess the kitchen," is the type of person who says, "I don't want to hear about it. I'm busy manufacturing a new enzyme in my head." Or at least a genius is not the type to accept a genius grant graciously. A real genius would be saying, "Thirty thousand dollars a year, huh? *What does Rona Barrett make?* And who's going to pick up my Blue Cross?"

Pandas. Can you imagine that? I should have gone into pandas.

EAT THAT WIG,
WEAR THAT SANDWICH

THE way people talk about the hell of the subways these days, you would think it is all a matter of municipal decadence, which is never the fault of the people talking. For my part, I often recall the time I did a bad thing on the subway, myself. And I still feel responsible, although it was owing to the difficulty of modern life.

In those days I lived in Brooklyn and worked in Rockefeller Center. I was on my way from the former to the latter on the D train. I had had the foresight to leave tardily enough that morning to get a seat. Still the car was fairly crowded, several unfortunates standing. (Even in those days, before sexism, I gave up my seat only to women who could show definite signs of dizziness *and* a doctor's statement that they were at least six months pregnant, or to anyone carrying a razor.)

We pulled into, I believe, the Grand Street station. I was absorbed in the *Park Slope News,* our weekly neighborhood paper, which reported the seizure of $200,000 worth of heroin in a house near ours (we didn't know them). Suddenly one end of the subway car was aflutter. It was the first time I had been in an even partially aflutter subway car, and I was bemused. I was accustomed to subway cars' having the interior atmosphere of cattle cars, or of quarter-ton trucks carrying enlisted men back at night from long, pointless exercises in the rain.

My end of this car, though, was filled suddenly with people gesturing, pointing to a spot just over my head and saying, "The window." Two men across from me had even risen from their seats and advanced in the direction the others were pointing.

I looked over my shoulder and saw what seemed to be the window in question — an adjustable horizontal vent over the big stationary pane. The doors had closed, the train was just beginning to move out of the station, and a young couple was running alongside, pointing at the window. It was open.

I can't *explain* my reaction very thoroughly. All I know was that I felt I had to react quickly, and I suppose that the only previous situations to which my mind could relate this one immediately were situations in which my automobile door was open and other drivers were shouting at me to close it. I knew, in my mind, that you couldn't be sucked out of a subway window the way you can an airplane window, but I may have assumed subrationally that there might be something nebulously hazardous about a subway window left open. And I loved New York, even including its subways, and I wanted to be a good citizen.

With one reflex motion of my arm, at any rate, I shut the window. The faces of the running couple outside fell as the train pulled away from them, and a paper bag hit the window and dropped back inside, onto the woman beside me.

"He closed the window," from another woman across the car, was the only comment on my action that I heard; its tone seemed moderately surprised, but too tired to be censorious. The man who had thrown the bag picked it up off the lady's lap and went back to his seat.

He and the man next to him opened the bag, revealing the

contents to themselves only, and the other people in the car murmured a bit and then lapsed back into their previous attitudes.

I couldn't put the thing out of my mind so easily. I went over to the two men, losing my seat to a blind woman as I did. "What was that all about?" I asked.

Both men shrugged, but then they showed me what was inside the bag. A blond wig and a sandwich.

It all came clear to me then. The young running couple had left his or her wig and lunch on the seat by mistake and had been calling for someone to throw them out through the window before the train departed.

The two men put the bag back down on the seat. They didn't want to wear the wig, and they didn't trust human nature enough to eat the sandwich.

By getting involved, not wisely but too well, I had prevented what might have been the only spontaneous and niftily coordinated friendly effort between strangers going on at that moment throughout the metropolis. I felt bad. I wanted to account for my actions. But nobody would look at me. I glared at the blind woman and stood there impersonally rattling and groaning on underground the rest of the way to work. Urban life is too complex.

I THINK IT WAS LITTLE RICHARD

I HAVE had a good deal of experience in stores. For instance, department stores:

I have accompanied a wealthy couple through Dallas's Neiman-Marcus (which meant fighting off little squeezes from floorwalkers); have been collared falsely and accused of shoplifting at Christmastime by a temporary store detective, a nervous middle-aged woman, on Lenox Square (which gave me the only opportunity of my life so far to say, "There must be some mistake!"); and have bought a plastic water-bottle (*un eau-flacon plastique*) in a big Brussels store that not long thereafter burned down.

Never, however, until one day a while back, had I been addressed by any salesperson as "Customer."

I chanced one day to be walking past a dimly lit clothier's, in a depressed area of the downtown, and noticed in the window some gum-rubber gloves coated with little bits of cork. They looked as though they had been rolled in crushed peanuts.

Somehow, they seemed at the moment to fill in my clothing needs a small void. I can't remember the last time that I did anything in rubber gloves, but there must have been some critical moment in my early youth when I was holding on to something valuable with rubber gloves, and it slipped out because there were no bits of cork for traction.

There was a time in my boyhood, I remember, when I was fishing off a dock in Florida, and an old lady fishing near me brought in a little fish, a nice whiting, which jumped off the hook, and I leapt up to grab it for her, and it squirted out of my hands into the water and the old lady cried.

At any rate, I felt a need for the gloves, and since they were cheap I went inside.

"Some of those . . . cork-studded gloves . . . caught my eye . . ." I said to a saleswoman who was leaning against a counter.

"Find those in the basement, Customer," she said firmly.

I did buy the gloves, but found no use for them until the wedding of my friends the Fants came up and I was able to slip them into the honeymoon luggage. More important, the "Customer" appellation struck me as a salutary convention; one that might well be widely applied.

Think of the hypocrisy that would be obviated, for instance, if it were established practice to say, "How about a little lunch with me Wednesday, Client?" Or "It's been awfully good getting to know you, Contact."

Then, however, I asked myself whether I could apply the practice to my own profession.

For instance, I talked to Little Richard, the rock-and-roll figure, on the phone some years ago. I think it was Little Richard.

Little Richard was certainly, or certainly allegedly, robbed in Atlanta, by his onstage valet, of $19,000 that he had in his hotel room in a sack, and since I happened to be on the police beat that day I called his hotel room to get the story.

But when someone answered, I couldn't bring myself to say, "Little Richard?"

I couldn't bring myself to say "Mr. Penniman?" either — which I knew from the police report to be his formal name. It is like interviewing baseball managers. "Herman" is too familiar, and "Mr. Franks" seems silly.

But neither, it occurs to me on reflection, would "Interviewee" have rung true. Or "Subject" — which would in theory have been appropriate not only as in "subject of an interview" but also as in the standard police-report usage: "Subject was located lying under bush and wouldn't move."

"Subject? This is a Reporter."

No, it is too cold.

The human element must be trafficked with. Or one must be a monk, or open a dimly lit store.

THE SOCKS PROBLEM

I WISH to broach a matter close to every man's, and most modern women's, feet: "Whatever happened to socks?"

Everybody I know agrees: It doesn't matter whether you are living alone in a tepee, or married to two different people in two different bungalows, or just floating around with no fixed address, or pursuing a career as a recluse in the family manse, or lying chained to the floor in a tiny basement room off the initiation chamber in a sorority house. The one result you can depend on is attrition of your socks. A person could stay in the same room with all of his or her socks for a month, never (except to sleep) taking his or her eyes off the drawer in which his or her socks are kept, and at the end of that period he or she would have three to seven fewer socks than he or she began with.

In my case, I believe I have considered all of the natural outlets:

• A member of my household, who is being blackmailed and can't make the payments out of the change on the dresser, sells them. I doubt this, because no member of my household can keep a secret. If they were involved in something that would worry me if I knew about it, they would tell me.

• The washing machine, or the dryer, digests them. This

may be. The dryer produces, I know for a fact, something that is very suggestive of socks. This is probably why so many of my washables are translucent — and if any member of my household were handier, a good many socks could no doubt be re-created annually from this lint, or fluff, three or four wash-loads' worth of which would cover a sheep. But this ongoing leaching of fiber from the nation's clothing, while it is some-thing that the Federal Trade Commission might well look into, appears to be a gradual process, which cannot account for the sudden disappearance of whole socks.

• The modern sock is made of a material designed to disin-tegrate, of its own accord, after a period of time. I would not put this past American industry, but in this case a sock would occasionally go poof while I was wearing it, or while I was holding it up to the morning light trying to decide what color it was.

• Dust is dead socks. If it isn't dead socks, what is it? Cer-tainly if you let the dust of two or three rooms accumulate for a while, you can shuffle your feet around the baseboards and have bedroom slippers that will serve in mild climates. But I have in my drawer, where hope springs eternal (and where, in fact, a sock has been known to resurface, magically, after up to eighteen months' absence), single socks whose ages range from three months to four years. Some of the older ones have been with me at seven different addresses. If the socks that match have gone to dust, why haven't they? Often, heartrend-ingly, it is almost-new socks that are missing. The poets have not written adequately of the near-erotic pleasure of easing your foot into a new, lissome, gladly yielding sock. And then one day it is gone, and you are left with shrunken, cankered old socks that may require lubrication.

Of course, one thing about socks is that they don't mate for life. You can buy fourteen identical black ones, and at the end of three weeks, even if they were all still extant in sock form, no two of them would quite match. It may be that people across the country should get together on socks. I have a newspaper clipping that tells of two one-legged ladies who, although one lives in Wisconsin and one in Ohio, have been sharing pairs of shoes for more than two years. (Incidentally, the report notes, both ladies "agreed they wouldn't want an artificial leg even if it could be easily fitted. The extended reach of a crutch is great for disciplining recalcitrant children, Mrs. Gruenbaum said, and Mrs. Harma sticks a cloth on the end of hers and washes ceilings.") People could advertise single socks in a newsletter and trade off by mail.

I don't know. Maybe one of my loved ones is saving all my missing socks to present to me, sewn together into an effigy of someone I admire, on the occasion of my retirement from active life. Maybe if the cat could only talk she could explain quite simply how it is that socks are transmuted into kittens. But I think it more likely that socks get off in some supernatural or wholly illegal way. I will not presume to trace the process by which they do it. But I think I know what becomes of them.

Every so often, usually at the change of seasons, when I dig into my closet for my summer or winter wardrobe, I find things I have never seen before in my entire life: a pair of pants, perhaps, that resembles a pair of pants only as a raisin resembles a grape; a sweater that a Red Guard might have denounced as too tacky; a knit tie with a horse painted on it.

Let us assume, then, in the absence of any compelling evidence to the contrary, that socks die and are reincarnated, perhaps in groups, as a variety of garments.

It is the work of the Devil — maybe — or maybe a sock-manufacturing-and-rummage-sale cabal, about which the media are so strangely silent.

ANIMAL AND
VEGETABLE SPIRITS

running, leaping dog-paws
and wagging dog-tails
and no dog in between

— Hans Arp
(translated by
Harriett Watts)

CHICKENS

I THINK there is more to the chicken than it gets credit for. We hear much about the dignity, mystery, and vulnerability of more alien, not to say less upfront, animals and aspects of nature. Chickens we only chew on or chuckle over. Some people probably hold the belief, whether they articulate it or not, that either a chicken sandwich or a rubber chicken is a purer representation of what it is to be a chicken, essentially, than a living chicken is.

Yet the chicken is as close to man and as savory as the apple, as full of itself as the lynx or the rose. A hen's feathers feel downy but organized when you lift her up. She has a peck like a catcher's snap-throw to first. A chicken *never* makes eye contact with a person. Who is to say why it crosses the road?

A good thing to read is *The Chicken Book,* by Page Smith and Charles Daniels, published by Little, Brown a few years ago. This book undertakes to see the chicken from all angles and to see it whole; to treat the chicken as an entity, multifarious: the chicken in literature, in history, in its own inner and outer workings, in the pharmacopoeia, in orange wine sauce. A fine idea, an estimable work, a rare advance in integrated thinking.

Then again, perhaps it is not the book (which required two authors, aided by a class of their students) that is integrated so much as the animal. Beyond the volume stands the fowl: a few feathers floating in the air, but far from exhausted. The chicken warrants further pursuit. It is hard, however, to discuss the chicken seriously. It is possible to talk about even the sheep seriously, or the badger; but you cannot reflect for sixty seconds, even to yourself, upon "the chicken" without something in the back of your head going "*Booo*-uk buk buk," dipping its head suddenly and pecking a bug. So I will not try to develop any thesis. I will just set down one person's Chicken Notes.

Which First, Chicken or Egg?

On this point, *The Chicken Book's* authors, without admitting it, throw up their hands: "Even when the chick is in the egg there are eggs within the chick, microscopically small but full of potential." And so on. That is like going through a daisy saying, "Even if she loves me, she might not. Even if she loves me not, she might." The chicken/egg is one of those questions like:

• Do the same tastes really taste the same to different people, and if so, in what sense?

• If you watched an area of your skin steadily for several hours while coming down with the chicken pox, could you discern the moment when a given pock appeared? And if not, why not?

• If you could get inside another person's head, would you know it, or would you think you were the other person?

One of those questions, I mean, that people have, with mount-

ing irritation, been wanting the *answer* to since early child-
hood.

Okay. No one is going to be able to track down an eye-
witness account of the moment when one or the other, chicken
or egg, first emerged. Lacking that best evidence, it is up to
each of us to make his own best determination. I say, the
chicken. If an egg were first, the chances are that Adam, Eve,
one of the beasts of the field, even one of the beasts of the air,
whatever was around then, would have broken and/or eaten (I
mean eaten and/or broken) it. We have no way of knowing how
many projected species were nipped off because they made the
mistake of starting out as eggs. I assume that the chicken was
first, and that it evaded destruction long enough to lay several
dozen eggs. This is just elementary Darwinism. Also, if the
egg came first, then what fertilized it? In point of fact, the egg
must have come third.

At any rate, talking about chickens gets us back to first prin-
ciples.

Chickens in Quotations

I've always figured that, when the time come I couldn't farm a
crop of cotton and a crop of corn and keep one woman faithful,
I'd get me a tin bill and pick bugs with the chickens.

> — from *Walls Rise Up,* a novel
> by George Sessions Perry

When I warned [the French] that Britain would fight on whatever they did, their generals told their Prime Minister and his
divided Cabinet, "In three weeks England will have her neck
wrung like a chicken." Some chicken; some neck.

> — Winston Churchill

How come a chicken can eat all the time and never get fat in the face?

— Roger Miller

On Fried Chicken: Goodness: Eating

My mother's (rolled in flour and dropped in *hot* shortening in a *hot, heavy* iron skillet, at *just* the right time, for just the right *length* of time) is not only the best fried chicken but it still represents to me the highest form of eating. It is crisp without seeming encrusted. In the best fried chicken, you can't tell where the crust leaves off and the chicken begins.

In the comic books they talked about caviar and pheasant under glass. I accepted these things as literary conventions. But in my thoughts they did not crunch, give, tear, bloom brownly. The richest brown — or sometimes *auburn* — in the synesthesial spectrum is well-fried chicken.

Which is not to say that the crackle is all. I once heard Blaze Starr ask an audience whether they would like her to uncover entirely her (larger than life) breasts. When the audience cried out yes, yes, ma'am, they certainly would, she froze; rolled her eyes; replied, with great, pungent reserve, "I reckon you *would* like some friiiied chicken."

The sweetest chicken pieces, though, are not the fleshiest. The wishbone — destroyed in most commercial cutting — and the "little drumstick," which is the meatiest section of the wing, are both delicacies. So is the heart. But when chicken is fried right, the tastiest meat of all — delicate, chewy, elusive — is between the small bones of the breast: chicken rib meat. I have never heard anyone mention this meat, and I have never spoken of it myself, even privately, until now. Fried chicken is a personal experience, like the woods out beside your house. But look for the rib meat. It's worth the trouble.

Another thing I recommend is to go off alone with the largely de-meated carcass of a roasted whole chicken and explore all its minor crisps and gristles for tidbits. You get to know a chicken that way. I'm not sure that tenderness and bustiness are the absolute virtues that Frank Perdue assumes them to be. I like chicken meat that offers some resistance. Meat should be earned, at each end. Chickens themselves, given the chance, are rangy, resourceful eaters. Remember, in the comic strip "Smilin' Jack," the overweight sidekick character who was followed around by a chicken that ate his shirt buttons as they popped off?

Chickens in the News

• I have lost the clipping on this, but it appeared in the *Cape Cod Standard Times* a few summers ago. Chicken growers, disgruntled at low chicken prices, had parachuted great numbers of ready-for-market chickens onto a town in Rhodesia — it was either Rhodesia or Rumania, and it wouldn't have been Rumania. The clipping said the original plan had been for live chickens to be dropped, but that project had been abandoned as inhumane. It would be nice to think that there was a local character named Sky Little who ran around shouting, "The chickens is falling! The chickens is falling!"

• On June 5, 1975, the *New York Times,* in a rare acknowledgment by it of this sort of thing, reported that on June 5, 1904, it had reported that "a Pochuck, N.J., man found a woodchuck that was raising four chickens." Even assuming that the woodchuck was raising them not for profit but out of maternal instinct, and even rejecting the possible inference that neither chicken nor egg came first but rather the woodchuck, this is quite a little story. So why doesn't the modern-day *Times* give its readers such news? When a chicken lays an egg in the shape of a heart, as sometimes happens, you never read about it in the *Times*. You will never come upon an individual chicken in the *Times*. Poultry raising, to be sure, and therefore chickens in the mass. But never one chicken singled out, nor one chicken's egg.

• In the *Batesville* (Mississippi) *Panolian*, there appeared several years ago a photograph of a woman displaying an egg and a sweet potato, both extremely elongated. The caption read: "NEVER AT A LOSS FOR natural phenomena is Mrs. Cordie Henderson of the Mt. Olivet community. Last week, Mrs. Henderson visited the *Panolian* with an extra large hen egg, which later proved to have two yolks; and an unusually long sweet potato." The *Times* is sometimes at a loss for natural phenomena.

• (Also to be filed under Most Surprising Thing a High-ranking American Official Ever Tried to Do with a Rubber Chicken.) According to *People* magazine, after Nelson Rockefeller delivered his graduation-day address at the U.S. Naval Academy, "outgoing midshipmen presented Rocky with . . . a rubber chicken (which the Veep vainly tried to inflate)." Rockefellers! There is no telling what the late Rocky would have tried to do with a live chicken. I can tell you what a live chicken would have let him do: not very much.

Keeping Chickens — A Personal Account

When I was about thirteen I got for Easter a baby chick that had been dyed pink. I now deplore the practice of dyeing chicks and ducklings, but this chick thrived and made a good pet. Some people don't believe this, but before all the pink had grown out of it this chicken was already running around in the yard after me like a puppy. I used to carry it around in my shirt or my bicycle basket. (I am not going to say what its name was. You can't win, telling what you named a chicken. The reader's reaction will be either "That's not a funny name for a chicken" or "He had a chicken with a funny name. Big deal.") I didn't really love it the way you love a dog or a cat, but I really liked it, and it liked me. We were talking about that chicken the other day. "I would think that would be embarrassing, being followed by a chicken," said my then-brother-in-law Gerald.

"No," said my sister Susan. "That chicken liked him."

But the chick grew into a pullet. It didn't look right, and might have been illegal, to have a chicken in our neighborhood; and we didn't have the facilities for it. We didn't want the facilities for it, because at our previous house we had kept chickens in quantity (six), in and around a chicken house, and my father was softhearted about wringing their necks (that is, he would try to wring their necks in a softhearted way). Or that is my recollection. When I asked my mother for details, she wrote:

> The chicken house was there complete with rather sad-looking and unproductive chickens when we bought the house. There was a rooster and five supposedly hens.
>
> The people we bought the house from had them because of the war and food shortage. I was sorry they were there, Daddy was glad. You were delighted with them. It also smelled bad and I hated cleaning it — so did Daddy and we tried to outwait each other. You can guess who won most often. We finally decided two eggs a week were not worth it. The chickens didn't look too healthy, then too they were all named and after one try we decided we couldn't eat them and gave them to a colored man.
>
> The one try was by Daddy. He assured me he could kill a chicken. His mother always wrung their necks etc. and he had watched. He violently wrung the neck (you were not told) —

real hard — and threw the chicken to the ground. It lay stunned and then wobbled drunkenly off to the chicken house. We spent the rest of the week nursing it back to health.

When the chickens were gone, the chicken house remained. It was made of scrap lumber and tar paper. I used it as a fort, a left-center-field pavilion, and a clubhouse for a while, but by the time I was eleven or twelve I had gotten off into other things, was playing Little League ball, and had peroxided the front of my hair. And my mother hated the chicken house. She said it ruined our back yard.

She said she burned it down by accident. One afternoon she was raking leaves and burning them, and the fire spread to the chicken house. When Mrs. Hamright, across the street, out watering her bushes, smelled smoke and heard the sirens coming, her reflex was to yell "Oh Dear Lord" and squirt the hose through the window of her house onto her husband, Gordy, who was inside reading the paper. We eventually had to give him our copy of that evening's paper. Even though we were the ones who'd had the fire.

Mr. Lovejohn, the old man who lived with his middle-aged daughter next door to the Hamrights, and whom we ordinarily never saw except when he was sitting in his daughter's DeSoto early on Sunday morning waiting for her to get dressed and drive him to Sunday school and church, came over in the dark-brown suit at about the same time the firemen started thrashing around with the hoses. He said he wanted to "counsel with" us. He said fire was the wages of smoking in bed.

"Now, Mr. Lovejohn," my mother said. "No one in our family smokes, anywhere. And there aren't any beds in the chicken house."

"That don't excuse it," he said.

By the time the firemen got there, the chicken house was

about gone, but they stretched hoses all over the back and side yards, trampled a dogwood tree, and eyed our house as if they would love a chance to break some windows. We didn't have many fires in our area at that time, for some reason, and the fire department was accustomed to igniting abandoned structures — chicken coops often, in fact — on purpose and putting them out for practice, playing them along for maximum exercise.

Mrs. Hamright kept trying to get one of the firemen to tell her whether the fire was under control. I think he hated to admit that it was. Finally, he turned around and asked her, "Whud they have in there?"

"Chickens," she said.

His eyes lit up. "Hit *them* rascals with the hose," he said. "They'd *take* off."

My parents didn't want to go through all that again, so we gave my pet chicken to Louisiana, who came every Wednesday to iron and clean and yell "You better not *bleev* 'at man, child" at the female characters in the soap operas, and who received a lot of things that we didn't know what to do with. The chicken was getting too big, I could see that. Having a grown chicken as a pet would have been a strange thing.

"How is the chicken?" Susan and I would ask Louisiana on subsequent Wednesdays.

"He wa— . . . He's fine," Louisiana would say. Finally, when we said we wanted to visit it, she said she had let it go see her granddaughter, who lived eighty miles away.

"Does she play with it lots?" we asked.

She said she did.

HIDE THE RAZOR ON APRIL FOOLS'

THIS may seem premature, but I think it is time we started getting ready for April Fools'. April Fools' rolls around on Monday, and most of us may think oh, well.

But those of us who have had occasion lately to read the *Atlanta Journal* for April 9, 1906, will not feel so casual.

"TRIED TO KILL HIMSELF," reads the headline on page one, "WHEN WIFE APRIL-FOOLED HIM."

"W. O. Roberts Slashed His Throat in Effort to End Life," a smaller headline goes on, "Because Wife Said There Was a Cow in the Front Yard."

The story begins: "As a result of brooding over an April Fool joke perpetrated upon him by his wife last Sunday, W. O. Roberts, a carpenter, residing on the Greensferry Road, Tuesday night attempted to commit suicide by cutting his throat with a razor."

Fortunately, it is explained, Mrs. Roberts restrained her husband, and with the help of some friends brought him by streetcar to Grady Hospital.

"Mrs. Roberts," the story continues,

who spent the night in the women's department at police headquarters, told Matron Bohnefeld that several months ago her husband suffered a lick on the head that affected his mind.

Sunday, while in a playful mood, Mrs. Roberts told her husband there was a cow in the yard. After learning that he had been fooled Roberts is said to have become morose and sullen and up until he cut his throat refused to speak to his wife.

Well. We are not told how Mr. Roberts suffered the lick on the head. Perhaps it was during one of his wife's playful moods. Perhaps it was during some involvement with a cow. That would give Mrs. Roberts's April Fool joke a little more point. "Here comes that cow again" is what Mrs. Roberts may have said in fact, or in effect, and Mr. Roberts may have been humiliated when Mrs. Roberts came to get him out of the closet, telling him she was only fooling.

We used to play a family joke on my old dog Chipper, I must admit, along very similar lines. Chipper used to hang out the window of the car when we drove up to Lake Burton, and she would bark at the cows along the side of the road.

Occasionally when things were slow at home we would yell, "Chipper, there are cows in the yard," and she would run to the front door and bark and cry. It would always get a good rise out of her, even though there were never any cows when we let her out. But she enjoyed it.

She enjoyed striking attitudes, and she believed cows were as small as they looked from the car window. In fact my father once stopped the car near some cows she had been barking at. "All right, Chipper, go on and *get* 'em," he said, and she jumped out and tore after them. She ran barking all the way up to the nearest cow, saw how big it was, turned around without breaking stride and ran barking back to the car, from which she continued to bark as we drove away. She never admitted anything.

Chipper has not only stayed away from suicide, she has defied veterinarians who gave her not much longer to live. She lives now in Avondale with my parents, and I expect she will still bark if cows are mentioned provocatively.

But there are those who, like Mr. Roberts, are less satisfied with illusions. If the reader is such a person, or is married to one, I hope he or she will think about the potential headlines before doing anything foolish Monday.

A NEAR-SCORE OF FOOD SONGS

Dream Song

I dreamt in the night I had gone on to Glory,
And found it was full of loose girls who weren't whory —

Whose faces were sweet, whose bodies incredible,
Whose sweat was white wine and whose few clothes were edible,

And all of whom naturally knew special arts;
And along with the wholes there were sumptuous parts:

Great legs, cherry lips, and deltas aglow,
And breasts you could nibble and cause them to grow,

And sirenlike voices expressing their gratitude
To me on account of my marvelous attitude.

And through the whole business I kept saying, "Look.
It's all very nice, but can someone here cook?"

Song to Pie

Pie.
Oh my.
Nothing tastes sweet,

Wet, salty and dry
All at once so well as pie.

Apple and pumpkin and mince and black bottom,
I'll come to your place every day if you've got 'em.
Pie.

Hymn to Ham

Though Ham was one of Noah's sons
(Like Japheth), I can't see
That Ham meant any more to him
Than ham has meant to me.

On Christmas Eve
I said, "Yes ma'am,
I do believe
I'll have more ham."

I said, "Yes ma'am,
I do believe
I'll have more ham."

I said, "Yes ma'am,
I do believe
I'll have more ham."

And then after dinner my uncle said he
Was predominantly English but part Cherokee.
"As near as I can figure," I said, "I am
An eighth Scotch-Irish and seven-eighths ham."

Ham.
My soul.
I took a big hot roll,

I put in some jam,
And butter that melted down in with the jam,
Which was blackberry jam,
And a big old folded-over oozy slice of HAM . . .
And my head swam.

Ham!
Hit me with a hammah,
Wham bam bam!
What good ammah
Without mah ham?

Ham's substantial, ham is fat,
Ham is firm and sound.
Ham's what God was getting at
When he made pigs so round.

Aunt Fay's as big as she can be —
She weighs one hundred, she must weigh three.
But Fay says, "Ham! Oh Lord, praise be,
Ham has never hampered me!"

Next to Mama and Daddy and Gram,
We all love the family ham.

So let's program
A hymn to ham,
To appetizing, filling ham.
(I knew a girl named Willingham.)
And after that we'll all go cram
Ourselves from teeth to diaphragm
Full of ham.

Song to Oysters

I like to eat an uncooked oyster.
Nothing's slicker, nothing's moister.
Nothing's easier on your gorge
Or, when the time comes, to dischorge.
But not to let it too long rest
Within your mouth is always best.
For if your mind dwells on an oyster . . .
Nothing's slicker. Nothing's moister.

I prefer *my oyster fried.*
Then I'm sure my oyster's died.

Song to Grits

When my mind's unsettled,
When I don't feel spruce,
When my nerves get frazzled,
When my flesh gets loose —

What knits
Me back together's grits.

Grits with gravy,
Grits with cheese.
Grits with bacon,
Grits with peas.
Grits with a minimum
Of two over-medium eggs mixed in 'em: um!

Grits, grits, it's
Grits I sing —

Grits fits
In with anything.

Rich and poor, black and white,
Lutheran and Campbellite,
Jews and Southern Jesuits,
All acknowledge buttered grits.

Give me two hands, give me my wits,
Give me forty pounds of grits.

Grits at taps, grits at reveille.
I am into grits real heavily.

True grits,
More grits,
Fish, grits and collards.
Life is good where grits are swallered.

Grits
Sits
Right.

Song Against Broccoli

The neighborhood stores are all out of broccoli,
Loccoli.

Song to Beans

Boston baked, green; red, Navy, lima;
Pinto, black, butter; kidney, string — I'm a
Person who leans
Toward all kinds of beans.
I hope that plenny

Of farmers sow them.
You're not any-
Where till you know them.

No accident beans
In common speech means . . .
Well, are you anything other than prim?
Have you keenness, spirit, vim?
Can you make all kinds of scenes?
Then we say you're full of beans.

"A fabis abstinete," Pythagoras said,
Meaning "Eat no beans." Where was his head?

Yankee, pole, mung; Kentucky Wonder;
Wax, soy, speckled; they all come under
The heading of beans. Flavor apart,
They are good for your heart.

Song to Grease

I feel that I will never cease
To hold in admiration grease.
It's grease makes frying things so crackly,
During and after. Think how slackly
Bacon lies before its grease
Effusively secures release.
Then that same grease protects the eggs
From hard burnt ruin. Grease! It begs
Comparison to that old stone
That turned base metals gold. The on-
Ly thing that grease won't do with food

Is make it evanesce once chewed.
In fact grease lends a certain weight
That makes it clear that you just ate
Something solid. Something thick.
Something like das Ding an sich.
This firm substantiation is al-
Lied directly with the sizzle.

Oh when our joints refuse to function,
When we stand in need of unction,
Bring us two pork chops apiece,
A skillet, lots of room and grease.

Though Batter's great and Fire is too,
And so, if you can Fry, are You,
What lubricates and crisps at once —
That's Grease — makes all the difference.

Song to Okra

String beans are good, and ripe tomatoes,
And collard greens and sweet potatoes,
Sweet corn, field peas, and squash and beets —
But when a man rears back and eats
He wants okra.

Good old okra.

Oh wow okra, yessiree,
Okra is Okay with me.

Oh okra's favored far and wide,
Oh you can eat it boiled or fried,
Oh either slick or crisp inside,

Oh I once knew a man who died
Without okra.

Little pepper-sauce on it,
Oh! I wan' it:
Okra.

Old Homer Ogletree's so high
On okra he keeps lots laid by.
He keeps it in a safe he locks up,
He eats so much, can't keep his socks up.
(Which goes to show it's no misnomer
When people call him Okra Homer.)
Okra!

Oh you can make some gumbo wit' it,
But most of all I like to git it
All by itself in its own juice,
And lying there all nice and loose —
That's okra!

It may be poor for eating chips with,
It may be hard to come to grips with,
But okra's such a wholesome food
It straightens out your attitude.

"Mm!" is how discerning folk re-
Spond when they are served some okra.

Okra's green,
Goes down with ease.
Forget cuisine,
Say "Okra, please."

You can have strip pokra.
Give me a nice girl and a dish of okra.

Song to the Lentil

If we are good basic people, then one can assume in us
An affinity for the leguminous.
And there is no more fundamental
Legume than the lentil.

Lens derives from lentil — due
To the flat/round shape. It is true
The lentil's opaque, but then who
Wants soup that he can look down through?

Lentil soup's as clear as fens,
But just as the ocular is eased by the lens,
So by the lentil
Is the gastric and dental.

That image may be inexact. However, what's meant'll
Glow through the lentil —
The hearty but gentle,
Almost placental,
Simmered-to-soft-focus lentil.

Song to Barbecue Sauce

Hot and sweet and red and greasy,
I could eat a gallon easy:
Barbecue sauce!
Lay it on, hoss.

Nothing is dross
Under barbecue sauce.

Brush it on chicken, slosh it on pork,

Eat it with fingers, not with a fork.
I could eat barbecued turtle or squash —
I could eat tar paper cooked and awash
In barbecue sauce.

I'd eat Spanish moss
With barbecue sauce.

Hear this from Evelyn Billiken Husky,
Formerly Evelyn B. of Sandusky:
"Ever since locating down in the South,
I have had barbecue sauce on my mouth."

Nothing can gloss
Over barbecue sauce.

Song to Catfish

To look at a living catfish,
Which is grey, which is whiskered and slick,
You may say, "Nunh-unh, none of that fish,"
And look away quick.

But fried,
That's the sweetest fish you ever tried.

Put a little dough on your hook and throw it out thayor
And pop you got a fish that cooked'll be fit for a mayor.

Close white fishfleshflakes, wrapped in crunch . . .
I couldn't eat all the catfish I could eat for dinner if I
    started at lunch.

Song to Bacon

Consumer groups have gone and taken
Some of the savor out of bacon.
Protein-per-penny in bacon, they say,
Equals needles-per-square-inch of hay.
Well, I know, after cooking all
That's left to eat is mighty small
   (You also get a lot of lossage
    In life, romance, and country sausage),
And I will vote for making it cheaper,
Wider, longer, leaner, deeper,
But let's not throw the baby, please,
Out with the (visual rhyme here) grease.
There's nothing crumbles like bacon still,
And I don't think there ever will
Be anything, whate'er you use
For meat, that chews like bacon chews.
And also: I wish these groups would tell
Me whether they counted in the smell.
The smell of it cooking's worth $2.10 a pound.
And howbout the sound?

Song to Onions

They improve everything, pork chops to soup,
And not only that but each onion's a group.

Peel back the skin, delve into tissue
And see how an onion has been blessed with issue.

Every layer produces an ovum:
You think you've got three then you find you've got fovum.

Onion on on-
Ion on onion they run,
Each but the smallest one some onion's mother:
An onion comprises a half-dozen other.

In sum then an onion you could say is less
Than the sum of its parts.
But then I like things that more are than profess —
In food and the arts.

Things pungent, not tony.
I'll take Damon Runyon
Over Antonioni —
Who if an i wanders becomes Anti-onion.
I'm anti-baloney.

Although a baloney sandwich would
Right now, with onions, be right good.

And so would sliced onions,
            Chewed with cheese,
Or onions chopped and sprinkled
            Over black-eyed peas:

  Black-eyed,
     grey-gravied,
         absorbent of essences,
             eaten on New Year's Eve*
             peas.

---

*Actually, black-eyed peas with onions chopped up in them are eaten on New Year's Day. On New Year's Eve, onion dip is eaten. I put *Eve* here for the sound, and so that I could go on in the next stanza to wonder what would have happened to human nature if "old years' Eve" had bitten an onion instead of an apple in the Garden of Eden. However, I was advised by a succession of readers, editors, biblical scholars and feminists that Eve had even less place in an onion poem that Antonioni. So out she went.

Song to Homemade Ice Cream

Homemade ice cream is utterly different,
Far more reviverant,
From that which you buy in the stores.
Homemade ice cream is something you eat enough of
     to feel for two days in your pores.

The peaches in homemade ice cream taste and chew like
     peaches,
And that's what they are.
And as for the milk and the sugar and egg whites,
     each is
Something that Mama brought home from the grocery
     herself in the car.

And Daddy goes out and brings home some ice
And salts it down in the churn,
And everybody knows the churn,
And each kid once or twice
Takes a turn at turning the churn,
Occasionally peeking in to learn
Whether the stuff is beginning to form,
Because the evening is certainly warm. . . .

You can't have any till after the chicken.
But, considering the chicken, who's kicken?

Homemade ice cream takes ahold of you,
Turns to young what's getting old of you —
And also what's warm into the cold of you,
But that at such an intimate level
It might be effective at blocking the devil.

The parents they may wrangle,
The kiddies they may roam —

But sitting round with their dishes of homemade,
They all make it home.

One Spot of Gravy
(*Thanks to Henry Taylor*)

Our happy home was clean and bright
Till he crept into view.
I'd come right home ev'ry night
To mop and scrub with you.
But you
        gave him
                one careless smile
And oh how my heart bleeds —
One spot of gravy
                is all a cockroach needs.

One spot of gravy
And the straight and narrow's wavy;
One spot of gravy
Is all a cockroach needs.

The sad thing was he came to sell
You insect spray that day.
But he was slipp'ry and you fell —
What's sure won't stay that way.
You let drop one sticky word.
Our garden's filled with weeds.
One spot of gravy
                is all a cockroach needs.

I happened to come home for lunch
To give you a surprise.
There were you and a cockroach scrunch-
Ing down before my eyes.

You dropped the dustcloth just that once,
And oh how trouble breeds —
One spot of gravy
                    is all a cockroach needs.

One spot of gravy,
And you cried out, "Peccavi!"
One spot of gravy
                    is all a cockroach needs.

Song to My Mother's Macaroni and Cheese

I wish that I
Were up to my knees
In my mother's mac-
Aroni and cheese.

Song to the Poet's Stomach

Stomach, as you know, I have
Had tonight some herring snacks,
Choco-chip ice cream
And Jack Daniel's.
Not all at once, certainly,
I was watching a long movie on TV with Herbert Lom in it
And I think Margaret O'Brien —
Is that possible? —
And Alison Skipworth,
And these things came to hand and seemed to go.
Stomach you and I have been together thirty years and I
Would honor you for all you've handled:
Anything the icebox can and more.
Stomach you stick out too far

But you have stuck with me
Through thick and thin. When I think
Of some of the times we didn't throw up!
Kielbasa, peppers, beer, shots and cigarillos
In Homestead, Pennsylvania, all night long.
Polish vodka, chili, pastries and champagne
In Forth Worth, Texas, at a wedding.
That was crazy, that night, but you know
You wanted it as much as I did.
Stomach you are my homestead
When I hunger, you are a fort
Worth support with such antacids
As you need.
Stomach here it is two A. M.
And I can't say about the soul
And do not know my mind,
But the dark night of an organ
Redoubtable as you are
Is scarcely more anxious than supper.
Stomach we can gut it out.
We'll have a glass of buttermilk or wine
And then turn in —
To what,
We'll see in the morning.
We may disagree,
But we will face our breakfast doughty,
Though you rumble like a fond
Put-out loyal bulldog, though
Our strange heart burn.

CORN PRONE

L ET me tell you something that happened to me in the Times Square Nathan's that still sticks in my craw.

I like Nathan's hot dogs, and Nathan's fried shrimp (which, strangely enough, are fried the way my mother used to fry them in Georgia), and Nathan's tartar sauce that you dip Nathan's shrimp in. And I like Nathan's corn on the cob.

I *prefer* — I would sell one of my relatives for — the sweet, white, exquisite little-crisp-kerneled corn on the cob that you get, if you know where to look, in Georgia. Or the just-off-the-stalk Butter and Sugar (yellow kernels alternating with white) corn that you can get, in season, in the New England country where I live. But the plump, yellow kernels of Nathan's are succulent too, in a cruder way.

So when, years ago, Nathan's opened its outlet on Times Square, I hied myself there with alacrity. And purchased fried shrimp, a vanilla shake, and a nice, juicy ear. And carried it all over to one of the many Formica tables in the place.

Now I know there are — I hate to use so harsh a term — scummy people that come into Nathan's. But I have a strong stomach. That's one thing I've always had, a strong stomach. The last time I threw up was 1969, and that was unusual circumstances, that's a whole nother story. Didn't have anything to do with what I ate, or at least it mainly had to do with getting hit in the stomach, and then I ate some stuff, but it was getting hit that made me throw up. I tell you what. I'd probably be a lot better off today, weigh less, have a lighter karma (if I understand Eastern religion at all; maybe I don't) if I threw up more often. But I don't.

So I can handle Nathan's. It was crowded and stirring in there, this first time I went in. People were milling around, the tables stayed full despite a rapid turnover, and they were shared by strangers. (And I'm talking about *strangers*. But that's all right.)

Everyone was fully dressed and no one was lying down, and no one was relaxing, but otherwise Nathan's was much like the beach at Coney Island, I thought. As I settled in for a substantial if not ideally digestible lunch, an exercised mother impelled her three busy children, aged about four, six, and eight, and hard-looking every one of them, into the three chairs opposite me.

So, okay. We all got to live. But.

"Now what you want to eat?" the mother queried over my shoulder — her intention evidently being to leave the young ones there while she went for the food.

"That!" said the eldest of the three, a girl, and she physically poked, with her finger, my ear of corn.

I sat there. Staring incredulously at my corn. As it rocked back and forth slightly in its butter. And then I stared at the trespassing girl, who sat — with an air about her of not having exceeded her rights, or even having begun to exercise them good — some fifteen inches away from my nose.

"*Cynthia . . . ,*" said the mother then, sharply. And I figured the girl was going to get a lesson in the inviolability, in a civilized society, of another person's ear of corn. ". . . that is *not* enough."

So, against her will, Cynthia ordered a hamburger and a large Coke to go with her corn, and the whole family continued to take no notice of me personally as I resignedly ate mine.

Okay. Okay. I *guess* I should have leaped up and seized either Cynthia or her mother by the throat and thrown her to the floor. I *guess* you could say that by not speaking out, by not standing up and saying, "Now listen here. Now listen here. People don't *do* that to other people's corn" — I guess by not doing that, I was as guilty of ignoring their personhoods as they were of mine.

But I was *astonished*. You don't poke another person's corn! Okay, it was a child. But my children wouldn't poke another person's corn. And if they did I would first turn to the owner of the corn and say, "Listen. If you want to have these children brought before charges, I understand. They deserve to be sent to the Tombs for what they did. But if you could find it in your heart not to saddle them with a criminal record, could you just let me snatch a knot in them?"

And I would snatch a knot in them.

I don't mean physically. I don't pound on my children. But I have, by word, gesture and maybe grabbing their arm or something, let them know when they have done an outrageous thing.

You know what I mean? I mean when Roy Cohn and George Steinbrenner and Alexander Haig and Jerry Falwell and John Simon were children going around poking other people's corn, if their mothers or fathers had just snatched them bald-headed (I mean figuratively), once, and said, "You can't get *away* with that shit," they wouldn't be such a problem today.

Of course their mothers or fathers would have been lying. You can get away with that shit. It sticks in my craw though.

ONE PIG JUMPED

Second Person Rural:
More Essays of a Sometime Farmer
By Noel Perrin
Illustrated by F. Allyn Massey
David R. Godine, $10

This is a dangerous book. It almost made me decide to go ahead and get pigs. The country, where I live less agriculturally than Noel Perrin, is full of such temptations: to go ahead and get chickens, sheep, ducks, a tractor . . . And I have resisted all of them except cats, dogs, a wood stove, a compost heap, a vegetable garden and a horse (who looked at me the other day as I was picking up a wheelbarrow full of manure and said, "Uh . . . You realize what that *is?*"). Still, Mr. Perrin makes pigs sound pretty inviting.

Of course, it is hard to write badly about pigs. But Noel Perrin makes pigs seem pretty inviting *anew*. He had one that jumped, and two more that were into earth art. He also had a diminutive farmyard-bred Bantam rooster that eventually (by proffering worms) befriended, but never managed to seduce, four imposing virgin Golden Comet hens that had been raised in a modern egg-factory and therefore lacked passion. The worms, and the bugs that two of the hens learned to catch, made their eggs' yolks much darker and more savory, though. This book almost made me decide to go ahead and get chickens.

Since I finally fought off these temptations, I would fail the immigration test that Mr. Perrin urges for the control of urban influx: When an upper-middle-class family moved to a rural area, "they would be issued visas for one year. At the end of that year . . . they would present evidence of having acclimated. For example, they show proof of having taken care of two farm animals of at least pig size, or of one cow, for at least nine months. Complete care would be rigorously interpreted. Even one weekend of paying someone to feed the pigs or milk the cow would disqualify them." This proposal may seem Draconian, but I like the spirit. I even favor some strictures; the country tends to become a place for weekenders, many of whom seem to think that it exists for the sake of their relaxation.

Even though Noel Perrin grew up suburban and his main work is literary (the book *Dr. Bowdler's Legacy: A History of Expurgated Books in England & America,* for instance, and teaching English at Dartmouth), and though he confesses with chagrin that "the two-by-six evaporator that we use to make maple syrup is called the Pleasure Model," he seems somehow to have become very nearly a farmer. Sometimes people, in fact, mistake him for the real article — thereby doing his soul good and providing him subjects for essays.

That's what this book is — a collection of essays about New England country living, a sequel to Mr. Perrin's equally felicitous *First Person Rural.* I have a high resistance to this genre, but here it is farmed well. If you are at all interested in splitting wood — as who with halfway decent instincts is not — you will enjoy reading Noel Perrin on various newfangled riving devices' inferiority to the good old maul. I think anybody, or at least anybody interested in leverage, will want to read Perrin on the peavey. ("How about Peavey on the perrin?" hardened urbanites may be snorting. Fine. Let them stay down on the pavement among the pigeons.)

Mr. Perrin does have an odd tendency to wrap up otherwise crisp essays a bit too bouncily: "Doesn't that sound almost as lively as the average conversation in a bar? Maybe even livelier than some? You know it does. If you want *real* talk, forget the city." And the dialogue he occasionally puts in the mouths of animals lacks pungency: "Oh, Mr. Teaser, what strong teeth you have! And that blond mane is so cute!" His sensibility seems less richly manured than those of two very disparate country writers, E. B. White and Harry Crews.

But Noel Perrin appreciates manure, and animals and wood and dirt, and the irony in the fact that he could have bought seven cows with the money that *Newsweek* spent getting a photograph of him without cows. (*Time* had run one of him with cows.) He cites any number of reliable friends and neighbors with whom he shares knotty chores. It might be more interesting if he were to characterize some of these folks more thoroughly, but then it might not be so neighborly. Though detached enough to be a student rather than an instinctive grasper of country codes, Mr. Perrin seems to belong where he lives, and it's always remarkable to read a good writer who manages to do that.

He says it is not true, incidentally, that farm kids grow up knowing all about the birds and the bees from watching farm animals. Farm animals, he says, are discreet. He has a Hereford bull who "must handle all his affairs between three and six on cloudy mornings." An affectionate nine-hundred-pound cow, however, once came within an ace of mounting Mr. Perrin.

This book did not make me want to go ahead and get cows.

USED WORDS

Just neat white paper covered with words
Or are they turds or are they turds?

— Elizabeth Smart,
"CBS and JBP"

IS THE POPE CAPITALIZED?

The Associated Press Stylebook and Libel Manual
Edited by Howard Angione
Associated Press, $2.95

The New York Times Manual of Style and Usage
Revised and edited by Lewis Jordan
Quadrangle, $10

The United Press International Stylebook
Compiled and edited by Bobby Ray Miller
United Press International, $3

The Washington Post Deskbook on Style
Compiled and edited by Robert A. Webb
McGraw-Hill, $10

It was under the heading "A Sense of Style" that the late George Frazier led off one of his columns in the *Boston Globe* with this sentence:

What I suspect may not be generally recognized is that beneath the sheen of hubris and swaggering insolence that colors my reflections on fashion there are a certain piety and high purpose — a caveat, a bit of consumer counsel designed to put you on guard against those who would exploit your naivete about clothes, cautioning you against submitting too sheepishly to the arrogance of ignorance of such cloak-and-suiters as the inexcusably tasteless Grieco Brothers, of such self-professed arbiters of elegantiarum as one Ralph Lauren, and of all such salespersons as tell you not to give it another thought, that's the way the lapels on a double-breasted jacket are supposed to look when the hell it is.

That kind of style, the joy of text, is rare in journalism these days. Occasionally, a nice touch crops up. A few years ago, Ray Swallow in *WomenSports* told of a day at Hialeah when jockey Eddie Maple was thrown by two different horses:

> "Eddie Maple [who wasn't] must be drunk," said a bettor behind us, who was.

Much of the pleasure — advancement of world socialism aside — that Alexander Cockburn takes in his *Village Voice* "Press Clips" column, I suspect, is in his own style:

> And I liked my Scottish public school too. . . . The fear was not really of bullying or homosexual assault so much as whether one's parents would make public spectacles of themselves on their periodic visits to the school, which was ten miles across the moors from the nearest point of civilization (Perth).

Nice, that "(Perth)," like a percussionist's closing, retroactively pervasive plonk.

But few journalistic stylists today are half so playful. Tom Wolfe's prose has flattened out considerably, and so has Hunter Thompson's. It may be that Thompson's full Fear and Loathing cry reached such a pitch that it is now, like the H-bomb, only unthinkably employable. In fact, he has fixed it so that *no one* can use such handy terms as *bull maggot, king-hell,* and *wolverine* with any real equanimity.

I don't mean to equate style with crazy shit. Mary McGrory's syndicated column, though cool and level, is eloquent, whereas Pete Hamill's, surging with intensified values, is usually schlock. On most news pages, vivid writing has made little headway, and that is doubtless a good thing. Certainly, writers of straight news copy are wise to avoid isolated special effects such as the one that closes this otherwise exemplary paragraph from the *New York Daily News:*

> Two correction officers, noticing his grandson, approached and asked: "David, what's the matter?" With that, Berkowitz began trembling and screaming. The guards walked him 50 feet down a hallway to his room and placed him in his bed, where he thrashed around. Wildly.

Now, the prose of the *Daily News* is generally a brisk, fluent, and pointed thing in the morning. That "Wildly" sentence is a break in form. However snappy it may become, daily-news-story English is quite a formal arrangement, almost as refined in its way as the language of "Mary Worth." It takes a straight face to pull off something like this, from the *Cleveland Plain Dealer:*

> Pianist Hilde Somer, her audience, and even the critics winced when she played a concert recently in Tarrytown, N.Y. The music was not the usual Somer perfection.
>
> The Baldwin Piano Co. checked the complaint and found that David Saphra, the technician who was supposed to have tuned the piano that day, was instead jumping off the Throgs Neck Bridge. . . .

The conventions of a personal column are somewhat different, of course. But, even there, I doubt that an American will ever be as rowdy and experimental as Flann O'Brien was in his *Irish Times* column (a column whose many felicities included the occasional intervention of a chorus, "the Plain People of Ireland," who would exclaim things like, "What in the name of goodness is all this about?"), or as "Li'l Abner" and "Pogo" were at their best.

Newspaper prose is too hard to control. For one thing, there is the problem of typos. A recent story by sports columnist Mike Lupica in the *Daily News*, about what New Jersey Nets coaches discuss while commuting from home on Long Island to work in Piscataway, New Jersey, ended like this:

> "You're always optimistic in this game," said Loughery. . . .
> "We beat them. It wasn't a situation where we got lucky. We beat 'em." I made pleasant conversation on The Ride.

One litle *t* is dropped from the first word of the last sentence and Lupica is rendered self-congratulatory. It is hard to say what gremlins caused the same paper's Dick Young to call Howard Cosell "an articulate diuretic" in a recent column. Since a diuretic is an agent that promotes the flow of urine, an articulate diuretic must be a well-spoken beer salesman. What Young doubtless meant was that Cosell had logorrhea, and what he intended to write — in euphemistic reference to the inelegant but functional phrase "diarrhea of the mouth" — was "an articulate diarrhetic." But that, too, would have been inapt, since I never heard of any such noun as *diarrhetic* and articulation properly implies almost anything but gush. "Articulate diarrhetic," ironically enough, sounds Cosellian.

But Young usually abstains from large phrases, and, though often objectionable, is a newspaper stylist of note. Unlike, say, Rex Reed, Max Lerner, or Steve Dunleavy, Young has worked out a crisp here-I-am-and-here-it-is voice, a prose that belongs on a tabloid page but also jumps off it. Style is presence, or, as Swift said, "proper words in proper places."

Style is also how many *e*'s in *employee* or *employe,* and whether or not to uppercase "the Pope."

"The Plain People of Ireland": Can there be any *question,* then?

No, I don't think there can be any question. If you are going to acknowledge the existence of the Pope at all, I think you have to capitalize him. There is only one, isn't there? "Is the pope Catholic?" looks funny. The new *New York Times Manual of Style and Usage* agrees with me "if a specific individual is referred to," but the new *Washington Post Deskbook on Style,* the new *United Press International Stylebook,* and the new *Associated Press Stylebook and Libel Manual* do not. They say it's "the pope," and "the queen of England," and "the president of the United States." I don't know, it doesn't look right to me. "The wizard of Oz." Sign of a faithless time.

The next thing we will see is the lowercasing of "Perth." But, however much we may quibble with them, these are important books. One or another of them is probably used by most of the papers in the country. What is the effect when millions of voters see "the president" uncapitalized every day? Maybe the effect is such presidencies as we have had lately.

At any rate, consistency is the hobgoblin of large publications. Can't have one correspondent saying "The Pope," another "the pope," another "th' poap." Personally, I resent the various stylebooks I have labored under, which have caused my *Okay* to become *O.K.,* my *grey* to be reshaded *gray,* my *barefooted* to go *barefoot.* Maybe such things don't bother you, but they make me feel messed with.

For the *New Orleans Times-Picayune,* I had to call Bourbon Street "Bourbon st." And I was *living on it.* I would have suffered emotionally, I believe, had I ever worked on the *Chicago Tribune,* writing *thru* and *altho* day in and day out. All those suppressed *gh*'s must back up on a person and fill his dreams.

The more I think about stylebooks, the more I wonder whether they should be imposed upon a free press. Just one minute before we get back to the specific books at hand. Read this excerpt from the *Saint Petersburg Independent*:

> . . . Elmore is retired from a lifework as a lather.
>
> He sat, worn work hands on each dark trousered knee, and looked up at the stage . . . with the grin always there. On came Welk in his plum double knits, looking down at the group, waving sometimes, talking with the homefolk talk which so many love.
>
> . . . then white lights, spots on drums and the full ensemble came out in watermelon pink to sing the Battle Hymn of the Republic while spots hit the mighty-size American flag stretched on the ceiling.
>
> "Look, Dad," said Solene, nudging him to see the flag. All their boys were in Service: "Jack, Dick and Bob were Navy. Herbie was Army. He was shot down in a helicopter and is full of shrapnel. Danny was a paratrooper and married a beautiful Eskimo girl. . . . Billy was Air Force and married a beautiful Japanese girl. She's the mother of my brightest grandchild." Then she looked at her crew-cut husband and put her hand over his. They smiled at each other then both looked back up at Welk.

Ah. You can't do a phenomenon like Lawrence Welk justice in institutionally styled prose. You've got to have prose with the spirit in it, even prose which raises questions such as how many worn work hands — or, once that question opens up, how many dark trousered knees — this Elmore has.

If they are procrustean, though, stylebooks are also helpful. There are other things to be written about than Lawrence Welk, and some of those things require a mastery of such distinctions as these four new books treat valuably — the distinctions between *phase* and *faze, apprise* and *appraise,* commas and colons, *fewer* and *less.* These books are devoted not only to uniformities but also to clarity. Thus we read, in the book of the *Post:*

> Use a colon preceding direct quotation of two or more sentences. *The President put it this way: "We shall win."*

The close reader will notice that, in the example, the direct quotation is only one sentence long. The closer reader will notice that *President* is uppercased, in violation of the *Post's* style.

Well, of course there are many things in these books more helpful than that. I shouldn't be so picky, even with regard to self-professed arbiters. But, while I am at it, I might as well point out a few other flaws in the *Post's* book. It is organized in such a way that looking something up in it is at least twice as much trouble as finding something in any of the other three books. It errs on the side of purism when it says *self-deprecating* shouldn't be used to mean *self-depreciating.* It errs on the other side when it says the use of *comprise* to mean *constitute* is no worse than *considered loose.* Editor Ben Bradlee, in his chapter "Standards and Ethics," makes a good point.

> No story is fair if reporters hide their biases or emotions behind such subtly pejorative words as "refused," "despite," "admit," and "massive."

But there is hardly any discussion in the book of just how these words are loaded and how they might be unloaded.

The AP book and the UPI book do explain the trouble with *admit.*

AP: A person who announces that he is a homosexual, for example, may be acknowledging it to the world, not admitting it.

UPI: A person who *announces* he is a homosexual, for example, may be *proclaiming* it, not admitting it.

The *admit* entry is a good example of how similar the AP and the UPI books are, and of how much sharper and terser the UPI book generally is. The AP book never breathes a word of what the UPI book acknowledges freely: that the two of them were, in large part, written by a joint committee. But the UPI's Bobby Ray Miller — which is a refreshing damn name for an authority on usage — evidently took the committee's draft home and tightened it up, and also added quite a few of his own touches. Of the four books, UPI's is distinctly the clearest on *among/between.* The *Times,* for instance, says

between is correct in reference to more than two when the items are related severally and individually: *The talks between the three powers ended in agreement to divide the responsibility among them.*

UPI says

use *between* for three or more items related one pair at a time: Bargaining on the debate is under way *between* the network and the Ford, Carter, and McCarthy committees.

The UPI book also has the best joke.

burro, burrow. A *burro* is an ass. A *burrow* is a hole in the ground. As a journalist you are expected to know the difference.

On the other hand, old Bobby Ray propounds some strange notions. His is the only one of these books, praise God, which approves *dialoguing* as a verb and *media* as a singular. "The news media is resisting attempts to limit its freedom" is acceptable, to Bobby Ray. This is just dumb. Would you say, "The people is resisting attempts to limit its freedom"? "The livestock is resisting attempts to limit its freedom"?

I like Bobby Ray's book, though. It's the only one of these stylebooks that has *style*. The *Post*'s is ill-focused, the AP's lacks personality, and the *Times*'s is about what you would expect. Sound. Avuncular. I don't suppose there is such a word as "great-avuncular." The *Times*, incidentally, seems highly conscious of its responsibility to dog shows. Entries such as *clumber spaniel* and *keeshond* abound.

The UPI is not going to get left behind by the evolving language, I'll tell you that. In fact, it may be out ahead of it. Bobby Ray goes so far as to say that *like* is "acceptable to mean *as* or *as if* " and that, aside from "certain idiomatic expressions" such as "for whom the bell tolls," *who* is acceptable in all references. "It was just like you said" is cited as correct and no bar is laid to "each of who." These guidelines are vulgar, but probably not too vulgar for the UPI (surely someone would find an excuse to fix "each of who"), and they do clear the air. After all, the most prevalent *who/whom* mistake — you see it even in the *Times* — is the undue *whom*, as in, "The Pope listed all those whom he felt would rise from the dead."

According to a friend of mine, who is a woman frequently mentioned in the press (not Elizabeth Taylor), the UPI is also ahead of the *Times* on the matter of *women*.

The gist of all four of these books' treatments of sexism (which are wholly called for, but as embarrassing in their necessity as laws against "Colored" restrooms) is that women should no longer be referred to gratuitously as mothers, wives, grandmothers, or objects of desire, as though the reporter felt obliged subtly and indirectly to imply an erection somewhere along the line every time a member of the female sex is taken note of.

But my woman source took one look at the first sentence of the *Times*'s *women* entry —

> In referring to women, we should avoid words or phrases that seem to imply that the *Times* speaks with a purely masculine voice, viewing men as the norm and women as the exception

— and said, "That's a man writing to other men."

The UPI and AP entries, on the other hand, begin simply.

> Women should receive the same treatment as men in all areas of coverage.

If I look at that for too long, I begin to sense libidinous undertones (what were the original post-Edenic areas of coverage?), but the undertones are evenhanded.

Not that I oppose bias in a book on words. I am all for bias openly arrived at, as in Dr. Johnson's dictionary. (He defined *pension* as, in England, "pay given to a state hireling for treason to his country.") But the *Times* book's bias is repressed, shrouded in dignity. Note that almost every time this book mentions a person's name in an example of usage, his or her last name is Manley. John P. Manley, Joan Manley, Honest John Manley, Air Chief Marshal Manley, John P. Manley of Queens, the Borough President.

The *Times* also says this:

> . . . it is no more appropriate to slide casually into parenthetical references to a woman's appearance — *comely brunette, petite, pert, attractive, bosomy, leggy, sexy* — than it is to speak of *the tiny Councilman.*

But these offenses are not parallel at all. "The Councilman with the sensitive eyes," "the compactly muscled Councilman" would be more like it.

A volume, or at any rate a feature story, might be written on why tininess occurs to the *Times* in this context. Do men or newspapers focus on women's bosoms, and so on, as a defense against their own secret feelings of smallness? I have always thought I did so out of sheer animal spirits. But it is worth noting that in usage books written by men a recurrent, telling example of the need for judiciousness in use of hyphens is the distinction between *small businessman* and *small-business man*.

Incidentally, both the *Times* book and the *Post* book are stuffy, not to say huffy, on such subjects as *obscenity, adultery* and *boyfriend/girlfriend*. Consider this from the *Times* book:

> *boyfriend, girlfriend.* Despite the wide currency these objectionable colloquialisms have attained, they should not be used until it has been definitely established that no other term or description will suffice. They are especially distasteful, as well as imprecise, in references to adults.

I still point to what Swift said about proper words and places. But then again who has ever been more distinctively improper than Swift? (And how could Swift have foreseen so proper a place as the *Times*?) I like Bobby Ray's book because it reads like *some particular person* styled it to suit himorherself.

GRYLL'S STATE

In *The Faerie Queen*, book two, *a number of men who have been turned into hogs by the enchantress Acrasia are turned back into men by the Knight of Temperance. Gryll is the one who makes clear his desire to become a hog again.*

Gryll
Had his fill
Of aspiring, falling short, and wearing hats.

Gryll
Had his fill
Of avoiding fats.

Gryll
Had nil
In the way of an attitude of holier-than-thou.

Gryll
Still
Enjoyed a good sow.

Gryll,
Until
He became a hog, was forever laying up everything he might
  need, and using everything he had laid up — or seeing
  that it was properly disposed of, or defended.

Gryll
Felt swill

Had things to recommend it.

Gryll
Felt ill
*At the thought of returning to a state of mind in which he
    had to think of himself as a probable threat.*

Gryll
Will
Be borne out by history yet.

HOW MISS WREN STOOD IN DE DO'

The Wren's Nest, home of Joel Chandler Harris, was being maintained as a museum, for whites only.

"You done year me say dat de creeturs is got mos' ez much sense ez folks, ain't you, honey?" inquired the old man, sighing heavily and settling himself back in his old seat with an air of melancholy resignation.

"Well den, one day when dey wuz a segashuatin' tergedder, Brer Rabbit up en 'low ez how he gwineter drap roun' down in town en see wuz Miss Wren ter home.

" 'Whuffo you wanter do dat?' sez Brer B'ar. En de yuther creeturs tuck'n sez 'mungs wunner nudder dat dey bleedzd ter ax de same Whuffo.

"Brer Rabbit he des sot der en sorter pull he mustarsh, en look like he know mo' dan he gwine tell. Twel bimeby he up en sez, sezee, 'Ef dis don't bang my times,' sezee, 'den Joe's dead en Sal's a widder.'

" 'Hit look lak,' sez Brer Rabbit, sezee, 'dat dem dat knowed de fust thang 'bout de pitchers en de pyapers 'bout de creeturs 'ud know dat Miss Wren's house is des bilin' wid 'em. Hit look lak,' sezee, 'dat de creeturs roun' yer done nat'ally tuck'n los' dey cultchul reckemembunce.'

"Wid dat Brer B'ar kinder got on he 'noyunce, en he up'n spon', he did, dat he knowed des ez much 'bout de pyapers en pitchers ez Brer Rabbit, en he 'low dat he gwine see 'em, if hit's de las' ack.

"En all de yuther creeturs up'n low dat dey wuz high up fer
ter fotch er look at de pitchers en de pyapers deyse'fs. Des den
Brer Rabbit lipt up en skaddle off down de road lak de dogs
wuz atter 'im, en de yuther creeturs lipt up en foller 'long.

"Well 'twant long twel dey fotch up at Miss Wren's, en Brer
Rabbit lipt spang up ter de do' en knock, blim, blim. En den
dar wuz Miss Wren, come ter see who wuz blimmin'.

"Brer Rabbit, he spruce up he years en sez, 'Howdy, Miss
Wren, we come fer ter fotch er look inter dem pyapers en
pitchers you got in yo' house 'bout de creeturs.'

" 'Howdy, Brer Rabbit,' sez Miss Wren. 'You en de creeturs mought des ez well des skaddle on back ter whar you
lives, kase we ain't open ter de cyolored.'

"Wid dat Brer Rabbit drap back he years en make er great
'monsteration.

" 'Now looker yer, Miss Wren,' he sez, sezee. 'Ez ter dat,
we is got black creeturs yer, en grey creeturs, en spackeldy
creeturs, en green creeturs, en creeturs 'bout zackly de same
cyolor ez yo'se'f.'

" 'En ah is b'ar-cyolored,' sez Brer B'ar. 'En b'ar-sized.'

"But Miss Wren she des scrootch back todes she pyarlor en
make ter shet de do'.

" 'Tooby sho,' she sez, sez she. 'Tooby sho. But dis yer house
is fer de creeturs ez knows who dey is, en dey gits in, en de
cyolored don't. En you is de cyolored.'

"En ker-flum, she shet de do'."

"And what did the rabbit do then, Uncle Remus?" inquired
the little boy at length, and with scarcely restrained impa-
tience, for the venerable darkey had relapsed into what gave
every appearance of being a deeply meditative silence.

"Now, den, honey, you er crowdin' me," he said. "Wen it
come down ter dat, I speck ole Brer Rabbit got ter projeckin'

like he natchul se'f, en Brer B'ar got he 'noyunce up, en sumpen er nudder come un it terreckly."

"I would surely like to hear about that," said the little boy. "Shall we make it this time tomorrow, then? Your place, of course."

ON HEARING IT AVERRED THAT THE WORDS *MONTH, ENGLISH, DIFFICULT, SILVER, GARBAGE, TWELVE, POEM* AND *WOLF* HAVE NO RHYMES

Oh two or three times or maybe just onth
A week or a couple of times a month,
I get to feeling a little tinglish,
And speaking all kinds of unusual English,
And things seem easy that once were difficult.
I feel that any old faith's a terrific cult,
And the sky looks gold and the landscape silver —
I run out the door to go wade in the rilver,
Get all tied up in the wirage and barbage
Of a barbed wire fence and a can of garbage,
Watch the old cow calve and the mama elf elve,
And eat a big lunch about quarter to twelve,
And grab somebody even though I don't know 'im,
And make him listen to a wonderful poem:

"Now ain't that a wonder-wonder-ful-f-
Ul dog over there, or is it a wolf?"

MORE LIKE A BUFFALO, PLEASE

T HE reviewer knows what you are thinking now: "Here is a guy who wishes *he* could guest-host *The Tonight Show* and *Saturday Night Live,* play the banjo, present his own network special, tie balloon animals, coin catchphrases like 'Well, ex-cuuuse me!' and have a live concert album go platinum despite its being banned from all K mart stores for strong language.

"But all *he* can do is review books. All he can do is *snipe* at wild and crazy Steve Martin, who on top of doing all these *other* things has authored *Cruel Shoes* (Putnam's), a five-thousand-word book of quips and quiddities that costs $6.95. Books, this *reviewer* probably thinks, should be written by people who can't do anything else: by members of some dusty literary clique who sniff at balloon animals and who ideally have been dead since 1930."

Pas du tout. The truth is that Edith Wharton could tie balloon animals, but she never did it publicly, for pay, because she couldn't do it *really well.* That is, she couldn't do it in such a fashion as to convey that she was great at it but had better things to do. She couldn't *toss off* balloon animals. So she tied them at home, alone, for her own reasons, until the sweat ran down her arms.

And no, one does not review books so as to *get at* anyone.

One does it for the satisfactions of (a) receiving free books *mailed to one's own home* and (b) being able, when asked at wedding receptions what one does, to say, "I review."

As a monologist, Martin is no Richard Pryor or Lily Tomlin (to name the two great stand-up comedians since W. C. Fields) or Lenny Bruce or Randy Newman or Bob or Ray. The best thing about his first big TV special was the *New York Times*'s preview of it. To read in the newspaper of record that a man was to deliver on prime-time network television a long sketch about turtle wrangling was gratifying; the sketch itself, one felt, was long. On his big-selling live album, Martin performs worn material rather perfunctorily for an audience that seems intent on getting hysterical without grounds. His appeal to the young borders on the bubble-gummy.

But Martin has done wonderful things: the original *Saturday Night* version of his "King Tut" song and dance (though if "Born in Arizona, / Moved to Babylonia" were the other way around, it would sound just as silly and yet have a point), his swinging-immigrant-guy character (though Dan Aykroyd is even more impressive as the brother), and various transcendent appearances on the Carson show.

Shtick detection is Martin's prime service. So despoiled is our culture by the false selves of Entertainment that anyone who can take off on show biz dreck as well as Martin does should be recognized — perhaps by a "roast" in which Don Rickles is actually cooked and eaten. Muhammad Ali and Menachem Begin can do *The Tonight Show* without succumbing to it, but only Martin seems capable of simultaneously doing it up brown and doing it in.

One recalls the night Martin was guest-hosting and Bill Cosby was guesting and Martin, without seeming mean, made it clear that nothing Cosby said was tongue-in-cheek enough. Cosby was reduced to apologizing for clichés. He looked as if he wished he could go off somewhere outside Hollywood and work on his moves. In his stride on the Carson show, Martin has as nimble a straight face under the circumstances as Donald Barthelme has in prose.

Prose, on the evidence of *Cruel Shoes,* is not Martin's element: "I decided to secretly follow this dog. I laid about a hundred yards back and watched him. . . . As I approached, I could hear the sounds of other dogs moving lightly. . . . I remember throwing them bones now and then, and I could recall several of the dogs seemingly analyze it before accepting it." The syntax is not that bad throughout, but only one bit ("The Nervous Father") in *Cruel Shoes* has what could be called happy feet.

Not that Martin need be expected to write as well as Woody Allen, the only audiovisual comedian whose diction knows what it is doing on a page. At times Allen's written humor may seem derivative — it needs his face and voice to make us realize "Oh, a *Jewish* Benchley" or "a *rumpled* Perelman." But even in its lapses, it has a ring, it is writing.

Writing is something many a book has done without. *Cruel Shoes,* however, lacks not only style but also character. Fields, Groucho Marx, and Fred Allen all spoke with decidedly less timbre and snap in print than orally, but each of them produced a readable book or two that at least evoke — if they fail quite to render — the author's voice. Precious little from Martin's slim volume would be funny, let alone original, even if fleshed out by Martin's bunny-ear apparatus and fine awful smile.

One chapter is called "Dogs in My Nose." It is three paragraphs long and seems to go on and on and on. Further nasal whimsy appears under the heading "Comedy Events You Can Do": "Put an atom bomb in your nose, go to a party and take out your handkerchief. Then pretend to blow your nose, simultaneously triggering the bomb." The reader who does not know five fourth-graders with better nose jokes than that is not traveling in a fast enough crowd.

Now, drolleries that do not quite come off may yet be estimable; sometimes not quite coming off is the better part of coming off. But some of these brief sketches suggest Richard Brautigan on a particularly languid day. There are several apparently straight, though furtive (but not furtive enough), poems. There are jibes at leaden philosophers that — although or because Martin was once a serious student of philosophy himself — are leaden (though thin). "Cows in Trouble" and "The Day the Buffalo Danced" are topics worth developing, but what Martin gives us is surely not the *way* discontented cows would act and definitely not how buffalo would dance.

An item about a nationality called Turds approaches risible flatness, but why "Turdsmania" for the country's name? Turdsey, perhaps. Turdwana. There is something to be said for this sentence from "Poodles . . . Great Eating!": "The dog-eating experience began in Arkansas, August, 1959, when Earl Tauntree, looking for something to do said, 'Let's cook the dog.' " But "experience" is not quite the word, the town in Arkansas should be given, there ought to be a comma after *do*, and "Tauntree" is not a funny name.

In this reviewer's estimation. Which is not to deny that one would perhaps give up all one's estimation for the ability to tie a balloon buffalo. And make it dance. *Like a buffalo.*

Since this review originally appeared, Martin has become a movie star. For the record let me state that I, unlike many tasteful Americans, loved The Jerk, *and I think Martin can dance like a son of a bitch. And let me say in all fairness that Bernadette Peters, with whom Martin has a close personal relationship, makes Edith Wharton look like Alfred, Lord Tennyson.*

WHOSE WHO?

A people-item journalist takes on the history of mankind.

Before last week, a couple of noted precursors reached the postcursing stage: for **Java Man** and **Java Woman**, it was the end of something. "We met in a tree," recalled J.M., "and just totally flipped over each other" — but then came twelve and a half years of rough-and-tumble. "We did the whole number, the bonking on the head, the dragging by the hair, the clawing and the biting and the names. 'Animal!' 'Troglodyte!' You know.

"Finally it dawned on us this was getting us nowhere. 'After all,' we said, 'we are two fully upright adults. Let's start acting like hominids.' Now I think we know each other better. Because we know *ourselves* better. And we realize we are two very different people."

So with jaws still ajut and brows still ridged, but personally more together, the Javas announced their separation. Observed J.W., who under terms of the settlement will keep the cave and brood (he, the club): "We were both evolving all the time. It's hard on a relationship."

Heliogabalus . . . **Jacob Riis** . . . **Magellan** . . . **Oswald Jacoby** . . . **Luke.**

Some millennia the third and second B.C. turned out to be for those **Sumerians!** That's the invention-of-writing people. In the old oral days, "ha" had meant "fish"; then came cuneiform, and the fish symbol meant "ha." No problem — until the Sumerians' northern neighbors passed from barbarism to civilization.

If you write, you share. The Sumerians, whose lower-Tigris-and-Euphrates stomping grounds lacked stone and metal, turned the new crowd on to Fish and Owl and all the other symbols. Pretty soon everybody was cuneiforming — and there were no more Sumerians to speak of. They'd been absorbed.

"They had the first 'ha,' " quipped an absorbent **Akkadian** as he hooked up a nice chunk of metal to a likely block of stone. "But we got the last laugh."

Eugène Sue . . . **Tito Fuentes** . . . **Elena Blavatsky** . . . **Georg Simon Ohm.**

And **I.** You heard me. I. I, by the standards of tidbit journalism, may not be a "person." I may not be "notable." But I am a . . . consideration. I occupy space, I breathe, black out; experience systole, diastole, longing, and a "zimmezimme" sound in my ears that I can't quite identify. I go home at night and face **Ciel,** and little **Uwe** and **Honoré** and **Willadean** and **Umbra** and **Fleming** and **Pud** and the dog **Tippy** and old **Uncle Pancoast** and our life together.

I voted for **Kropotkin** in the recent mayoral contest.

And I write the items.

Remember that tooth dislodged from **Hammurabi** by Babylon's then-minister of brick during their late-night "all in fun" bout of tackle-the-man-with-the-tablet? Well, it seems the tooth will not be compensated for along the usual lines. According to a government spokesman, the code does not apply to officially recognized sporting events. In any case, the minister's teeth were termed "much smaller and browner" than the King's, after each was removed and considered. The minister was reportedly placed under 777 new bricks, where he will await reassignment.

Maud Gonne . . . Mary I . . . George Romney . . . Jubal Early . . . Epaminondas of Thebes.

And **You?** Dear idling soft-news reader. Maybe an electrician? Maybe a Burmese woman? With soft translucent eyes? You can reach me here at the office. We'll meet, we'll talk, we'll grab a couple of Blimpies and get *out,* get *away* from all these . . . snippets of vicarious popularia. This "people."

And have you noticed that "the people" went out as "people" came in? Bringing with it "people issues," the kind of person who describes himself as "a people person," the expression "he's good people," and the neutron bomb?

Or have I lost you already? Has your attention span been brought to this — that it can no longer take in more than thirty-five words without **a name** and a

slug of white space?

Apparently the Yuletide was not all triumph for **Charlemagne.** What with all the coronation commotion, remarked the Holy Roman Empire's new head, his family didn't get a chance to open presents together. "It just didn't seem like Christmas," he has confided to friends. "I know it disappointed the boys."

Vespasian . . . Wolf Mankowitz . . . Eva Marie Saint . . . Li Po . . . Al Lanier of Blue Oyster Cult.

Back to **You.** Don't just sit there reading with your head bent forward: bad for your neck, makes you look like a serf.

Take sides. Let them go at it, one on one, and tell me, who do you like? **Gato Barbieri** or **Lazarillo de Tormes**? **Cher** or **Moussorgsky**? **Lon Nol** or **Hughie (Ee-Yah) Jennings**? To this observer, it is Kropotkin over any or all, though Uncle Pancoast plumps for **Thutmose II**.

What of **Napoleon Bonaparte**? The former French Emperor, reached in Elba, said he was working with aides on his forthcoming memoirs, stretching his 24-inch-inseam legs with daily strolls on the beach, and puttering around the governor's mansion. '*Mais maintenant, il faut courir,*" he concluded. "*Il faut 'cultiver mon jardin.'* "

Listen, this "people" stuff is not the bargain it seems. It's fast folks, makes its way into the bloodstream like bacon substitute. But — we are not *obliged* to nibble away submissively on processed "people." We can take a hand.

Pick somebody — anybody: **Carmen Basilio** . . . **Saint Crispin** . . . **Leon Trotsky**. Think about him. "Oh, yeah, Trotsky — better-natured kind of guy, wasn't he, than **Stalin**? Communist, though. Hit with an ice axe in Mexico . . . but how'd anybody look innocent carrying around an ice axe, down there, oh well what the hell, etc., etc." And on to the next "person," be it **Elihu Root** . . . **Colley Cibber** . . . **Imre Nagy** . . . **Ned Buntline** . . . **Herod** . . . **Julia Ward Howe** . . . **Gorboduc** . . . or **August Gneisenau**.

But wait a minute. Would you have hit Leon?

If so, with what?

We headline our columns "Notes on People," or "Newsmakers," or "Names . . . Faces," but are these in fact the lowest common denominator? Are they even units? In the process of some random paragraph's filtration through your household perhaps you have caught a glint of this microbiological hypothesis: that all of us, even **Henry L. Stimson,** have been host organisms for that master race by which we are, so to speak, peopled — those wee, ineffably knowing, intimate, unconfrontable intracellular bodies that live our inner lives, even carry our genes, the **Mitochondria.**

Are the Mitochondria just laughing up our sleeves? They must have hummed to themselves while those scientists at Brookhaven National Laboratory bred a person-plant: cancer cells from a Baltimore woman fused with cells of hybrid tobacco. And what has she/it developed? No doubt foliage, ratiocination, limited enthusiasm for the Orioles, and a hacking cough. But the Mitochondria don't care: to them it's just a kicky new split-level home.

The reunion after sixty years of **Dr. Sigmund Freud** with his school soccer team was a hit with all concerned except Freud himself and goaltender **Sandor Ferenczi,** whom Freud steadfastly maintained he didn't remember, even after Ferenczi did a certain droll thing with his ears and fingers that had made him highly popular in school, then donned an old team jersey and produced a ball that he kicked toward the father of psychoanalysis.

Freud ignored the kick, and seemed to be incensed by the thing with the ears and fingers. Ferenczi said he found the Freudian lapse "interesting."

Atatürk . . . Dana X. Bible . . . O. E. Rölvaag . . . Sacagawea.

His "Principle of Uncertainty" he called it, in no uncertain terms. It is impossible to determine exactly and simultaneously both the position and the momentum of any body, stated **Wer-**

ner Karl Heisenberg, thereby weakening the law of cause and effect.

"What makes *you* so hot? What makes you so *sure?*" exclaimed a policeman in the audience. In the ensuing confusion a series of shots was heard which struck the rostrum.

But Heisenberg was gone.

Vasco da Gama . . . Vaughn Monroe . . . Huey, Dewey, and Louie.

It's a brand-new White House pet for Amy Carter: a baby chimera swapped to her by an unnamed classmate. The President's daughter would not reveal to reporters either the quid pro quo or the chimera's name, or whether it liked peanuts or understood the role of the press.

Diderot . . . Capucine.

I slim. I put on weight. My belt also shrinks and stretches. Ajax. Alaric. (I sometimes feel that someone on the copydesk made up Al Kaline and Dr. Armand Hammer out of whole cloth, just to see if I was paying attention.) Bhutto. Qaddafi. I am paying attention. To what is there. To what is not there. To the people who move their lips concerning me, in such a manner that I can't quite make out the words or the tone. To the media. Which engross us in taglanguage, which take us for granted, which never remember our name.

Eugène Delacrois.

SYNTAX'S TACK

SYNTAX RETURNS HOME AFTER DISAPPEARANCE

Michael P. Syntax, 62, Maple Heights advertising executive who disappeared May 24, is back home. He returned Sunday, according to his wife, Doxie, who said he has resumed working.

Syntax was not available for comment. But in a prepared statement he said he did not recall how he "strayed to the Veterans Hospital in Houston, Tex."

He said that no political threats were involved in his disappearance. He had attended a political meeting the night he disappeared. He is a Democratic precinct committeeman.

Mrs. Syntax told The Plain Dealer she did not want to say anything more about the incident because she is still "too upset." She said her husband's spirits were good.

— Cleveland Plain Dealer,
June 13, 1971

Syntax is back,
And Doxie's got him.
She would know
If it were not him.

Loose, he strayed,
Unlike he useta, 'n'
In a while
Popped up in Houston.

Spirits good,
He lay with vets,
Ruling out
Political threats.

Did he tire
Of constant tense
Agreement? Take
His leave of sense?

"The answer needn't
Be rabbinic.
Simple error,"
Says the cynic:

"He preferred
[I don't agree]
Sin tactics to
Doxology."

I say, he left
Ohio bound to
Make some point
He will come round to.

He may have been
To Maine, or Mars.
Give him time.
Syntax will parse.

THE NEW WRITING AIDS

THERE may still be those who think it is just: look into your heart, study the markets, pull on your moleskin trousers and write.

Wrong. We who do write know better. Some mornings it may be more than you can do to plug your typewriter in. As a word person, you are not electronically minded. You tend to get the prongs wrong. And with your special sensitivity, you may regard the word *plugging* with a deep ambivalence. You are drawn into this work by a love affair with the English language, or perhaps with an editor somewhere. You resist the connotation of "plugging away."

But just as there are marital aids, which need not foreclose romance, so too are there aids to writing.

For the writer who balks at plugging: turn on every morning with the new solid-state power-pack Afflatus Apparatus, $64.95 retail. With a slight pressure of either foot, this elegantly engineered Penn Inc. product can be nudged smoothly along the oiled cambered grooves of its felt-backed burnished blue-steel housing to lock securely into any office or residential socket. Not only is your keyboard now thrumming, but as contact is made, lagniappe: a subtle electrical charge enters your body through the specially conductive accessory sock ($4.95, fits all sizes 10–13). Gets those mot juices flowing.

"Facing that blank sheet of paper" is an agony all of us know. Available from O'Fiction House are Pic'n-Scribe preworded sheets, $49.50 the ream. Just start crossing out the words you *don't* want and pretty soon you've built up enough momentum to shift bing bing without skipping a beat to freshly guilt-free virgin recycled bond. Specify if special Gothic, Newsweekly or Critical sheet is desired.

Are you a writer who hears in the hum of your fluorescent desk lamp a mocking, antihumanistic tone? You sit there trying to summon up something and what you hear, the still small voice, is *nnnnnnnnnnnnnnnnng*? Check out Tu-ne-on, which modulates your light's sound into whatever pitch and tempo suits *your* rhythms best. It's $19.95 at Better Noise.

But sometimes gear is not enough. You need a service. Has it been four and a half years since you promised delivery "early next week" of "the first big chunk" of that novel of Liberal Republicanism which was even then overdue by twenty-six months? And are you still struggling with that big opening scene, in which Whisenant receives the troubling phone calls on both extensions from Evans and Novak at once?

That big opening scene, versions of which you have worked out not-quite-convincingly from seven different points of view, including those of Whisenant himself, Evans, Novak, Evans *and* Novak, a fly on the wall, the omniscient narrator, the omniscient narrator's doctor-friend and a shamus hired by Senator Jesse Helms, Jr.

That big opening scene, several key pages of which slithered down into the dark recesses behind your long-unfinished basement game room's paneling when you were changing a fuse while distractedly holding those pages in your fuse-turning hand (as several members of the family loudly demanded to know whether they were ever going to be able to *play* in the game room, and the dog stood behind you making a nagging catarrhal sound), in March 1975? And you don't want to pull the paneling *down*, it's the only part of the game room that's finished? And the publisher's legal firm is on the phone?

Enter Inter Inc. (motto: We're Inter Everything). "Mr. Beddoes [should your name be Beddoes] is unable to be reached," says your Inter rep into the phone. "In fact, he is . . . gone. Done in by valueless goons while averting their interference with an elderly nurse. Gone, but remembered fondly. Many a one — many a man, woman and corporation at every level of society — now regrets plaguing Mr. Beddoes with *subliterary concerns* while he . . . was . . . among us."

That buys you some time. But say that you also badly need at this point a new advance of funds from the same publisher. And when you phone to urge your literary agent to negotiate this advance, the switchboard operator answers, and says that your agent's secretary is in a meeting. And when you phone again, a recording device answers, and says that the switchboard operator is unable to be reached.

Enter Inter Inc. (motto: New Modes of Middle) again. Your rep proceeds physically — dressed as a fireman — to your agent's offices, confronts your agent's switchboard operator face to face, gives his ax a brandish and exclaims, "The building is fully involved!"

Then, as the operator flees, your rep dons the discarded headset and performs whatever plugging is required (you needn't know the details), then changes to plaster-dusted workman's garb, walks physically up to your agent's secretary, revs his pneumatic drill meaningfully and exclaims, "Today's the day it comes down!"

Then, as the secretary flees, your rep sits down at the abandoned desk, buzzes your agent on the intercom, disguises his voice skillfully and says: "Ready on your call to Mr. Beddoes." (Should your name still be Beddoes.)

What is the cost to you? Inter Inc. bills on a basis of coming into your home and looking around among your possessions and taking whatever seems right. (Motto: What We Do Is Between Us.)

But — while Inter Inc. is working for you, what are *you* doing?

Writing? No? Perhaps, then, you share with many writers another problem: no one, at home or office, is willing to believe that you are just about to start working. Or that you *have* to start working, right now. "Just help me repot this sweet william, and then write," you will hear. Or, "Come on, let's stop by Production for Gibbie's going-away pouring. You'll be back at your typewriter before dawn." Or, "Why *can't* you put my B.J. and the Bear Go to Namibia Action-Rama Kit together for me this very minute?"

Yet no one doubts that an athlete or a bus driver is just about to do some work. "Well, here I am in War Memorial Coliseum where at 8:05 my mates and I are slated to lock horns with the streaking SuperSonics," observes the former. "Well, I have to go drive the Number 8 Cromie Heights–117th Street–McArdle Avenue bus now," notes the latter. And off they go to it, no questions asked. Why? Because they have put on their uniforms.

Now: *a uniform for writers.* Not quite a bushjacket, not quite a smock, the rumpled-deerskin top allows plenty of play yet ample surface tension. Ingeniously engineered bias-cut pockets hold pens, notes, snacks, reference materials, ampules of whiskey and your smoking preference — and for that loosely regimental, staunchly unregimented look, a hint of piping down the vents subdued. Don't forget the hat: a modified slouch, perma-stained, with just the suggestion of cavalry braid. The pants? Comfort and a hint of nostalgia as well: Victor Charlie pajama. By Mr. Ernest for Leon of Russia, about $250.

Unless you would rather repot the sweet william. Because of the way your prose doesn't move. You want it to come at the reader bim bim, bimbimbim, bim like some mythic animal. You don't want it to be like

> I am rigging up a paragraph here. Wait . . . let me work my way back, around, here to the point, wait a minute wait a minute if I can just get this . . . one more second — to the point that
> I am rigging up a paragraph again.

No, you want that first paragraph suddenly to *be* there. And then as the reader murmurs "*What* th' . . . ?" you tug its thread and it all unravels and ravels again, and all unravels and ravels agai, nan dal lunravel sand ravel saga, inanda llunrav . . .

What has gone wrong here?

You forgot, or were unaware, that *ravel* and *unravel* mean the same thing.

For God's sake. Get yourself a little three-dollar dictionary. Are you sure you write?

TOTAL NUDES AND
BUBBLING BABIES

THOSE people who shook their heads at the news that there were "topless" dancers in California, who shook them even harder at the news that there were "bottomless" dancers in California, and who keep wondering "What will they think of next?" will be interested to learn that a nitery on the Sunset Strip now has its outside covered with this summing-up of the girls inside: ONE NUDE, THE REST TOTALLY NAKED!

It heartens a writer to see that it is language — energetically if loosely applied — to which we turn for a sense of revelation when we run out of actual veils to strip away. After "One Nude, the Rest Totally Naked" there is always "One Totally Naked, the Rest Buck Nekkid and Barefooted," and so on.

Another Language matter has enlivened my stay here. I have just been reading a magazine called *Story of Life*, whose cover story, "The Art of Walking," tacks on the following claims:

• "In two-footed walking, a limb is off the ground longer than on it."

• "Medical statistics record a case of someone with 12 toes on each foot."

I am willing to accept the second claim, though I wish there were a picture backing it up.

But I don't know what to make of the first claim. To begin with, I don't know what to make of the phrase *two-footed walking*. Is there, in Portugal or Tunisia or among the Horseguards, one-footed or three-footed walking? Maybe by *two-footed* is meant "real, unadulterated" walking — as in "pure, unadulterated smut." If I ever have to promote a walking show, I will bill it as "One Walking, the Rest Two-Foot Striding."

Furthermore, I don't think that feet in any number are limbs. A limb is an arm or a leg. And I don't think it is noteworthy that either an arm or a leg is mostly off the ground during walking. If it isn't, the walker is so drunk or in such a hurry as to be more nearly tumbling.

Now, if we eliminate all the fancy wording — if we assume that *two-footed walking* is walking more or less as we know it in this country, and that by *limb* is meant "foot" — I don't think the claim is true. In all the walking I have done or seen, at least one foot is always on the ground. A photograph of the article's author, John Hillaby, walking, shows portions of *both* his feet on the ground. Unless Hillaby springs straight up into the air for a moment after every step (and if he does I think he would have mentioned it), each of his feet must spend slightly more time on the ground than off it. That is nothing against him, in itself; in fact it contrasts favorably with the way he writes.

However, that is not the language matter I have in mind. The same magazine carries an article entitled "Why Babies Cry," in which it is stated:

"Winding a baby may stop him crying, but. . . ."

Well, I am tempted to imagine a wife asking a husband, "Have you wound the baby?" But the context indicates that the *i* is short and that *winding* is a euphemism for *burping*. Another euphemism for *burping*.

Do you know who else has found a polite term for this amiable exercise? Dr. Spock. Dr. Spock, in his no doubt otherwise great book, tells you how to "bubble the baby." When I came upon that expression three years ago I quit reading Dr. Spock, except on the war. In the first place *bubbling* suggests inflation, which is the opposite of what is desired. But the big thing is that *bubble* is inadequate to denote something that sounds like the collapsing of a great log in the forest, or the broaching of a ripe watermelon.

At a time when everything is done to make nakedness sound extravagant, we play down the pungence of babies.

LIGHT VERSE

You also write about things that an ordinary person would pass by, like the jump of a fish, or the movement of trees, or light.

— *Paris Review* interviewer, to James Dickey

Though it brings them more than TV does or ever might,
Ordinary people pass by light.
The poet takes it as a theme.
You should see light beam.

LOVE AND
OTHER INDELICACIES

Dowered, invested and endowed
With every frailty is the poet —
Yielding to wickedness because
How the hell else can he know it?

> — *The True Confession
> of George Barker*

YOU MAKE ME FEEL LIKE A NATURAL PERSON TO TRY AND COME UP WITH A TERM BY WHICH A PARTICULAR WOMAN MAY BE REFERRED TO FAVORABLY AND WITH FEELING IN TIMES SUCH AS THESE

Woman *is either political or merely generic;*
A doll *or a* dame *is a dullard.*
Femme *and* lass *are crass or esoteric;*
Lady, *I guess, is like* colored.

Girl, *it is argued, is too much like* boy.
Broad *is just used for effect.*
A bird, chick *or* frail's *like a pet or a toy;*
Tomato *connotes disrespect.*

Eve the Eternal *is too rich and fruity;*
Damsel's *as loaded as* wench.
For you: add a touch of patootie
To a cross between siren *and* mensch.

SO THIS IS MALE SEXUALITY

Of the sum of human misery, that part caused by sex research is probably small. But there was a period when I had a hard time, at certain moments, getting Masters's and Johnson's faces out of my mind. If you think that God is watching you, it may be limiting but it also lends timbre. To think that Masters and Johnson, in their white coats, are watching just gives you the creeps.

You know what I mean? (Which is like asking, "Was it good for you, too?" And nobody answers. Don't ever let anyone tell you that writing isn't strange work.)

Now we have Shere Hite to contend with. She looks a little wasted in the news photos, but that's because she is on a book tour. (To promote a book you are expected to get it up eight or ten times a day, sometimes in Philadelphia.) It may also be because she is so tired of reading about scrota and anuses.

After a few pages of her book on male sexuality — based as we all know on 7,239 questionnaires filled out (and how) by the type of man who likes to write about his anus and scrotum and parents in questionnaires — I was tired of reading about them, I know that.

The first question should have been, "*Do you get off on questionnaires?*" The second, "*Do you get off on questionnaires alone,*

or do you also require manual stimulation?" The third, *"Is it really
necessary for the general public to read your questionnaires, in order
for you to get off?"*

Don't get me wrong. I am as prurient as the next man, as
long as he isn't sitting too close. If someone were to tell me,
"That photograph lying face down there on the table shows
Abraham Lincoln lying naked with John Wilkes Booth and a
slave woman thought to be named Elviry," I would turn it
over. If I were told that it was *any* naked people — with a few
exceptions that leap to mind — lying together, I would turn it
over. The only movie I ever walked out of on grounds of dis-
gustingness was Pasolini's *Salo,* in which Nazis . . . take my
word for it. I sat through all of *Animal Lovers.*

But I would regret having turned the Lincoln photograph
over. If in fact it seemed genuine, I would spread the word —
that's my job — but I wouldn't enjoy it. I am coming to the
conclusion, these days, that there is a lot of stuff I don't want
to know. I don't want the government to keep me from knowing it; and I don't mean to suggest that there is anything *bad*
about anuses and scrota, it's just that I don't want to know
specifically what 7,239 people like to do with theirs.

I like to read about sex as much as the next man, as long as
he isn't making loud noises. But I don't want to be told by
every Tom, Dick, and Harry how it feels to him, and where.
I like to read about food, but I don't want to read a lot of "I
like to chew a bite of green peas three or four times and then
just let it rest on the very back part of my tongue where it
arches up a little and . . ."

I do not presume to judge this male Hite report as a whole,
because I have read only three pages. (In *Scribner's,* which is
no place to wade through a lot of scrota and anuses.) However,
I have taken the trouble to read several of the reviews with
care, and I gather that one of the study's conclusions is that

men are tired of being expected to be the dominant one: the host.

Yeah! A woman is never expected to know how to fix the vibrator, for instance — which is why I won't have one (a vibrator) in the house. We guys get tired of standing like a Colossus night after night, year after year, even if we have a cold. I used to know a little filly down in Raleigh, North Carolina, who wouldn't let me even start to *think* I was being dominant enough for her to start getting *interested* until I had whipped two or three truck drivers and written her a bar-napkin sonnet (always strictly *abab cdcd ef ef gg*) that caused a certain physiological reaction. That's tough in one night. I got to where I stopped going through Raleigh.

But then there is this direct quote that keeps popping up in the reviews — Hite's conclusion that men are oppressed by being "brought up to feel that a vital part of being a man is to orgasm in a vagina."

Well. Not a *necessary* part. I don't guess everybody can recommend it to everybody. I wouldn't want to have to do it every twenty minutes. There are many, many other things in life. But . . . did those 7,239 guys think it *wasn't* vital? Of course *I* was brought up to think it wasn't vital to "fill out" questionnaires.

Okay. I guess it isn't vital to orgasm in a vagina, and I have been a fool all these years. I guess I just took too much for granted.

BUT I DO KNOW ONE THING. That is the nastiest term for fucking I ever heard.

I'D RATHER HAVE YOU

I'd rather have you than all Europe,
Including Paree and Madrid.
I'd rather pick you than Lamour up
Back when Lamour was a kid.

> *Rather have riches or fame or debauchery?*
> *Naw, cherie —*
> *I'd rather have you.*
> *Rather than two*
> *Of anyone other,*
> *Rather than Daddy and rather than Mother —*
> *Rather than living in Hono-lu-lu,*
> *Rather than being immune from the flu —*
> *I'm here to tell you that I am one who*
> *Would rather have you.*

I'd rather have you than Virginia,
And I mean the state not the girl.
I'd rather have everything in ya
Than everything else in the world.

I'd rather have you than a million

Dollars, racehorses or friends.
I'd rather have you than Lillian —
My wife — and her stock dividends.

Rather than owning three Porsches, all new,
Rather than knowing exactly what's true,
I'm here to tell you that I am one who
Would rather have you.

DON'T BE RAMBUNCTIOUS AROUND YOUR GRANDMA, SHE'S A LITTLE TIRED THIS MORNING

> What in heaven's name is strange
> about a grandmother dancing nude? I'll
> bet lots of grandmothers do it.
>
> — Sally Rand at seventy-one

Night is when the grannies dance,
Late toward dawn when juniors sleep.
Quietude and greys enhance
A nude grandmother's dip and sweep.

In heaven's name and heaven's eyes,
Nothing's strange; what would surprise
Us here where none see Grandma bare
Is taken on its merits there.

Saints beam out from glowing bushes,
Cherubs twitch congenial tushes,
Hermits turn from festive fasts
To view the old ecdysiasts.

Naked as the day, they're borne
Up through negligees of cloud.
How life's made you isn't porn.
They've transcended "well endowed."

Bobbly dancers, or thin as fans,
No body stemmed or globed the same.
Every mother's mother sans
Stays, stockings, station, shame.

How transported Larchmont's Mrs.
R. Coles Trowbridge, Sr., is! Is
There a soul back home who'd know her?
Grannies samba, wheel and soar,

Spin, unwind, then gather, knitting
In the altogether fitting
Gram finale curtain: rich
In folds without a single stitch.

One more time! The Granny Ramble!
Stirred-up unborn lambkins gambol!
Wide-eyed stars neglect their twinkles!
Grannies show them all some wrinkles!

Then they slide down pearly ramps
Back to unsuspecting Gramps
Or (if he's gone, he's up there crying
"Encore!") one more hour of lying

Solo. Then . . . get up, get clad,
Get peevish, restless, rattled, harassed.
"Grandma," people say, "looks sad."
She's itching to be hoofing bare-assed.

THE *TIMES:* NO SH*T

T HE other day I was interviewed (*Interviewed, were you?*) by a large newspaper (*Out with it: which one?*), the *New York Times* (*That large, was it?*), about Humor (*Well now*), and one thing I said was, I like writing for *Soho,* here, because I can say *shit.*

I had never been interviewed by the *Times* before, and perhaps I got carried away. The next day, I saw *Absence of Malice,* noting in particular the scene where Sally Field tells the woman whose suicide she will cause, "You're not talking to me, you're talking to a newspaper." And I began to wonder. Should I have said what I said to the *Times?*

I don't suppose it will *appear* in the *Times,* whose policy continues, I believe, to be as follows:

> All the news that's fit
> To print, and that ain't *shit.*

The *Times* has printed *Shiite,* and *Johnny Wadd,* and I myself have used — by no means sniggeringly — a *penis* (Elvis Presley's) in the *Book Review.* But in a sports column I wrote a couple of years ago, the *Times* (after graciously tracking me down at my in-laws' house to explain that it was, after all, a family newspaper) changed *jockstrap* to *glove.*

And *Sports Illustrated* once turned my *crap* to *baloney,* and *Esquire* my *fuck* to *forget.*

Actually the *j* word, the *c* word, and the *f* word were none of them mine, but had been spoken to me by some interviewee or other. Which is what I was the other day, for a few minutes, in the eyes of the *Times.* What if I am quoted in the *Times* as saying that I like to write in *Soho* because I can say *feces?*

I believe there was already one *fuck* in that issue of *Esquire.* So, okay. I doubt that Joe McCarthy, the old Yankee manager, ever said, "Forget a duck," but it has a certain ring I guess. But *baloney?* In fact, the *crap,* which I attributed to a basketball coach in whose mouth butter wouldn't melt, had been pronounced by him as "shit." I had done years of clean work for *Sports Illustrated,* and I thought I had a *crap* coming. Especially if it was marked down from a *shit.* But no.

I am reminded of the World War II correspondent who was on a ship attacked by Japanese planes. He saw a sailor run out onto the deck — which was burning and strewn with parts of his buddies — and shake his fist at the strafers and yell, "You fucking Japs!" Aware that no such expression would make it into his paper, the correspondent filed it as "You damn Japs!" The copydesk changed it to "You darn Japs!" Today, of course, it would be "You darn good industrialists!" and properly so.

I am no coprophiliac (or "shithead"); I do not feel the need to say it (note the impersonal pronoun) over and over. But if I am rattling along and a *shit* crops up and I have to start thinking, "I mean *stuff,* I mean *do-do,* I mean . . . ," then a voice in the back of my head starts chanting, "You can't say *shi-it,* you can't say *shi-it,* nyah nyah nyah nyah nyah." These inner embarrassments take their toll.

An interesting sidelight to the interview of me (*Back to that again*): it was held in the Van Dyck diner, across the street from *(Yes, yes)* the *Times.* And a man two booths down objected when I raised my voice in criticism of Ronald Reagan. (Reagan has a terrible sense of humor, but he is so secure in it that no one has been able to get his goat. I proposed taking an expedition all over the country, if necessary, in pursuit of a Goatgate.)

This man two booths down began to shout, "Get out of here with your bullshit! I don't want to hear your bullshit!" In other words, people can say all kinds of *shit* all around me, and I — who am being interviewed by the *New York Times,* and who am expected to be mightier, day in and day out, than the sword — am too often reduced to *stuff* or, just maybe, *excreta.* It isn't fair.

In *Armies of the Night,* Norman Mailer, referring to himself as "he," observed: "He had once had a correspondence with Lillian Ross who asked him why he did not do a piece for *The New Yorker.* 'Because they would not let me use the word "shit," ' he had written back. Miss Ross suggested that all liberty was his if only he understood where liberty resided. True liberty, Mailer had responded, consisted of his right to say 'shit' in *The New Yorker.*"

Since then, there has been a *shit* or two in *The New Yorker,* and other publications have eased their dung restrictions. *Newsweek* recently quoted the *Sunday Times* of London as saying *shat* — a more elegant word, especially when imported, than the present tense.

But of course every freedom carries with it certain responsibilities. For one thing, there is the risk of running *shit* into the ground. So many people cry "Holy shit!" in movies these days that it has come to be like "Zounds!" Perhaps, then, the *Times* practices a wise conservatism. If anyone ever does say *shit* in the *Times,* that person will resound across the ages.

And although the word is a very comforting one to many

people, we should not forget that there are cultures — Nice Southern Methodism, for instance, in which I was reared — that take *shit* even more literally than they do, say, Adam. The best policy to follow is perhaps the one enunciated by my daughter when she was seven, and had to be careful around her grandmother: "I never say *fart* in front of anyone until I've heard them say it first."

So why didn't I think of that, before saying *shit* to the *Times?*

After this appeared, a reader named Mark Sloane sent me an astonishing clipping from the September 22, 1975, issue of the Times. *On that day in history, it would appear, the* Times *reported that an Englishman named Lord Reith had spoken in his diaries of " 'that bloody shit Churchill.' "*

Later, the Times *printed the story on humor for which I was interviewed. In it, I was referred to as "an amusing Georgian."*

Shucks.

TO LIVE IS TO CHANGE

At a great distance, William Barrett's memoir may look like one of those reactionary outbursts that so often occur when one's idealism has withered with age and one's knee has lost the power to jerk liberally.

After all, in the course of his text, the author manages to cancel the subscription of his youth to both Marxism and literary modernism. . . .

If his logic is correct, then we should be ready to die for anti-communism.

— Christopher Lehmann-Haupt

Shee-it. That ain't nothing. If *my* logic is correct — and you better not say it ain't and I hear about it, because me and Doyle Cathcart will come over there and beat the pure shit out of you. If my logic is correct, we should be ready to kill anybody that says anything smart-ass about General Westmoreland.

And you're listenin' to a man who used to get on Jean-Paul Sartre's ass for bein' a tool of the interests.

Shit yeah, I knew old Sartre. I remember the night before I graduated the Sorbonne, he come over to my table in the Deux Magots and said he'd heard about me, did I want to help him write a leftist screed. "I doubt it'd *be* 'leftist,' " I snapped. I could reely snap in them days.

Cause I had been raised in a household where we strangled Spanish priests. That's right. Believed in assassinatin' anybody in America who'd ever been as high as cabinet-level. Saw Trotsky as an agent of the Big Railroads. Advocated the nationalization of mom-and-pop stores.

Yeah, I was born in Greenwich Village one night while my momma was trying to get the floor so she could demand less shilly-shallying at a Com'nist bomb-throwin' meetin'. They threw them round, cannonball-looking bombs with the fizzy fuses, like you used to see in the cartoons. My momma could throw one of them things twenty yards. Yeah. And my daddy, he knew Emma Goldman before Maureen Stapleton was *born*. In the summer they'd go to Provincetown and do modern art.

Nude theater. Hell, I was in my first nude theater when I was three months old. Crawled out on the stage while Edna St. Vincent Millay was just as nekkid as a jaybird bein' mounted by Eugene O'Neill in a cutaway swan suit, and my diaper slipped and the audience loved it. My folks, why they threw off their clothes so they could run out from the wings and grab me, but the audience made 'em leave me out there. Course O'Neill got the red-ass and stomped off. He wasn't no modernist, no more'n Sartre was a leftist.

By the time I was seventeen or so, I had composed an anti–Wall Street opera that lasted two and a half hours and had only one note in it, sung twice.

And acourse as the years rolled on I was right there at the barricades on everything, right on up through colored rights, Veetnam, Abstrac' Impressionism, and antinucular. I took all the right stands and said all the right things and wrote poems that I defy anybody to this *day* to explicate. I was writing stuff that made Ezra Pound's *Cantos* read like "Dan McGrew," and at the same time throwing sheep's blood at Nelson Rockefeller and doing more acid than Timothy Leary. I had my hair down to my ass and was sleeping with a gunrunning Guatemalan nun and an auto-parts sculptor from Chad and was writing long letters to *The Nation* in defense of Alger Hiss *because* he was guilty. My ex-wife was organizing hookers in Nuevo Laredo, my son was doing out-of-body travel in New Guinea, and my three daughters were down in Angola with a Cuban brigade.

And then one day I was listening to the weekly Forty-eight Hours of Rage broadcast on this underground Maoist radio station I pick up — I believe it was an Albanian reggae group singing a song against Adlai Stevenson — and eating some tofu I'd bought at a Whole Grain Weatherpeople rally and making some nonobjective silk-screens for the Debourgeoisization of Poland Committee, and somehow something jist, I don't know, I just sat down and said, "Fuck it."

You know. I mean, maybe Warren Beatty got a movie out of it, but where had it all gotten me? Where had it all gotten the world? And I turned on the TV and there was this preacher, Brother Luther Bodge, he was saying "Brother, if you have not found the light, you had better leave off your un-American ways. You had better move on down here to Sudge, Arkansas, where for the furtherance of this gospel I will sell you a lot in my Closer Walk Developments and soon as the Com'nist-inspired interest rates go down you can build yourself a nice house, and meanwhile you can vote against the forces of godless atheism and shout Hallelujah!"

And I did. And I started tawkin' like this. And shit, you know, it felt good. And me and Doyle Cathcart go out dynamitin' fish and puttin' up signs saying "Don't Nobody Better Think about Buildin' No Synagogues in This County" and readin' the Closer Walk Industries Simplified Holy Word ever' mornin' about four A.M. and then I come home to my lot here and think for about twelve or fifteen hours about how great a country this is, and about how much greater it's going to be after I go back up North for a couple of weeks and pitch scaldin' water on ever'body I used to know that ain't a Christian, which is *ever* 'body I used to know and specially that nun. She was awful. She'd do *inny*thang.

I got to work on not saying *shit* so much. It feels so good sayin' it when you're a conservative. But I know it's a sin. And I got to stop bein' tempted to read old Ezra Pound. It's all right for the *content,* Brother Bodge says, the *content* is fine. There wasn't no foolin' Pound on social issues. But the *form* is Satan-inspired. You can tell that by comparin' it to Billy Graham's column in the paper.

Course Billy Graham ain't no Christian. No more'n this William Barrett memoir is truly reactionary. Course it's not something I'd buy anyway, being it ain't put out by Closer Walk. But it sounds to me like this William Barrett has got a ways to go yet before he's reely part of what's goin' on.

THE ORGASM: A REAPPRAISAL

IN this time of revisionism and indictment, as sunshine stands accused of causing skin cancer, marijuana of making men grow breasts, and Uncle Sam of giving LSD to soldiers, there has remained one sacred cow: the orgasm. You can tell people you had eleven of anything *else* last night — tequilas, heart attacks — and people will say, "Big deal," or "No wonder." Tell them you had eleven orgasms, though, and it doesn't matter who they are — Henry Kissinger, Tatum O'Neal — they will say, "Wow!" Or, at the very least, "Aw, come on" — to which you can always reply, "Sorry, not this morning."

Oh, there may have been those who argued people ought to put less emphasis on the climax and more on the horsing around, but that is just urging travelers to notice the scenery along the way; the basic assumption has always been they'll only be happy when they get to where they're going. Whatever the current credit rating of vitamins, Julie Andrews, the Easter Bunny, or college degrees, no one has ever arisen to deny that the orgasm, at least in its place (wherever, according to preference, that might be), is a good thing.

Until now. Two new studies have appeared which challenge the orgasm's inviolate status. The first of these, a book entitled *But My Head Is Bending Low,* by the Wisconsin erotophysicist

M. O. Naseberry, argues not only that orgasms are far less important, popular, and salubrious than they are made out to be, but that those people who do have them have them wrong. To wit:

• The orgasm is not really ideal for everyone. "After all," he writes, "orgasms exhibit the same problems as modern-day cities — they are loud, violent, and hard to govern. Many people would rather belch discreetly, or go off into the woods somewhere and scream."

• Lack of communication has generally been thought to interfere with orgasm — as when one partner cannot tell whether the other is exclaiming, "Quick, quick, quick!" or "Quit, quit, quit!" The orgasm, however, may also be something that interferes with communication. For instance, when one partner springs high into the air crying, "Holy sweetleapinggreatjumpingcrawlinghoppingmotherof *Joseph and Mary!* Ngah! Um! Whooo!" . . . or simply lies there and says something dumb, like "Gee whillikers" — the other partner may be put off, feel left out, and refuse to discuss the matter further.

• Fish do not have orgasms, and, so far as we can determine, neither did the late J. Edgar Hoover. Whenever he was asked whether he did or not, he would just wink puckishly and have the questioner sent up the river on some especially sticky federal rap.

• Government figures show that people who have orgasms commit almost 80 percent of those crimes the perpetrators of which law enforcement officials are able to apprehend (usually by staking out their molls). Furthermore, orgasm limits production. Almost *no work* was done by Americans last year in the twenty minutes following orgasm — excepting those achieved after 12:45 P.M. on weekdays in massage parlors.

• Towns where orgasm is extremely common, even during

city council meetings, were compared with towns where people had forgotten all about orgasm until the canvasser brought it up. People in the latter class of town seemed just about as well off, and far less exhausted, than people in the former. "I don't know," said a spokesman for Impassive, Montana. "Nobody around these parts ever *goes* anywhere much either, so it kinda balances out. There's a sight of other things in this area to enjoy. Long walks. Sitting on the sofa. Rototilling. Torturing mice."

Orgasm may not be harmful in itself, Naseberry concedes, "but all the facts are not in yet. There is no doubt, for instance, that it can lead to harmful other things, such as smoking in bed, raiding the icebox nude, and acrimonious property disputes after the earth moves." He advises that people considering orgasm not rush into it but consult a physician first, and then "Dear Abby." "And then count to ten. And then think of boils and warts."

The second recent noteworthy assault on the orgasm is a study, which many regard as seminal, by V. N. Menander Spurgeon, professor emeritus of classics at DesPond Junior College, DesPond, Alabama. Spurgeon begins by looking at the word *orgasm,* which derives, he says, from *Orgasmos,* the Greek god of playing with dynamite, who lived way off back in a deep cave and only emerged to rain bad trouble and cold sores upon whoever had stirred him up (or was handy). *Orgasm* did not enter the English language, Spurgeon notes, until 1684 — a full 884 years after *cheese-lip,* and 49 after *grout.* (Before 1684, apparently, what we call orgasms did occur, but people just said, "Ods bodkins!" or "What was *that?"*) Nor has the word always represented anything particularly great. Among the early written appearances Spurgeon cites are "When there appears an Orgasm of the humours, we rather fly to bleeding as more safe," and "Vain, ah vain the hope / Of future peace, this orgasm uncontroul'd!" Only since Americans stopped studying Greek in high school, contends Spurgeon, has poetry begun "to treat the orgasm as a romp," as in Personica Bumpers's "Poem for Me":

> Orgasm, orgasm,
> Right up my chasm;
> Orgasm, orgasm,
> Undo my Not!
> I want to have a lot!
> Clit'ral and vaginal,
> Not to mention spinal,
> Is not enough. I'll settle
> For that and also dental,
> Ad'noidal and bipedal!
> I'll demand, I will stockpile,
> I'll
> Steal and I'll solicit 'em —
> Orgasm!
>   Oroilum!
>   And orelectricitym!

Spurgeon's argument, say his critics, is undercut by his imperfect grasp of present-day vulgar idiom: He speaks, with some distaste, of *getting one's socks off* as a current term for orgasm. Few people, though, will look upon orgasm — their own, their loved one's, or anyone else's — in exactly the same light after being exposed to Spurgeon's dismissal, syllable by syllable, of the very word itself: "*Or* is an indecisive, optional word. *Gas* is a vapor. And though *m* is, to be sure, a sound of pleasure, it is a very small one indeed."

"That's just 'cause you're seventy-eight years old, fool!" cried a student heckler during Spurgeon's controversial lecture at Notre Dame last month. Spurgeon retaliated by breaking off right there, fifty-five minutes into his scheduled two-hour talk, and starting all over again from the beginning.

Whatever the merits of this mounting new skepticism toward the orgasm, there is little doubt its impact is being felt. Anti-Excitement Leagues are already being formed on college campuses, and there is even talk of going further, all the way to the downplaying of all muscular contractions. As the saying goes, there is no delaying an idea whose time has . . . arrived.

I submitted this piece to various men's magazines, thinking their editors might find it amusing. None did. However, Cosmopolitan accepted it, added a few italics, and ran it. Several years later, I was asked to discuss it on Helen Gurley Brown's cable television show. I was joined in the greenroom beforehand by an expert on male impotency, an expert on the myth of female frigidity, and an entrepreneur of sexual-enhancement items. When asked what I was there to discuss, I impressed them all, I believe, by saying, "The orgasm."

But then I was taken aside by a producer, who said that he had just read my piece a couple of times and concluded that it was "a spoof." It seems Ms. Brown had been thinking of it in terms of a series in the magazine — which my piece, unbeknownst to me, had inaugurated — on "The New Orgasm." The producer wondered whether I would discuss the orgasm, specifically the new orgasm, in more "substantial" terms. I declined. I said I didn't know what the new orgasm was. I said I didn't think I had ever had one. I suggested that I just go on and be, in an agreeable way, spoofy. The producer didn't know how Ms. Brown would react to this. I suggested that he warn her. He didn't think that was a good idea.

So I sat down next to Ms. Brown on-camera and we talked for a few moments cordially but at cross-purposes. Then she asked how it was that I had become an expert on orgasms, since "men don't have them."

If we had not been at sea before (mutually, but not at the same sea), we were now.

"Men," I said after swallowing hard, ". . . do."

"Well," she said, "I know they ejaculate, but . . ."

I looked at her. She looked at me. We both — in my case pleadingly — looked at the camera.

"Imagine!" she said. "Me talking to a male writer, on television, about something like this!"

I have worked with many a TV host, but never one more poised. She changed the subject to my book Crackers, which I plugged.

VALENTINE

When silverfish have eaten up
Your backless dresses' fronts,
And frankly even what is left
Is not what it was once;
And a man approached with pity
Attacks you with his crutch —
You think life has no meaning,
Or at least not very much —

 Oh then it's time to rally,
 Then it's time to shine.
 Then you might remember
 You are my Valentine.

When both your fiancés depart,
And cite your double chins,
And what was ecstasy à trois
Is you, expecting twins;
And someone's tied you to a chair
And no one hears you yelling,
And all the golden plans you've laid
Appear not to be jelling —

 Oh then it's time to rally,
 Then it's time to shine.
 Then you might remember
 You are my Valentine.

THE FAMILY JEWELS

In the garden of Eden lay Adam,
Complacently stroking his madam.
And loud was his mirth,
For on all of the earth
There were only two balls, and he had 'em.

Those were the days. Now everybody has balls, or claims to. Fellows used to seek ladies of sensitivity, gentleness and full blouses. Now the "ballsy" woman is in. The stereotype of gay men as people with exquisite taste in home furnishings is giving way to that of people with full baskets. There are even signs that ballsiness is regaining widespread acceptability in straight men. And it was no slur on Billie Jean King when people said it took balls for her to go on TV and admit to having had a lesbian affair.

In New York, the cable-TV personality who calls himself Ugly George — his own pair rendered clearly if unwelcomely evident by tight pants — roams the streets of Manhattan "looking," as he mutters in voice-over, "for goils with balls." Which is to say girls willing to pose naked for his TV show, which, whatever else may be said of it (*yuck, ptui*), has . . . balls.

Balls are a politically, morally, sexually neutral quality. Israel has them, and so does Qaddafi. Billy Martin and Reggie Jackson. Roy Cohn and Mother Teresa. Barbara Walters and Abbie Hoffman. J. R. Ewing and Dolly Parton. Balls' wholesale dissemination may have begun in 1959, when Norman Mailer, laboring in the two-"fisted" shadow of Ernest Hemingway (who wrote often of castration), described Truman Capote as "a ballsy little guy," and Capote began quoting Mailer on that point with high-pitched relish. Or maybe it was in 1960, when Jasper Johns executed a work called *Painting with Two Balls,* an encaustic and collage on canvas "with objects." The objects were a pair of metal spheres stuck into a crevice of the painting. If a painting can have balls, why not a woman? Now an Australian New Wave group called Mi-Sex sings:

> *It's got balls,*
> *It's got balls,*
> *It's written on the walls,*
> *Graffiti crimes in the shopping malls.*

There are dildos these days with balls you can fill with hot water and squeeze.

Nuts, grapes, stones, testes, testicles, *cojones, huevos,* gonads, the family jewels. *Testis,* the singular, is Latin for "witness." The ancient Romans, it is sometimes explained, held their hands over their genitals when taking an oath. But if that were true, you'd think you'd run across, in perusing ancient texts, such expressions as "Cross my balls and hope to die" (*testes meos traicio et mori spero*) and "I swear on a stack of testicles" (*per cumulum testium juro*). Serious dictionaries prefer to speculate that testes got their Latin name from being deemed witnesses of virility. And yet what are balls shaped like? Eggs. It works out neatly, in a way. Balls have a feminine shape, and they send the male off in search of other feminine shapes.

Of course, Shere Hite has made the highly debatable assertion that it is only conditioning that makes men "feel that a vital part of being a man is to [ugh] orgasm in a vagina." But there is no denying that each ball contains eight hundred convoluted, threadlike seminiferous tubules (altogether some eighteen hundred feet in length), wherein sperm are produced by the hundreds of millions. And between the tubules is interstitial tissue whose job is to secrete testosterone — a hormone that stimulates mustaches, aggressiveness and heavy muscularity, all of which have traditionally aided men in their quest for places to sow the sperm. Still rather neat so far.

But that is not the whole story. All those sperm cells, those teeming halves of little babies, impel the male not only to show up at female doors with corsages (incidentally, *orchid* is Greek for "testicle," which may account for the pride with which girls used to wear them on prom dresses, sometimes called "ball gowns") but also to kick ass, climb, wander, make money, jack off, outdrink friends, build high-rises, drive Alfa Romeos very fast, and force some less hairy prisoner to do the laundry. They impel the male to do nearly everything, in fact, except settle down and help take care of whole little babies. So things don't always work out so neatly. Especially when women, too, get heavily into balls. (The average human testis weighs one ounce; fortunately for the underendowed, they are all but impossible to weigh. A sperm whale's run around fifty pounds apiece.)

As a matter of fact, with androgyny all the rage, balls in straight men have lately been looked down upon. *Macho,* every bit as invidious a term as *bitchy,* has been used to take the bloom off of everything from shotguns to law enforcement. Alan Alda, a prime example of unpushy, sympathetic, increasingly boring seventies masculinity, has described machismo as "testosterone poisoning." But androgyny has not always been regarded with favor. Herculine Barbin, a nineteenth-century French girl, was found at the age of twenty-two to have a woman's urethra, and something approaching a vagina, and an organ that might have been a small penis or a large clitoris, but also two undescended testicles. So she had to be reclassified as a man, who eight years later killed himself. Balls, at certain periods in history, are identity. Now, once again, as Jimmy Carter has given way to Ronald Reagan, and social services to bombers, balls in the male have come back, along with jelly beans. Moderates are called wimps in the Congress. Wayne Newton, mustached, throws his weight around in Vegas.

Meanwhile (even though Rosalynn has given way to Nancy), the *macha* woman continues to be, you might say, the nuts. In her book *Machisma*, Grace Lichtenstein hails "the scent of power, of female potency, catered to by advertisements for perfumes with names like 'Charlie' and 'Babe.' It is the reason for the television commercial that shows a young woman leaping in triumph after a racquetball victory over a man." The "adventurous, ballsy, gutsy . . . voracious . . . fierce" *macha* woman, says Lichtenstein,

> jumps at the chance to climb Annapurna. . . . She picks up the check at lunch with a male companion in an expensive restaurant and flashes a gold American Express card. . . . She subscribes to *Field and Stream* and hides *Vogue* in the bathroom. . . . She lets male campers know that her backpack is five pounds heavier than theirs. . . . She prefers Clint Eastwood movies to Dustin Hoffman ones. . . . She manages to let slip how many men she's dated in the past week. The *macha* woman "goes for it."

A touching tackiness in all that, as in a newly freed slave wearing spats. The *macha* woman should bear in mind balls' down side. They can make you want to stockpile armaments, screw sheep, and pound the piss out of somebody for no good reason. What war boils down to is who's got the most balls.

"Get them by the balls and their hearts and minds will follow."
"Nuts." "Eyeball to eyeball and they flinched."

> Hitler, he only had one ball.
> Göring had two but they were small.
> Himmler
> Had something similar,
> But Goebbels had no balls at all.

If people of every persuasion are going to go around having balls, then we had better examine the whole testicular concept rigorously, in the round. (Now, cough.) But gently!

Gently! For, as everyone knows or should quickly be advised, balls are not only potency's source but also the tenderest things known to man. Achilles' mother made him 99 percent immortal by holding him by the heel and dipping him in the river Styx. Mother Nature makes the average Joe 99 percent tough by holding on to his 'nads. Back when these were a jealously guarded male property, the standard riposte to women who claimed that men knew no pain like that of childbirth was "You ever get kicked in the balls?"

Actual testicles are also *homely*. Of all the external organs of man or woman, they look most like they ought to be internal. (No wonder that a starkly nude man is described as "balls naked" or "standing there with his balls hanging out.") If they grew on the backs of our necks, we would grow our hair long and wear high (soft) collars. Bulls' balls, hanging down like a heavy-rinded gourd and swaying gravely with the pace, are prepossessing, but human ones look like vaguely pulsing yolks inside a pouch made of neck wattle. Sort of fetal, yet sort of old. And here resides the force that through the green fuse drives the flower.

The surface of that pouch, the scrotum, is described by

Gray's Anatomy as "very thin, of a brownish color and generally thrown into folds or rugae [not to be confused with reg-
gae]. It is provided with sebaceous follicles, the secretion of
which has a characteristic odor, and is beset with thinly scattered, crisp kinky hairs, the roots of which are visible through
the skin." In spite of all this, a fellow may well share, with a
kindhearted friend, an affection for his balls at times, and may
also take pleasure in them quietly at home, alone.

> *A desirable thing for McHeather*
> *Was tickling his balls with a feather.*
> *But what he liked best*
> *Of all the rest*
> *Was knocking them gently together.*

Folks have been known, I have *heard,* to put fish food on
them and lower them into a guppy tank. Still, they are not the
kind of thing you want to wear on your sleeve, or to take out
and wave, in and of themselves, at strangers.

Testes might be prettier, but would be even more vulnerable, were they not cloaked five times anatomically. The scrotum comprises two layers: the integument (the thing with the
odor and rugae) and the dartos tunic, which is made up of
muscular fibers that are — I would say unregrettably — not
striped. Then come three membranes: the cremasteric layer,
the internal spermatic fascia and the *tunica vaginalis* (which,
interestingly enough, is Latin for "pussy jacket," I believe).
The outer layer of the testis itself — and this will come as no
surprise to anyone who in adolescence suffered a condition of
unrelieved excitement known as "love nuts" or "the blue
balls"— is bluish white.

The reason males get sterile if the mumps "go down" into
the balls is that this outer layer, the *tunica albuginea,* is so

inflexible that when the inner ball swells against it, the tubules are damaged. Ovaries, on the other hand, can expand and ride mumps out. Another thing that can happen to balls is hernia — the intestinal lining ruptures and crowds down into the scrotum. One more thing before the male reader's stones creep out of sight (they do rise toward the abdomen in response to fear): There has been nearly a 70-percent rise in testicular cancer in the United States since 1972. Some researchers suspect that too-snug bikini briefs are the cause. (Are you listening, Jim Palmer?) The good news — quickly — is that victims of this cancer can be cured in 95 to 100 percent of cases if it is caught early enough. (Look for lumps.)

Sumo wrestlers do exercises enabling them to retract their balls at will. The question remains: *"Why* are the testes located *outside* of the body?" I am quoting now from *The Missing Dimension in Sex,* by Herbert W. Armstrong, pastor general of the Worldwide Church of God.

> The Great Architect had a very good reason — but men never learned this reason until quite recent times. . . . Today it is known that the cause was, simply, that these marvelous and mighty little "factories" generating human life do *not* perform their wonderful operation of producing *life-imparting* sperm cells at bodily temperature. They must be kept at a temperature several degrees lower! . . .
>
> The scrotum . . . is made up of a kind of skin *different from any other* in man or woman! It is a non-conductor of heat! It is made up of folds. [Remember the rugae?] In cold temperatures . . . these folds shrink up, and draw the testes up tight against the body . . . lest the outside temperature become *too cold* for these marvelous little "laboratories."
>
> But, in very *warm* weather, they stretch out, until the testes are dropped down a considerable distance farther from the warmer-than-normal body.

Thus, this scrotum . . . acts as an AUTOMATIC TEM-PERATURE GAUGE! . . .

If you think "mother nature," blindly, and without mind, intelligence or knowledge, planned and worked all this out, you are welcome to your ridiculous opinion! It was not dumb and stupid "MOTHER nature" — it was the Supreme *FATHER-GOD* — who instructed CHRIST, who "spoke" and commanded, and the Holy Spirit was the POWER that brought it into being.

Men — even pastors general — tend to get defensive when discussing balls. And understandably so. Women, said Margaret Mead, are "much fiercer than men — they kick below the belt." That opens up a large area of discussion. You can look at it this way: Since decent men refrain from physically bullying women, and since they ungird their loins before women, it is cruel and perverse of women to undermine those loins, to be "castrating." Or you can look at it this way: Men have it both ways in the battle of the sexes by exploiting their testosteronic strengths, on the one hand, and by using their balls' sacred inviolability as a defensive weapon on the other.

Woman has been known to keep man down by self-fulfilling disparagement of his masculinity. Man has been known to batter woman and then to expect her not to damage his fragile ego (down there beneath the rugae) by telling anybody. A man who abuses women often justifies himself by calling them "ball-breakers." A woman who takes pleasure in kicking men in the crotch, literally or figuratively, often justifies herself by calling them insensitive to any other kind of feeling. There is a real sense in which women have men by the balls, and there are real grounds for a cultural imperative against women's taking that advantage. But there is also a sense in which men have women by the lack of balls. Freud said that the female equivalent of the male fear of castration is fear of the loss of love.

Maybe, if enough women wear Charlie perfume and get gold American Express cards, that will change.

It's a complex matter. Men may speak with relish, among themselves, of "real nut-cutting politics" — or at least I know a man to whom Richard Nixon once spoke thus. Nothing gets so surefire a laugh in a certain kind of movie as somebody getting kneed in the balls. There is something almost macho about a baseball catcher rolling in the dirt around home plate from having caught a ball in the balls. (The Middle Irish for testicle was *uirgge*.) As long as he is not crying.

Balls are big in sports. IT TAKES LEATHER BALLS TO PLAY RUGBY. To make every effort is to "go balls-out." Ballplayers are probably the only people who often scratch their balls, and adjust them, and hustle them, on national television. Baseball players sometimes amuse themselves by tapping teammates in the groin with a bat and crying, "Cup check" — if the tapped teammate is wearing his aluminum cup, he is all right. Another thing a player may do is to take the cup out of a teammate's unattended jockstrap and replace it, in the little pocket where the cup goes, with something like a live frog. (A frog's testes, by the way, are attached to his kidneys. That may explain why he pees a third of his body weight every day. If frogs ever found out about beer . . .) Pranksters may also put hot liniment in the part of the jockstrap that makes contact with the rugae. In *The Bronx Zoo,* his memoir of a year with the Yankees, Sparky Lyle recalls what he once did during batting practice in Anaheim.

> The gates had just opened, and I was in a crazy mood, so I zipped down my fly and took my nuts out. I was standing in the outfield in my uniform with my balls hanging out, shagging flies, having a good old time, and I must have been doing this

for about five minutes until Cecil Upshaw noticed me. He cracked up. He was laughing so hard, he was drawing a lot of attention, so I stopped. I put my nuts back inside. The next day when I came to the ball park, [Manager Bill] Virdon called me into his office. He said, "I have a favor to ask of you." I said, "What's that, Bill?" He said, "Please don't shag balls in the outfield with your nuts hanging out anymore."

Balls are, I believe, the only sexual organ that people remove from animals and eat. Zorba the Greek ate goats' balls raw. Less ballsy people get together and enjoy the fried testes of calves (mountain oysters, prairie oysters, calf fries), roosters (rooster fries), pigs (hog nuts) and squirrels (squirrel nuts). All of these are good and taste different.

Schoolboys talk about balls a lot. "You got a ball?" "Yeah, I got two of them." How do you tell if a woman's ticklish? Give her a test tickle. *The Ruptured Chinaman,* by Wun Hung Lo. Man overboard yelling in a deep voice, "Help, help!" Then, in a high voice, *"There's sharks in these waters!"* Somehow or another, every boy by the age of ten has seen photographs of African natives with elephantiasis (always pronounced "elephantitus" by boys) of the balls. And he has heard stories of men who were tortured by having their balls clapped between bricks. And he knows of a teacher or a coach who is so big, and peculiar, because he elected years ago to have one ball removed — which is probably not what Andrew Marvell had in mind when he wrote, "Let us roll all our strength and all / Our sweetness up into one ball."

Students of the liberal arts also know ball lore. Errol Flynn gelded lambs with his teeth. Henry James's asexuality, if not his prose style, may have been the result of a genital injury suffered in youth. Jean-Luc Godard lost a testicle in an accident right before making the movie *Numero Deux.* The Hollywood producer Walter Wanger shot off one of the balls of an agent, Jennings Lang, in an L.A. parking lot, with regard to Wanger's then-wife, Joan Bennett. The French title of the Bertrand Blier film *Going Places,* in which one of the two leading characters is shot in the balls, is *Les Valseuses,* which literally means "the (female) waltzers" but is slang for "balls." Picasso is said to have remarked of Michelangelo's *The Dying Slave,* "Look at the balls. They're so tiny. It says everything about Michelangelo." Picasso's are said to have been bigger than average.

Balls abound in figures of speech. Don't get them in an uproar. Wouldn't give him the sweat off mine. Get your rocks off. Pocket pool. Brass ones. Nuts to you. Don't bust my balls. Make a balls of something. "Ballocks in brackets" is, according to Eric Partridge, "a low term of address to a bowlegged man." (The way orchids got their name, in case it has been bothering you, is that their roots look like testicles. Having only one ball is monorchidism. Having undescended balls is cryptorchidism.)

According to Stuart Berg Flexner in *I Hear America Talking,* men in this country commonly called testicles "balls" by the 1880s. Flexner cites such other terms for ballsiness as *gumption, spunk, grit* (from the early 1800s), *sand* (1870s), *guts* (1890) and *backbone* (1905). "Balls has meant manly courage since about 1935," says Flexner, who doesn't mention *ballsy. The Underground Dictionary,* 1971, defines *ballsey (sic)* as "very forward, aggressive and impulsive. When used to describe an aggressive female, it can have a negative or positive connotation, but it is always complimentary to males." Times change. *Aggressive* is still, I think, ambivalent when applied to women, but *ballsy* now is not only favorable, it's almost tender.

When, around 1924, American newspapers came to grips with the "rejuvenation" craze (older men seeking renewed vigor through injections of goat-ball essence), the papers "found it necessary," wrote H. L. Mencken, "to invent a new set of euphemisms. So far as I have been able to discover, not one of them ever printed the word *testicles*. A few ventured upon *gonads,* but the majority preferred *glands* or *interstitial glands,* with *sex glands* as an occasional variation." Not even Mencken ventures upon *balls.*

So perhaps it is not surprising that throughout most of American literature, balls have been conspicuous, if at all, by their absence. You have to read *The Sun Also Rises* carefully to gather that Jake Barnes has had his shot off in the war. "What happened to me is supposed to be funny," says the Hemingway man, keeping his cool, but he also mentions that an Italian officer saluted him in the hospital by saying, "This man has given more than his life."

But balls' low literary profile is more than a matter of prudery. You don't run into many testicular symbols, even, in literature. Oh, maybe Tweedle Dum and Tweedle Dee; East Egg and West Egg; the first two strikes against Mighty Casey. But what are those few instances compared with all the dragons, snakes, mushrooms, fairies (the male ones that wear red caps, get into everything, and shrink and grow unpredictably), trees, towers, guns, poles, rocket ships and umbrellas (not Mary Poppins's, I guess) that betoken you know what.

Not even Freud finds much drama in balls, per se. He does propose that tripartite symbols such as the cloverleaf and the fleur-de-lis represent the whole male cluster. And he had a patient, "the wolfman," who was so afraid of being afraid of what he was *really* afraid of — being castrated by his father — that he preferred to be afraid of being devoured by a wolf. (Today, of course, analysands avoid vulpine-ingestion phobia for fear of being diagnosed too brusquely.) But castration complexes run to dreams of long, upstanding things being lopped off. To Freud, "the more striking and for both sexes the more interesting component of the genitals" is "the male organ."

The male organ, is it? So why doesn't anybody want to be called a prick, a schmuck or a real hard-on? Why is it *ballsy* that everybody wants to be?

Maybe we are just going through a phase. Maybe it will pass. Maybe the Balls Boom grows from a dawning awareness that the world cannot afford, now that the phallic warhead has grown so overwhelming, to let truly potent nations exercise their balls anymore. So everybody talks about balls. But real balls, as we have seen, don't call attention to themselves. It may be that all this talk is just a lot of balls.

I might point out, however, that it takes some balls to leave this business dangling on such a low double entendre.

THOUGHT SHE WAS EVE

We were good together,
Nothing up our sleeve.
She didn't know me from Adam
And I thought she was Eve.

Those were the those were the those were the days,
Oh what a beau- what a beautiful phase,
When I said, "Hello, Madam,"
She didn't know me from Adam
And I thought she was Eve.

We met in an upstairs shower
At a friend's home New Year's Eve.
She entered through the curtain
As I was about to leave.

And I stayed, I stayed, I stayed for a while
Because she gave me, gave me a smile
When I said, "Hello, Madam,"
She didn't know me from Adam
And I thought she was Eve.

The two of us were naked,
I thought we were free.
If she knew anything different,
She didn't let on to me.

Oh those were the, those were the, those were the days,
Oh what a beau- what a beautiful phase. . . .

But then a snake came creeping,
And I, at least, knew shame.
It turned out Lois Ambrose
Was actually her name.

And there was Adam Ambrose
And also Art McKee
And eight or nine more fellows
That she didn't know from me.

Oh that was the end, was the end of the days,
Oh what a beau- what a beau-tiful phase,
When I said, "Hello, Madam,"
She didn't know me from Adam
And I thought she was Eve.

AFTER PINK, WHAT?

EVEN when we were kids and *navels* were really something, Eddie Utterbund foresaw that the kind of magazines we perused in his garage would go further than the rest of us dreamed. The day would come, he kept telling us, when we could walk right into a nice drugstore where everyone knew us, put down half a dollar, and see *everything*.

"Aw, naw," we'd say.

"Yeah, yeah, they will. They'll show the hair and everything."

"Of old hoars and things." That was the way we thought you spelled it. Because we'd never seen it spelled.

"Naw. Of majorettes." We didn't believe him. I don't think we even wholeheartedly wanted to believe him. It was too much. But Utterbund, except that he didn't figure inflation, was right.

And he grew up to be a media consultant, so I still run into him occasionally. He has maintained a strong interest in skin magazines. I remember he predicted a couple of years ago, "Next they'll show pink."

I was ashamed to admit I even understood what "show pink" meant. "Aw, no," I said. "Who really wants to *look at* pink? Anyway, pictures of it."

"Hm," he said, as if to imply that I protested too much. "They'll show pink. They'll show purple."

"*Why?*"

"Because it's there."

Utterbund's concern with that kind of thing has always struck me as too explicit or something. But after all, one does wonder these days — just as one once wondered about logical positivism or dissent — where dirty magazines can go next. So when Utterbund called me the other day and said he was himself planning to start a new "breakthrough" dirty magazine and needed a contributing editor, I agreed to meet him for lunch.

"What is *left* for dirty magazines?" I asked him.

"Well, obviously," he said, "there are lines that still haven't been crossed." He was having the huevos foo young. He likes Cuban-Chinese restaurants because they remind him of an act an uncle of his once saw in pre-Castro Havana, featuring a donkey and bound feet. "We haven't had glossy intromission yet. Or even a full erection in the slicks.

"I'm talking over-the-counter right-there-next-to-*Commentary*-and-*McCall's* now, of course. At that level, frankly, I don't know that magazines will ever go to screwing. No. I'll tell you what the next *big* thing is. I'll tell you what the next *breakthrough* skin magazine is going to be." Utterbund pushed aside his beans. His eyes were unusually bright. He said, he hissed almost: "*Inspired.*"

He looked off into the distance, such as it was in the restaurant there. "*Felt. Complex.*

"*Achieved.*"

There was a pause. In keeping with the cuisine, he looked both inflamed and inscrutable.

I got the feeling Utterbund had been working on his prospectus.

"Let me just give you an idea of what could be done. A class act. Name of the magazine: *Myrrh*. We get that, as we make clear every month beneath the masthead, from the Song of Songs:

> *I rose up to open to my beloved;*
> *And my hands dropped with myrrh,*
> *And my fingers with sweet-smelling myrrh,*
> *Upon the handles of the lock."*

"You'd use the Bible?"

"Who's going to sue? And incidentally, you could sell a lot of actual myrrh itself, mail order. But that's incidental.

"Features. A little *imagination*. Re-create a 1936 'Life Goes to a Party' spread, same hairdos, same decors, same skin tones, only it gets out of hand. Everybody loses their heads and gets naked, right?

"Here's another. Modeling session, right? Starts out okay, first page she's going along, gradually slipping out of things and rubbing herself with a velvet pillow and a bunch of grapes and musing; but then, turn the page, *she's outraged*. 'You want me to *what*? What kind of girl . . .' *Furious*. Eyes flashing, hair rumpled. Shot of her throwing her blouse and skirt back on; shot of her stomping out half-buttoned with bra in hand. *She's gone. She never gets naked.* For months, letters. 'Can't you talk Candy Veronese of your August issue into coming back?' 'Who does this Candy Veronese think she is, holding out on us? Signed, The Sixth Fleet.' Does she come back? Maybe. Maybe not. Negotiations ensue. Some months, we report, she seems mollified. Sometimes she's pouting.

"I know what you're going to say. We'd never find a model who'd actually get outraged. But the readers don't know that. We could find one who could fake it.

"Letters. No more 'I never believed any of those letters you print about prolonged bouts of passionate oral lovemaking right on top of the teacher's desk while everyone in the room looked on, that is until my History of Western Civ class yesterday.' That stuff is played out. You need to attract a different tone of letters. You might get a few that sounded like letters to the *Times* of London on sighting the first cuckoo of the spring, only they would be about vulvae. We could get lively controversies going between top authorities, in which they could call each other filthy names.

"Service articles. Edible panties — how are they nutritionally? Simple methods for keeping count of your climaxes in a swimming pool. What to do for snakebite of the cervix. How to regain your footing on Wesson Oil. Again: imagination.

"Advice column. It's 'Ask Our Amy.' All kinds of gamy questions come in — *and Amy doesn't understand any of them.* She has grown up sheltered, refers to beaver as 'down there,' gives incredibly naive advice. Gets so embarrassed finally she says she thinks she's going to cry. So now everybody is writing in, explaining things to *her.* Nicely. Gently. Affectionately.

"Gradually, gradually, over a course of months, she begins to get hip. Opens up to things. Wears more and more revealing clothes in her picture. Even gets a little rowdy in an unaffected way. Everybody is *hot.* Everybody's heart *opens. She drives everybody in the country CRAZY!*

"Then . . . she begins to go over the edge. Bit by bit her advice, her features, coarsen. She gets into and advocates hard liquor, drugs, every kind of group and individual debasement. People write in: 'Amy, don't cheapen yourself!' She advises them to shove it. Finally, above her last column, she sits there brazenly spread and smeared all over with margarine and making a pun about it. Well. It's what America for so long has been dying to see. But now, somehow, it isn't so great. Her face is not the same. Her advice has become jaded, glazed over.

Next month we announce we had to let her go. She is reported doing French Dominant in a Newark massage parlor, for free. Then she drops out of sight entirely. So many people haven't been moved to tears since the death of Little Nell."

I didn't know what to say.

"It's tough," Utterbund conceded. "It's life. Her kid sister takes over the column."

I told him I thought a job on a magazine like that would be too much for me emotionally. "But, Eddie," I said, "you're a visionary."

"That's not what you said," he replied, "when I told you they were going to show pink."

BETWEEN MEALS SONG

I want to gnaw your ankles,
Root behind your knees,
Nip your bended elbows,
Browse your forehead, please.

   Oh, let's make love and supper with-
   Out washing off our hands.
   Eat prairie oysters, turkey breasts and
   Other sav'ry glands.
   Let's make love and supper with-
   Out washing off our hands.

I want to wrinkle your neck's nape
And stretch out your back's small.
Go "This little piggy" on your toes
And darling that ain't all.

I want to heft your two prize calves
And play like you're a farm
And I'm the farmer and my house is
Underneath your arm.

I'll cultivate your collarbone,
Achilles' tendon, palm
And ears inside and out and lobes
And hair on end or calm.

I like your eyelids and your hip
And relatives and friends.
Your navel is a constant source
As are your finger ends.

The bottoms of your feet rate high
Before and after bath;
I want to reckon on your ribs
Whenever I do math.

I'm taken by your vertebrae
And back behind your ears,
Your adam's apple, temples and
Most of your ideas.

Oh, let's make love and supper with-
Out washing off our hands.
Eat prairie oysters, turkey breasts and
Other sav'ry glands.
Let's make love and supper with-
Out washing off our hands.

JEALOUSY SONG

My darlin is dancin with some asshole.
It burns my behind, I must confess.
I think I'll go see if he can wrassle,
And if he can I'll think of somethin ess —

I'm goin to . . .
                          get that stupid shit
Who's dancin with my darlin,
Stomp on him with the strength of ten —

I'm goin to . . .
                          kick the livin shit
Out of my darlin's partner
And fix him so he'll never dance agin.

THE WAGES OF FUN

THANK God I am married, is all I can say. I walk the streets of the city and see poor, single, promiscuous wretches, with these slightly-less-tight jeans and hangdog looks: their genitals have either fallen off or imploded. I was single once. I know what goes on.

Stumble out of one partner's bed; don't wash; have a couple of vodkas, a number, maybe a little *fnf, fnf*; meet some strange piece of stuff at Sam Goody's and off you go again. Whammity-whammity. (How do you ever get any work done? When do you write your mother?) *I* know.

Seem like fun, don't it? Seem like heaven.

It ain't heaven, brothers and sisters.

It is Hell.

They told me, when I was growing up in Georgia, in the Methodist Youth Fellowship: it would be Hell. And I believed them. Then I saw a series of French films and got divorced and met all these . . . *partners* and I didn't believe it anymore.

Hey, you know, the body is a holy thing. And the ecumenical message is: There are a *lot* of holy things. With these really neat swells and declivities, and the most essential of oils, and barely perceptible down.

And the Methodist Youth Fellowship message is (I remember a talk we heard about how you may think the Duke and Duchess of Windsor are cool, but *wait a minute,* she was *divorced*): you screw around and okay, buddy, you get a vile disease. You're lucky you get to screw *at all.* Back off — *way* off — from *around.*

And the Methodist Youth Fellowship was right. The Pill gives you cancer and the herpes never dies. Lord! Lord! Ain't nothing that fills your soul and don't eat your nose out and don't rot your vitals but Jesus.

Or Moses. Or Jesse Helms, Jr.

Lord.

It don't pertain to me anymore. I'm settled down a family man once again, in the country. I wouldn't doubt we have a certain amount of paresis up here in our town but I don't think there's any herpes, yet. Though who knows? Who after all knows? I'm worried about going down to the post office, afraid of who on up the line somewhere has been handling my mail.

Talk about Communism!

It is a hell of a note when you can't be a roving port-in-every-girl bandito anymore. You notice the U.S. secretary of state hasn't been running around with bimbos, now, for a number of years. Kissinger swore it all off and married a clean woman. Cyrus Vance had a bad back. Alexander Haig has other things on his mind.

But forget about the federal level. We got to get down to the *personal* level. We got to accept that the sexual revolution is over and a certain number of people, if they don't watch out, going to be caught standing outside the Bastille waving their swords and grinning, and waving their swords, and grinning, and beginning to wave their swords a little slower, and beginning to grin a little narrower, and checking out what is accumulating in the atmosphere around them, and letting their swords kind of decline, and beginning to mumble, well, I wasn't

really *revolting,* you know, I was just, I just thought . . .
*Oh please have mercy oh God I didn't know, I was just young
you know and bliss was it then to be alive and, and, I see now I
should've realized but, oh, I'll . . . can I join a convent or something, please . . .*

You know why a dog licks his balls?
No. Why?
Because he can.
And you know why we would do every vileness and call it
sweet?
Because we could.
Yes. But. We can't anymore.
And do you know why, now, they will look at our every
sweetness and call it vile?
Because they can.

I had a conversation the other day with a guy in Pittsburgh
who said he had *psychosomatic* herpes. From worrying about it.
"You know it came to this country from Peru," he said.
"No. I didn't know that."
"From llamas."
"*Fernando Lamas!?*"
"No. *Llamas.* From guys screwing *animals.*"
"No!"
Who knows how much truth there is to that? But I'll tell
you this. My friend Slick Lawson of Nashville once visited a
Cajun home, and it was time for supper, so the father hollered
to the eldest son, who was up on a ladder painting one side of
the house:
"Alphonse! Unclimb that ladda! It's dinna time!"
Sisters and brothers, the time has come. We got to unclimb
that ladder. We got to get down off our high libidinal horse.

We got to look toward new yesterdays. We got to *stop* . . . being . . . *loose*.

Thank God I am married, is all I can say.

Don't be coming up here where I live in the country looking for salvation, with your infections, your carcinogenesis, your . . .

You know a word that is going to come back in vogue?

Pox.

NO BIGGER THAN A MINUTE

Maybe you're like six foot four
And I'm just four foot ten,
Maybe I'm just a little bitty woman
And you're all great big men,

But you think you can outgo me?
I'm tempted just to laugh.
I ain't no bigger than a minute
But I can go like an hour and a half.

Oh I ain't no bigger than a minute,
I'm cute as a newborn calf,
But when it comes to going, boys,
I can go like an hour and a half.

Set your watches ticking, boys,
Swing that old long hand.
Mine may be a whole lot shorter
But it's got a longer span.

When it comes to watches, boys,
I'm right there fore and aft.
I ain't no bigger than a minute
But I can go like an hour and a half.

(Chorus)

Oh I don't punch nobody's clock,

Ain't nobody's maid.
Ain't nobody's play-toy either,
They're the ones get played.

I've held longtime positions on
Many a high-level staff.
I ain't no bigger than a minute
But I can go like an hour and a half.

(Chorus)

SPORTS AFIELD

Then ye returned to your trinkets; then ye contented your souls
With the flannelled fools at the wickets or the muddied oafs at the goals.

— Rudyard Kipling, "The Islander"

FIVE IVES GETS NAMED

J IM! Me! Calling from the *big* leagues! You know, them leagues Ty Cobb and Warren Spahn was in! Woooo!

I *know* it's great. Jim, you would not believe tonight. I got a nickname, I — Yeah, I'll call Pop. But I can't tell him all of it. Don't want to disillusion Pop about the BIG LEAGUES.

No, it's not — Just let me tell you. It is late, isn't it? Is that the baby crying? Shit, I'm . . . You shoulda been up here, Jim. Waiting to show me around. Like in Little League and high school. If it hadn't been for your knee. Yeah.

I'm *going* to tell you. Yeah, *sort* of drunk. In New York. Jim, I ain't going to get mugged. You're worse than Pop. No, I just mean — listen, I walk in this afternoon. Right? Visiting clubhouse YANKEE DAMN STADIUM, Jim. Summoned up by the Techs.

Course, yeah, we didn't exactly grow up drooling to be Techs. Cause there wasn't any then. But if the Dodgers'd held on to me I'd still be in Lodi. Techs pick me up, this Perridge breaks his leg, and I get a CALL, Jim.

Only thing, to get here, I have to grab two buses and a red-eye. And I walk into the dressing room with zip sleep. And first thing, this Spanish guy jumps on my back. Yelling, jib-dyjibdyjibdy, ninety miles an hour. Then this bald black guy with a big gut who is stepping real painfully into his pants yells across the room, "Ju-lo get off the man's back! He don't even speak Spanish!"

"Jibdyjibdyjibdy espik Esponish!?" the guy yells. And he gets off me, like he's pissed I'm not bilingle, and he goes to his locker and I see the name, it's Julio Uribe! You remember, played second for the Orioles a couple years and bounced around, yeah. And — Jim, the fat guy is Boom Holmes! "God DAMN my feet!" he yells, and that's my greeting to the Techs.

Except just then I meet my Peerless Leader. Berkey. Yells out from his office, "Who you!" Jesus who'd he think I was, I'm the only guy got sent up. I go in, kind of salute, like reporting to duty, only he don't laugh. He is sitting there eating a — looks like maybe a Franco-American-spaghetti sandwich, real wet, and there's a big bottle of Maalox on his desk, and he looks at me like I'm already overpaid. "Can you mbunt?" he wants to know. Is all he wants to know. I don't know whether he can manage, but he has a lot of trouble with his *b*'s.

"Yeah," I say. He's a big sumbitch but a real old sour-looking guy, Jim, looks like Mr. Wiedl used to teach us history and be pissed all the time because we didn't care about the broad sweep of the great human saga. Only Berkey I guess is pissed because the Techs just about got a lock on last place in June. Yeah.

Anyway, what Berkey does, he grabs me by the arm and drags me back out into the dressing room and hollers at everybody, "This guy can mbunt! He prombly can't play, but he can mbunt!" And he goes back in his office with his wet sandwich.

And I'm standing there. Clubhouse guy shows me my locker — I'm dressing next to Hub Kopf. Yeah, right. He is talking to Junior Wren. Yeah, used to have the crippled-children commercial. And here's what they are saying:

"Your *niece!* How could you . . . ?"

"Axly it was more my half-niece," says Junior Wren.

"How the fuck . . . ?"

"Anyway she was adopted, I think."

"You *think*. You didn't *know*?"

"Anyway she was in these little shorts and halter and she had this raspberry wine . . . and I gave her a little bump. Next morning I felt so bad, I quit smoking."

Here I am hearing this shit from guys was All-Stars once, and meanwhile I am *wasted*. "I'm Reed Ives," I say. Cause I'm new in this whole organization, they don't know me. "I'm wasted," I say.

"Welcome to the AL," says Junior. "Have one." And he gives me a pill.

So — no, I wouldn't ever depend on it, no, but anyway I pop this thing, and then I ask, "What is it?"

You're right . . . but — anyway, "Five milligrams," he says.

I never did half that! And I'm sitting there thinking, "Oh Jesus. Five milligrams."

And the next thing, I'm on the field running all over like I've had twenty hours sleep. Playing pepper, taking grounders, little b.p. — yeah, I got ahold of a couple pretty good — and then, though, the game starts.

And I'm sitting. And I'm, you know, VAW-AW-AW-AWM. There's these billions of dollars' worth of Yankees out there a few feet in front of my face, and I'm jumping up, getting water, sitting back down, jumping up, taking a leak and thirty thousand people are screaming all up above and behind me and Junior Wren is looking over and nudging Hub Kopf, and they're giggling, and Berkey is glaring at me. Cause I'm not even *seeing* the game. I'm sitting there exploding thinking, "Five milligrams!"

And suddenly Berkey grabs me, drags me off into the tunnel. I can't believe it, I'm about to fly into smithereens and

Berkey is yelling, "If you tell anymbody what I'm mbout to tell you I'll mbeat your ass."

I'm going Whaaaat and he's saying, "Mbefore I was mborn my father was hunting with a preacher named Harding Earth. That preacher stood up at the wrong time and my father shot him in the temple, killed him outright. Preacher was to mblame mbut my father swore right then he'd have a son, and name him Harding Earth mBerkey and have him mbe a preacher. He had that son. It was me. Only he never told me. Till the day he died. He told me then. He told me he had done everything in his power, without telling me, to make me grow up to want to mbe a preacher. Mbut I grew up to want to play mball. That's how much I wanted to play mball. If *you* don't want to play mball, I don't want you *around*."

And he leaves me and I ease back to the bench with my brakes jammed on, and I'm sitting there dazed next to Roe Humble — yeah, he's okay — Humble says, "He give you the shoot-the-preacher story?"

And I just nod and I have no idea the status of the game and next thing, Berkey is standing in front of me, trembling. And he says, "Let's *see* you mbunt."

And he's sending me up! I don't even know who I'm hitting for. I'm in the game! Against — you know who pitched tonight for the Yankees?

Tommy Damn John. My first up in the big leagues. Only, I'm not thinking Tommy John. I'm thinking, "Five milligrams!"

And here comes this pitch — well, you know Tommy John don't waste any time but it seems to me he is idling *very* low, and I'm jumping up and down and "Five milligrams!" and here comes this dippy-do sinker, wandering up to the plate like its heart's not in it, and I square off to bunt, which in my present state means I am holding the bat like it's an alligator, and, dum, de dum, Sink, the ball drops and I miss it a foot.

Yeah. I *know* Pop taught us. But — and the same thing happens the second pitch. "Five milligrams!" is blasting in my head and then, oh-and-two, he wastes a fastball up and away. And you know, Jim, I like that pitch. I could even hit you, when I was nine, and you threw me something up there. Went *with* it. And Jim, I got it all.

Jim, I took Tommy John out of Yankee Stadium at the three-eighty-five in right center. Two men on, we're only behind one run for some reason, and WOOOM I put us ahead. I'm circling the damn Yankee damn Stadium bases, and you know, on the postgame shows they always ask 'em, "What were you thinking about, rounding the bases?"? I'm thinking, "FIVE MILLIGRAMS!"

And I cross the plate and Boom Holmes gives me a high-five — Boom Holmes gives me one, Jim — which, a *high*-five, is appropriate as shit. And he says, "I didn't know you was that *strawng.*"

And all I can think to do is, now everybody's slapping at me, is open my mouth and holler, "FIVE! FIVE!"

And Junior Wren and Hub Kopf are rolling around in the dugout, and acourse, what the hell, we don't hold the lead, Jim. But in the dressing room afterwards everybody is hollering, "Five!" "The Big Five!" "Five Ives!"

"Why're you calling him Five?" this reporter asks Boom, and he says, "Well, that's ghetto talk, you know. That's some *street* talk, there. Means . . . Means he got the full five faingers on it, you know," and Junior Wren and Hub and Uribe and everybody else except maybe Berkey knows the truth — they're yelling, "*Full* Five." "F. F. Ives." And —

Well, yeah, I guess it is a shame, sort of. Never know, yeah, whether I could've done it just straight, first time up. Yeah. But, Jim, you know, if I'd been straight I'd've *sacrificed*.

You're right, that'd been sound baseball.

So, yeah. So, sorry I woke the baby — tell Sharon. I guess I better go, I'm in this restaurant somewhere. I'm *still up*, Jim. And Jim, there's this honey at the bar —

Yeah, maybe they don't call them honey in New York. I'll call her something else.

I took Tommy John out of the Stadium, Jim! No, not all the way out, nobody ever — I know. But that's the expression . . . uh-huh.

So . . . Well, thanks. I will. I'll watch it. Yeah. Hey Jim, don't, you know, don't tell Pop.

WHY THERE WILL NEVER BE A GREAT BOWLING NOVEL

I HAVE agreed that from time to time the weight of this column will be thrown behind, or on top of, or just slightly to one side of (due to unavoidable human error) some "participant" sport. God knows why. Oh, there is some notion in the magazine business that participant, as opposed to spectator, sports are the coming thing. Myself, I would define a participant sport as one that is not being done very well. When you write about such a sport you must either advise people on what is the best shaft for a niblick, pay tribute to some anonymous fool, or write about yourself. And I hate to expose myself to my pitiless scrutiny. It is true enough that I have at times been as good a softball player as I have ever seen. But by and large as I participate in a sport, I watch myself with no pleasure other than the perverse satisfaction one might derive from reading, years later, one's high-school diary.

But what the hell. Bowling. A bowling alley was where Jack Nicholson picked up Sally Struthers in *Five Easy Pieces,* but I'm married now so that's out. I once talked to Satchel Paige at a party following one of Willie Stargell's sickle-cell-anemia-benefit bowling tournaments. Paige said something about liking fried chicken. "I thought you advised people to avoid fried foods, which angry up the blood," cut in a listener.

"I said, 'Avoid 'em.' I didn't say I avoided 'em," explained Paige.

That's about all the bowling lore I have to offer from my own experience. But I figured I could come up with some by consulting friends in the media. Here are the responses I received to the question, "Know any good bowling stories?":

• "My roommate's mother was bowling champion of West Virginia."

• "I was *forced* to bowl in the Army."

• "Good *boring* stories?"

• " 'Rip Van Winkle.' "

Bowling just doesn't seem to come alive somehow. There has never been a great bowling novel. (What would it be called? *Three Finger Exercise. Rumble!*) There has never even been a great bowling song, to my knowledge, except of course for "Proud Mary keep on bowling."

Even my friend and mentor Vereen Bell in Nashville let me down. Usually Vereen will tell you a good story. For instance, when he was playing basketball for Quitman High School in south Georgia, his team traveled to a larger school, walked out on the court, and saw, for the first time, transparent plastic backboards. "They don't have a backboard!" cried one of his teammates. "I can't play without a backboard!"

Just the other day Vereen was at his health club watching one of the instructors there advise a man on bench pressing. "Take deep breaths," said the instructor. "That's good in bench presses and in *all* walks of life."

But the best Vereen could come up with in the way of a bowling story was: "The other day I overheard a woman telling about how tired she was the night before. She said, 'I was so tired I couldn't go bowling!' "

Well. My friend Kim Chapin did say that he once heard a professional bowler tell about a party at his house at which the bowler's mother wound up getting thrown into the bathtub, nude. His *mother?* "The bowling tour is wilder than people realize," said Kim.

"Also, bowlers go to séances. To find out how they're going to do. Race-car drivers' wives and professional bowlers — big on séances."

Now I can't imagine a livelier column than one that would accompany a bowler to a séance at which, while he is trying to divine whether he will convert a 1-10 split in the big tourney tomorrow, the spirit of his drowned mother appears crying, "You son of a bitch!" But remember, this month we're into *participant,* not professional, sport.

All right. A friend of the family, Maggie Johnson of New Zealand, disclosed that she had never been bowling. Never been bowling! And people from New Zealand talk funny — say "Git it togither" instead of "Git it together." Ought to be something in that. To make sure, we took not only Maggie but also the kids out bowling. Kids add a lot to a bowling evening. It may take five minutes for the ball to reach the pins. While it is rolling, they ask for another Coke. We hit the nearest alley, which at the time was on the West Side of Manhattan.

Stepping through the street-level door, we were confronted with a narrow staircase. The word *Kill* was scrawled prominently on one wall and a scrofulous-looking shopping-bag lady was sitting crumpled on the first step.

My children challenge all direct orders. When the television tells them, "Eat Wheaties," they cry out immediately, "Why should I eat Wheaties?"

"Why should I kill?" said my son Kirven.

"It is easy enough to take moral stances at your age," I told him. "Now step over the shopping-bag lady and —"

"Why should I step over the shopping-bag lady?"

"Because she is there. Now let's go upstairs and bowl."

When we reached the alley, however, the proprietor said the kids could watch but not participate. "City ordinance," he explained. "No kids can bowl after six o'clock. Inspector comes in and checks, we get a ticket. Thirty-five dollars. *Kid* gets a ticket. Thirty-five dollars."

"What's the point of that?"

"One of these old blue-laws," he shrugged.

We all left. The shopping-bag lady was still there. Writing a good bowling story in a puritan society is not easy.

But wait. I hadn't given up. My brother-in-law Rick Ackermann once got his name posted on the bulletin board in an alley in Ibiza for his achievements on a lane which sloped sharply off to one side for part of the way and then sharply off to the other side for the rest of the way.

When I heard that I thought: Perhaps what bowling needs is a more interesting terrain. Maybe even bridges or water obstacles, like in miniature golf.

Or psychological obstacles. Ah. Bowling as an existential act. If I'd been in Paris when all this came to me I would have hotfooted it right over to the Deux Magots and challenged Sartre to a few lines. Unfortunately I happened to be in a small town in southern New Mexico.

I was interviewing a horseman. "I think I'll go bowling in town tonight," I told him.

"Huh. Watch out for sharpies," he said.

Sharpies. What would a bowling sharpie — a *cowboy* bowling sharpie — look like, I wondered as I stepped into the Bowl-a-Matic that evening. I don't know about you, but when I walk into someplace like a bowling alley in a small western town, I expect to be pounced on and stomped any minute. And if some kind of heavy hustling was going on to boot . . . If I beat somebody, what measures would be taken? Would somebody try to break my fingers? *Inside* the ball?

Oh, no. I couldn't *type* with a bowling ball stuck on my hand. One hand would be all right, but my lead might go something like: "(Smash)(Smash)t(Smash)(Smash)(Smash)ed aga(Smash)(Smash)st a b(Smash)(Smash)e(Smash)gra(Smash) (Smash)ct(Smash)ber s(Smash)(Smash) . . ." The best doctors in the country would be trying everything — scooting my hand and the ball with a hose — to get me loose.

There were some rough-looking old boys, and girls, in there, all right. They eyed me. I rented some shoes. I put them on. I went over to the ball rack, started sticking my fingers into the town balls. Sure that any minute a chill would fall over the room. Somebody would come over with his hand on his gun. "Stranger, that's the *sheriff's* ball. . . ."

I made my selection. I began to bowl. Nobody said anything. Well. Maybe I have the kind of presence that keeps sharpies away. I knew I didn't have as much presence as a guy back home who once, after knocking down only two pins with two balls, slowly walked the length of the lane and kicked all the others over with his foot; but maybe there was something about the way I blended all those hard surfaces in one fluid interface climaxing in explosion, vum vum vum vum rml rml rml rml ESCHATOLOGY!, that earned the homespun respect of these people.

I bowled several lines. The crowd thinned out. At last, it was just me and the two guys I figured must be the sharpies. They both had toothpicks in their mouths.

My confidence began to wane. Maybe they would try to stomp me *with* a bowling ball.

Why stay on, then? To test myself. When I was but a lad shooting baskets by myself in the back yard in bad weather, I would say, "Okay, sink six out of ten and then go in." I would hit five. That would piss me off. "All right, I'll show you — *seven* out of ten. Or we're not going in. Ever." My hands would get cold and wet and muddy. Darkness would approach. Swish. Thunk. I would grow to hate myself, and the ball, and the rim, as strongly as one is supposed to hate an opponent in order to win. I learned a great lesson out there on that small muddy court: Don't participate seriously in sports.

But here in New Mexico I had my column to do. How many games would it take to prove something? Going into the last frame of the seventh game, I decided to forget about it. It looked as if nobody was going to try to sharp me.

"I make this spare," I said, "I call it a night."

I missed it.

And when I looked again at the two guys I had thought were sharpies, I realized what they were: the guys who had to close up. They had changed into their boots and they were squinting at me hard. They wanted to go home.

Pressure.

"Okay. You got to bowl a one-forty before you quit," I told myself.

Eighth game: one-thirty-seven.

Ninth game: one-twenty.

Frankly, now I'm worried. It must seem to the two guys that I am trying to be a smart-ass or something. They aren't saying anything. Just chewing their toothpicks. What if they make me back down from myself?

I start the tenth game. Pick up a couple of spares. Couple of strikes — great sounds in bowling, I'll give it that: vum vum rml rml rml rml DEBACLE!

Sweating. Arm very tired. Come to the last frame. Hear one of the two guys call the other one "Vern." *Never* let a cowboy named Vern think you are having fun at his expense. Vern, I swear to you, I'm not. I am bowling blood.

Need a spare. Rommel rommel rommel rommel KRAKA-TOA!

One pin left.

Rmmmbl-l rmmmbl-l rmmmbl-l rmmmbl-l P . . . L . . . ONK!

Pick it up.

Last ball, all I need's a couple of pins, I don't even concentrate. Nonchalant it. Get four.

One-forty-three. By God, don't nobody go around saying I'm scared to come into your town and bowl.

Vern doesn't say that. "Quat a little workout," he says when I pay. He says it hard.

I'm tempted to say, "Well. Where was all your sharpies at tonight?" But don't push it. Gracious in victory. " 'Ep" is all I say.

I start my exit.

"Uh," Vern says. I freeze. I have nothing, not even a ball, to throw at them. I turn.

"Them're ars," he says.

I look down.

I don't guess anybody out there has any good "Why I am walking out onto the mean streets of New Mexico wearing the house's green-and-red-striped shoes" lines.

After this first appeared, Docteur Georges-Guy Maruani of Paris wrote to inform me that there is in fact a great bowling novel: La truite, by Roger Vailland. Imagine my consternation to find that this novel is written entirely in French. Which I read slowly. So as this goes to print, I am taking Dr. Maruani's word for it. There is one great bowling novel. La truite. And nothing but La truite.

BALLOONING WITH SLICK

THE faithful reader of this column, hapless dupe though he be (be? is? were? am?) — hapless dupe though he am — will have noticed that I have not fulfilled my promise to write at frequent intervals on participant sports. I have not done it because — what are you going to say about them? "A large group of us went skiing in Vermont last weekend, including my friend Mayo Whitsett and his wife Amber and several other people you never heard of either, and the snow was good — well, it was pretty good — and we all went *wheeeeeeeeeeeeeeeee*, and it looks like more and more people are into these Montagnard X-2's that will release your feet only when you scream but then will let go of them in two-tenths of a second, according to the specifications, but then there are a lot of pros and cons on that. . . ." It's either that kind of thing or you have to get *really* serious, because spectator sports are fantasy but participant sports — let me put it this way: nobody is watching but God.

Well, anyway, *I am up in a damn balloon.* I'm skimming the top of a persimmon tree and pulling off a persimmon and biting it. There are only eight hot-air balloons in Tennessee and I am up in one of them, *The Ubiquitous Serpent.*

Voilà. The above is another first for this column. Last month we participated in a holdout, and this month we have blocked out our lead in a damn balloon. I didn't have my typewriter up there, to be sure, but I did block out the above lead in my head while, yes, veritably brushing the crest of a hundred-foot Franklin, Tennessee, persimmon tree and looking straight down on the backs of startled rabbits, deer and cattle. And looking down on a man, standing next to his pickup, who hollered, "How y'all boys doin'?" and we hollered down, "Got three gret big persimmons."

We were in Slick Lawson's balloon — Slick, my sweet wife Joan and I. Slick, whose formal name is W. E., maintains that he was nicknamed Slick from birth because of his expeditious departure from the womb. He's a Nashville photographer — shoots album covers, gubernatorial candidates, Tennessee-whiskey ads, beautiful bare-breasted women waving speared catfish and running from an inflated shark (to illustrate the invitations for his annual catfish fry). In his living room he has a picture of himself *taken by* Johnny Cash. That is the level of Music City photographer Slick is. Also he is the author of the song title "Last Night I Won the Dance Contest (But I Can't Take the Trophy Home)."

That's another thing about participant sports. I'm afraid I'll lose my sense of sin in them. That's why you didn't catch Faulkner waterskiing or doing some other damn thing. He'd go out and chase animals and shoot at them, but that's different — that's at least about half wrong, and therefore pertinent. The only thing I can think of that is wrong about riding a balloon is that if the Devil had taken Jesus up in a balloon instead of onto a mountaintop — but no, the Devil don't ride a damn balloon, I don't believe. Even though Slick, with his frizzly greying hair and beard and nimble, chunky trunk-forward carriage and his face like a mobile bag of little apples, looks more like Pan than anybody else I have ever known personally. And even though the balloon's burner is like a dragon's mouth, puts out fifteen million BTU's an hour, which is enough to heat a small building, and makes this *raarrghph* sound. Off to our right we could see the other two balloons of our party, Butch Stamps's and Allen "Deux Rite" Sullivan's. They were floating, looking prettier than lighter-than-air Easter eggs, and off and on roaring like hoarse lions.

Slick first went up in a balloon a few years ago, in the balloon of Eric Sosbe, who as a Vanderbilt football player distinguished himself by his response to a disparaging remark he heard while coming off the field against the University of Tennessee. His response was to go up into where the UT band was sitting and whip the piccolo player. (If that had happened at the time I was at Vanderbilt in the early sixties, it would have been the high-water mark of a whole era of VU football.)

Slick crewed on the balloon owned by Allen T. Sullivan, a stockbroker, and Franklin Jarman, a shoe magnate, until finally at his own insistence they certified him trained, and now he's an FAA-licensed aeronaut and the owner of *The Ubiquitous Serpent,* which has huge serpents of Pueblo Indian design emblazoned around the surface of its envelope, the part of the balloon that inflates. The envelope, made of Dacron, is the size of a seven-story building.

The part you stand in is the basket, made of wicker and suede, about three feet deep and big enough around to hold three propane tanks and three people standing. The basket is tough; we dragged and jounced through the treetops in it, and Slick once entered the annual Atlanta raft race by landing the basket in the Chattahoochee River.

The part that makes the balloon go up, by converting the propane to hot air, is the burner, which is suspended over the basket and is about the size of a chain saw. Sometimes you "gimble the burner." Or *gimbel.* I asked Slick's ballooning confrere David Eastland how you spell *gimbal* and he said, "Hell,

I don't know. Why would a writer ask me how to spell something?"

Gimbal the burner is the only technical ballooning term I picked up. It sounds like the title of an Isaac Bashevis Singer short story, but it means to rotate the burner at an angle, because the wind is pushing the envelope out at an angle and you have to direct the hot air into it.

There isn't any part that steers the balloon. You can cause the balloon to soar by turning on the burner and to subside by turning it off, and you can make the balloon sink abruptly by pulling on a rope that opens up a big hole in the top of the envelope, and you can navigate by soaring or subsiding into the wind currents that ease and swoop and shift along valleys and up and over slopes, but you can't sail into the wind. You usually don't even feel the wind, because you're not resisting it, you're in and of it. There are "hound and hare" competitions that entail following the hare balloon's course as closely as possible, but you don't know where you're going to wind up. You've got a chase car following you to pick you up, and you just aim not to come down on power lines or interstates or farm animals. Or barn roofs. Or bonfires. The best ballooning stories are about coming down.

When another Tennessee balloonist landed in a farmer's field, the farmer got off his tractor and came up to him and said, "Where you headed?"

"Nowhere in particular," said the balloonist.

"Well, you made it," the farmer said. Then he went back to his tractor and resumed plowing.

Six people were killed ballooning in this country during the past year, Eastland told me before I went up, "but in every case it was pilot error." He acted as though that point should reassure me. "But my pilot is going to be Slick," I told him.

"That's true," said Eastland. After all, Slick is, by his own account, a man who once seized a fire extinguisher at a black-tie affair and covered two prominent Nashvillians with foam because they were taxing him for his informal dress and then on leaving the party went to a restaurant called The Gold Rush, did a backflip through the front door, whirled and exclaimed, "Who in here wants to fight or fuck? Either one, because I don't get out much."

Slick, however, gave us an orderly ride. Someone had stolen the stereo and headphones out of *The Ubiquitous Serpent's* basket, so we weren't listening to Mozart, but I didn't need any Mozart, myself. I must have flown five hundred thousand miles in my life and that was the first time I ever felt like I was *flying* — and I mean really flying, like in a dream. We came over those hills easy and smooth as the moon.

The first man who ever achieved flight in anything, you know, was Jean Pilâtre de Rozier, in 1783, in a hot-air balloon whose paper-and-cloth envelope was made by the Montgolfier brothers, who burned wet straw and wool on a pan and thought it was the smoke that made the balloon rise. Ballooning moved from hot air to gas, and Pilâtre de Rozier was later killed when another Montgolfier balloon exploded while he attempted to cross the English Channel in it. It wasn't until the 1960s that people started getting back into hot-air ballooning. Hot air is a lot cheaper than helium; you can have a nice hour-and-a-half flight for just eight dollars' worth of propane.

"What's yer initial cost getting into a balloon?" some curious old boys hollered up at us once when we swooped low. "About six or seven thousand," Slick cried. For the price of a station wagon, you can move like the down of a thistle.

Another Tennessee balloonist once came down way out in the middle of nowhere, didn't know where he was. His chase car didn't show up. He waited and waited. It got dark. He saw two big headlights bearing down on him. Realized, then, he was standing in the dirt bed of an unfinished stretch of highway. Saw the headlights start to tumble. Saw them smash into a bank a few feet away.

Ran to the car and found the driver, who was of a race different from his own, badly hurt. Wondered whether he should do mouth-to-mouth. Resisted the notion. Saw the driver die.

Another car approached. The balloonist hollered at the driver to come help. The driver, who was of the victim's race, got out of his car and saw a man in a fancy flight suit beckoning. "Come on, I need to show you something," the balloonist said, casting about for the appropriate words.

The driver edged close. He finally peered into the car. There, where the balloonist was pointing, was a corpse. He ran back to his car and drove away.

And there was the balloonist, no more lights of any kind in sight, a downed balloon and a dead man on his hands.

Peasants, thinking they were seeing either a demon or the moon that had fallen because of something they had done, would set upon the early French balloons with pitchforks when they landed. But nothing like that happened to us in Slick's balloon. Our chase Jeep showed up right away, and Slick went and introduced himself to the man in whose field we'd landed — a Mr. Frazier, who sociably opened his fence gates for us so we could get the Jeep and trailer in and load up the *Serpent*. Then we were off to a nearby restaurant for steak, eggs, grits, turnip greens, beer and, in my case at least, a sense of dissatisfaction over not still being afloat, not still looking intimately down into the trees the way I used to think only birds and angels could.

MY B.P.

IF you get caught, pummeled by security police, and hauled before Commissioner Kuhn like a common Finley, don't say I told you this was legal. All I'm saying is that if you're very discreet and act like you know what you're doing, you can probably get away with it. Pick a nice unspectacular weeknight game. Get to the park early, at least two hours before game time. Buy a field-level ticket, avoid ushers once you're inside the park, stride purposefully past your seat to one of those little gates in the fence near the dugout, walk right onto the field, proceed to the batting cage and lean against it.

Now remember, you're not out there to solicit autographs, cop baseballs or broach business propositions. Try any of that stuff and you deserve pummeling. You are out there as a student of the game who can't really nurture his feel for it without a close-up view of batting practice.

Often batting practice at close range is more impressive than the game. In bad weather at home the Reds hit in a small netted enclosure under the stands. Just a pitching machine, a bunch of baseballs, sixty feet six inches, a home plate, and Morgan and Bench and Rose and all those guys, one after the other, swinging away. Deep in the cellarlike bowels of Riverfront Stadium. It's dark under there. FOOP of the machine, hiss of the offering, grunt of the Red, ineffable sound (*Crack* will have to do) of sweet vicious contact, CLONK or THWOP or SSNK of the ball stopped by metal, pad, or netting. FOOP sss unh *Crack* CLONK. FOOP sss mf *Crack* THWOP SSNK. (Sometimes the ball bounces off the pad and into the net and you get both a THWOP and a SSNK.) Stadium mice dig deeper into their holes and the concrete walls resound. Vulcan at his forge doesn't touch it. It is like Joan Sutherland singing in the shower.

Normal outdoor live-pitching batting practice (or b.p., as players call it) is airier and more social. Journeyman outfielder Jim Gosger used to do an imitation of Babe Ruth. He would put batting helmets in his shirt to simulate the belly, and he'd take mammoth swings and little prancing pigeon-toed steps. Once in Yankee Stadium the Angels' late Chico Ruiz, a light hitter, drove a b.p. pitch over the fence. Immediately he dropped his bat, ran into the right-field corner, vaulted into the stands, and wrote his name and the date on the seat where the ball had landed. When humorist/ex-catcher Bob Uecker threw batting practice for the Braves he would do his impressions of various odd-looking pitchers around the league. "Dick Hall!" Braves around the cage would cry, and Uecker would give them Hall's strange turkey-neck delivery.

Even outdoors, however, b.p. is not just whimsy. Standing behind the cage you appreciate the *force* of a pitch, even a relatively easy one. The lower half of the batting cage is covered with canvas. When a pitch strikes that canvas it makes a loud FOMP! On television the ball is a thin white streak. In the cage it is not only sudden but *strong*. It puts up *resistance*. Getting into a high inside fastball and pulling it for distance is like snatching an outboard motor off your chest and horsing it up onto a chin-high truck bed in one smooth move.

Not that heft is all. To see the young whippy wrist-hitting

Henry Aaron flick his bat out to arrest a ball's momentum and convert it into a long carrying streak in the opposite direction was to see a form of power. . . . Well, to me *power* has negative connotations — armaments, bossism, throwing weight around, Michael Korda. The young Aaron's power was fine like dancing.

But fiercer. *"Rip city,"* you might hear a crowd of onlooking hitters cry in admiration of a b.p. cut that produces a savage line drive. The ball a batter slashes into is something that under game conditions might come at him and fracture his head.

Some players don't like batting practice. The Dodgers' John Roseboro thought it was bad for his timing, the Mets' Art Shamsky was bothered by it in cold weather ("You hit a ball on your fists and it stings, then you go into the game psyched"), Richie Allen disapproved of it because "your body is just like a bar of soap — it gradually wears down from repeated use."

But most hitters eat b.p. up. One will say to another, "Go long ball with you," and then they will see who can hit farthest. Willie Mays would ride one way up into the seats and younger Giants would whoop, "Are you that *strong?* Are you really that *strong?*" Not many people in this country regularly get to whang away at something as hard as they can with a good stick. The hitters jump in quickly when it's their turn so as not to waste a second. They accuse each other of taking too many swings. They berate the pitcher when he doesn't get the ball over the plate. They keep looking anxiously over at the nearest coach and asking, "How much time?" — meaning when will the groundkeepers come to roll the cage away. The coach, dumpy and aged, says, "Pretty soon."

B.p. is also a boon to the fan. Even from the stands you can watch the batters moving around like horses in the paddock. Dave Kingman may strike out four times in the game, but in b.p. he is bound to hit one several miles. Once in Montreal I watched Ron Hunt, a distinguished bat-control man, take b.p. one-handed, holding the bat with his left hand in a right-handed stance, and rap out fairly sharp, though quickly dying, little grounders. Once in Vero Beach, Florida, at the Dodgers' spring training camp I watched Jim Lefebvre work on the all-but-lost art of place hitting. Tom Lasorda, then a coach, would say "Harrelson" or "Kessinger" or "Beckert" or "Tito Fuentes" just before the pitch reached the plate and Lefebvre would try to hit the ball toward the position — shortstop or second base — played by that man. Dixie Walker, another Dodger coach, was also giving Lefebvre advice. As he was leaving the cage Lefebvre said, "I enjoyed that, Dixie. I got a lot out of it."

Dixie said, "Well, you don't just swing your head off. You take *batting practice.*"

An old lady who used to live in Brooklyn watched all this with me. "You know, in Ebbets Field, Dixie Walker hit a foul ball that hit my late husband. Oh, yes," she said.

"Who was pitching?" I asked her.

"Howie Pollet."

The best thing of all about b.p. is that it can be a participant sport. B.p. is available to the civilian. I don't know whether there is a batting cage near you, but there is one fairly near me, which is the main thing I care about, if you want to know the truth. There should be one nearer me, though. I have to drive forty-five minutes. But it's worth it. B.p. is the only sport I can engage in at the highest level.

That's right. I hit the big-league machine. The place I go to is on U.S. 7 just south of Pittsfield, Massachusetts. The Batting Cage has three compartments, three machines. The slow machine is for Little Leaguers. The medium machine is about high-school level. The fast machine can *bring* it.

"That thing throws eighty-five miles an hour and it'll put

you in the hospital!" the lady who was supervising the Batting Cage told me on my first visit. "You put that helmet on."

"Actually it'll get up into the nineties," says Bill Mickle, whose wife owns the Batting Cage. Mickle never played professional ball himself, which is a shame. He and somebody named Claude Dine could have been scrappy little guys batting first and second. Their manager could have said of their opponents, "We're going to Mickle and Dine 'em to death."

Up into the nineties! Think of that! That's a good deal faster than Randy Jones and only ten m.p.h. off Nolan Ryan. Put a quarter in the machine and you get ten approximating-major-league fastballs. I spend about five minutes working out on the medium machine, just to make up for all the high-school pitching I didn't hit while in high school, and then I put in a chaw of Red Man, spit out, tp, tp, two little flakes that have gotten on my tongue, and then I head for the big time.

Because I can get around on the ball. I am not going to knock down many fences but I am going to make contact. The day they put down the rubber three feet too close to the plate and Kent Shalibo, the fastest guy in intramural softball, was hurling, *I was the only person in the entire Sigma Chi lineup who fouled a ball off.* Finally after three innings and nine Sigma Chi strikeouts somebody realized that the rubber was too close, so we will never know whether I might actually have grounded to the second baseman off that incredible speed. I did some calculations after the game. I figured that fouling off Kent Shalibo from that close was the equivalent of hitting .180 for three weeks in Class D professional ball. And I was out of shape.

Well, I'm going to tell you the truth. At the Batting Cage I don't wear out the big-league machine right off the bat. I'm into it fifty cents by the time I'm hitting anything fair. But this is something I am willing to put some time and effort into.

I'm there for six, seven, eight dollars' worth of pitches. That's what, over three hundred cuts?

That means blisters. And the blisters break. And the ball is past me and I'm just kind of dabbing at it, it's taking the bat out of my hands. The planes and vectors of hitting are more real and terrible even than under Riverfront Stadium.

And then I *pop* one. Not a blister, a pitch. Now I'm getting some of *my* weight into the *ball*. It's like I've been trying to bang a dull splintery stake into hard ground and all of a sudden I'm driving a clean blue nail into a soft pine board.

Then I start figuring my batting average. I count every swing except fouls as a time at bat. Out of the last hundred at bats I generally get thirty-one, thirty-two *clean* hits. Some of them bloopers, yes. Certain bloopers do fall in. But no leg hits. Let's face it, I never got a leg hit in Little League, why should I start getting them in the majors? When I'm going good, I don't need them. Thirty-two hits in one hundred at bats is .320. Joe DiMaggio's lifetime average was .325.

All right. I know what you're saying. There's a big difference between hitting .320 in a batting cage, at however advanced a level, and hitting .320 against real major-league pitching. I know that. I am willing to adjust for that.

The pitching machine doesn't throw breaking balls. I figure that's worth a hundred points — now I'm down to .220. Doesn't change speeds. Down another fifty. But then the machine does throw *crazy wild* pretty often. Goes for your head, your feet. And in the big leagues every twelfth ball doesn't have a split cover. So put twenty points back. Then there's the ATRBDEJOB, or A Three-month-old Rubber-coated Ball Doesn't Exactly Jump Off the Bat, factor. Give myself twenty more points for that.

A number of other factors enter in. If I were really in the big leagues I'd probably be writing a book about it, and the other players would forever be worrying about what I was going to disclose about them. They'd call time every now and then to ask me, and that would probably affect my hitting. Of course it would probably affect the pitchers, too.

So it isn't easy to figure, but I've spent a lot of time on it. I figure, give or take thirty points, I would be hitting .117 right now in the major leagues. In the American League, anyway. If I could run and field well enough to play.

At thirty-five that's not bad. In my prime, around '71 or '72, I possibly would have hit .195. I can live with that. Of course I've lost out on a lot of intangible benefits, passing up a career in baseball. But some of them I can get at the Batting Cage. Leaning against the screen watching other fast-machine guys hit, waiting for my turn, comparing notes with other guys who're watching.

"Thing git to be an addicition."

"Eah."

"Machine'll cross you up. Move it around on you."

"Thing'll bad-ball you."

"Th'ew one behind me."

"Hit on one in Rhode Island. Christ, that thing caught me right on the *wrist!*"

Then, wups, the machine lets fly with a duster. Guy in the cage doesn't hang in there too well. He goes down, bat flies, the machine is inexorably pitching on, he's thrashing around on the ground, people are scurrying around to pull him away.

As he leaves the cage disgruntled, his last pitch is thrown. WHANG it goes against the screen. "Scuse me," I say to the writer who is interviewing me for this column. "I got to go hit."

MERELY SHOT IN THE HEAD

ONE of the few good reasons I can think of for running twenty-six miles would be to escape being shot in the head. But Dennis Rainear, twenty-eight years old, of Midland, Michigan, runs such distances for his own gratification. And when somebody did shoot him in the head, after ten miles on November 4, he kept on running.

The .22-caliber slug in his scalp slowed him down enough over the last sixteen miles, though, that he took 3 hours 9 minutes to finish the Grand Valley Marathon in Allendale, Michigan. That time was nine minutes too slow to qualify for the Boston Marathon next April.

"I was all prepared," Rainear was quoted as saying when he finished the race. His best previous marathon time had been 3 hours 31 seconds. "I was sure I could knock 31 seconds off my time, and then this silly thing had to happen."

On reading this statement, I finally had to break down and admit that I was impressed by the running state of mind. Just when running was becoming more boring as a sports topic than what is wrong with the Giants, just when the average non-running American was firming up several good reasons why he was not out there pushing past pain barriers in perfectly fitted shoes himself, here comes Dennis Rainear. Here comes a runner who is so absorbed in biting the bullet that he can't be bothered by the bullet in his head.

"This silly thing," he calls it. It seems to me that being shot in the head, when it occurs, should be a big thing in a person's life. To a nonrunner, it would make more sense to hear someone say, "All my life I have been trying to avoid getting shot in the head, and here it has to happen while I'm running this silly race."

I wanted to know more about Dennis Rainear. Maybe all this was a hoax, and I could stop worrying about it. I called him at the Dow Corning Company in Midland, where he works as a chemist.

He said he had been having trouble getting much chemistry done lately — not because of his wound but because of his fame.

"You've been getting a lot of calls on this thing?"

"Is the sky up? I'm hearing from about every newspaper and magazine and TV show in the country."

The story was true, he said.

"I don't know exactly where the bullet came from, because I don't know which way I was facing or what the angle of my head was when it hit. But it landed just to the right of the top center of my head. I remember there being a thud when it struck me, and it damn near took me off my feet. I thought I'd been hit by a brick or something.

"I looked around to see who'd thrown it, but there was nobody there. Other than yell a little bit, I probably wouldn't have wanted to take the time to do anything anyway. But I had trouble focusing my eyes. It was like I was drunk. I kept blinking. And I kept opening my jaw, trying to get my ears to pop.

"I've had worse races, in the heat, when I really felt wracked. But I ran through a really bad period at the twenty-two-mile mark. I was wobbling, and my eyes were going in different directions. I assumed it was undertraining, or over-fatigue, or dehydration. So I slowed down to a walk, but that made it worse. I thought: 'The blood must be pooling in your legs. Running will help pump it back up to your brain.'

"So I started running again, and I felt better. I thought, 'I must have run through whatever it was I was in.'

"When I crossed the finish line my wife knew immediately I was disappointed. 'By the way,' I told her, 'somebody clobbered me with a brick or something.'

"I had a big goose egg. So we had the physician who was there look at it. 'I can see something shining in there,' he said. All of a sudden things really made sense. It wasn't just muscle fatigue."

At the hospital Rainear was taken to, X rays showed a slug flattened up against the skull. "The doctor had to use plastic tweezers to pull the bullet out so it wouldn't be damaged for the ballistics tests. He had a hard time. He kept jerking my head, jerking my head."

Fortunately the slug had hit a solid part of the skull and hadn't penetrated at all. "All I've got now is a small scab. I've been out running every day. The other day I was out on a new road, and I heard a gunshot crack. I hightailed it out of there. I figure I've used up my luck."

Rainear assumes that the bullet that hit him was a stray. "I could as easily have been hit sitting in a bar somewhere. Some of the stories that have come out have concluded that running is no longer safe — that if you go out running, ipso facto you're going to get shot."

Rainear deplores such conclusions. It's true that when he is training, people occasionally try to run over him, or they open their car doors as they drive past to try to bowl him over, and he is a bit worried that "some nut" watching his next race will say, "Okay, you took a twenty-two bullet; try this thirty-ought-six." Still, Rainear thinks that "running is the best thing going."

"It's free-form exercise. It's great for cardiovascular fitness. And it's cheap. Anybody can do it. I'm just the average Joe on the road, and I've run races with Bill Rodgers, Lasse Viren, Frank Shorter, all the big shots."

I suggested that he would be something of a celebrity himself at the next Boston Marathon, in which he will compete by virtue of a special invitation.

"No," he says, "I still consider myself a little shot."

A BAIT BOX OF GREEN JADE?

YOUR chances of seeing a show of cricket cages and other cricketing paraphernalia are apparently slight. The Asian Gallery on East Eightieth Street in New York claims its current exhibit is the first in the United States to feature "the unique art forms associated with the ancient Chinese sport of cricket-fighting."

I don't know much about art, but I know one form of cricket-fighting. Nearly every time I go fishing with crickets someone turns over the tricky wire bait box they are kept in, and in a flash everyone in the boat is covered with crickets. Fishing is relaxing but wrestling with crickets is exercise. My friend Vereen Bell once came home from a fishing trip, sat down at the table, and a cricket hopped out of his shirt pocket into his chicken gumbo soup. The Bells' Siamese cat Beep saw the cricket jump and went after it. A cricket can add a lot of shouting and grappling to your life.

The Chinese fought crickets, however, in the sense that the Vanderbilts race horses. According to *Insect-Musicians and Cricket Champions of China,* a 1927 pamphlet by Berthold Laufer, which Richard Ravenal of the Asian Gallery showed me, it was a peculiarity of the ancient Chinese that they "were more interested in the class of insects than in all other groups of animals combined." Hence, silk; and hence also the great enthusiasm, as early as the tenth century, for watching prized crickets fight each other in a pottery jar. As late as 1927 the sport was so big that wagering on a single cricket-match in Canton might go as high as $100,000 and a national *shou lip* (winning or victorious cricket) would bring his home village as much honor as Johnny Bench brings to Binger, Oklahoma.

I am not making this up. Crickets with black heads and grey body hair, Laufer says, were held to be the best fighters. Next were those with yellow heads and grey hair. The trainer of a first-class cricket would keep the temperature in its cage just right. If the cricket's mustache started to droop, it was too warm. Fighting crickets were fed rice mixed with fresh cucumbers, boiled chestnuts, lotus seeds and mosquitoes. Sometimes a cricket fancier would allow himself to be bitten by mosquitoes, which he would then feed to his cricket. When time for a fight drew near, the cricket might be deprived of food for a while, until its movements became slow, whereupon it would be fed small red insects in water. A cricket enthusiast might carry a caged favorite around in his breast pocket so that the fighter could keep warm and all the world could hear it sing. A strong chirping voice was an attribute of the best cricket gladiators.

How it was possible for more than a few fans to watch a big cricket bout Laufer does not explain, but the event would take place in a demijohn-sized jar placed in the middle of a public square. Opponents were matched according to size, weight and color. Before each set-to they were carefully weighed on a pair of tiny scales.

Crickets are natural fighters in defense of their own turf, but in the ring, or rather the jar, they had to be provoked. The referee, using a device made of hare- or rat-whiskers inserted into a handle of bone or reed, would twiddle first the contestants' heads, then the ends of their tails, and finally their

large hind legs. Then the crickets would stretch out their an-
tennae and jump at each other's heads. An antenna would break
off, then a leg. Usually the struggle would end in the death of
one fighter; often the winner would manage to land with its
full weight on the other's body and sever its head.

The sport has died out, at least on the mainland, since the
revolution banned gambling; who wants to watch crickets fight
if you can't bet on them? But in the old days emperors and
other high officials put a lot of money and artistry into cricket
cages and accoutrements, and these are the objets that the
Asian Gallery is showing. In winter the crickets were kept in
cages made of gourds that were about the size of a swallow.
The beauty of these cages resides in their perforated tops and
in the designs on the gourds themselves. The caps were carved
into flowers or dragons or intricate vinelike tangles, from san-
dalwood, elephant- or walrus-ivory, coconut shell, green jade,
white jade, ebony, bamboo or tortoise shell. Some of the designs on the bodies of the cages were etched, but most were
raised. Molds with indentations on the inner surface were fas-
tened around gourds while they were still on the stalk, so that
the gourds would grow into patterns.

Some of these gourd cages are exquisite antiques, and they're
more interesting to explain to guests than, say, a Tiffany lamp.
Their prices range from $250 to $550, and the gallery will
continue to sell the objets after the exhibit closes. Ravenal im-
plied that he might well throw in one of the cricket ticklers,
cricket water bowls, cricket beds (singles), porcelain cricket-
bout scorecards or hard-to-describe small decorative items (apparently trophies or memorials to cricket champions) that are
also part of the collection. Another interesting piece is a sash
worn by a cricket-fight referee. Evidently, judging from the
size of this sash, the referee was a man. I had hoped he was a
field mouse.

JOCK LINGERIE

ALL I can say is, the thing I wanted most when I was a kid was to be a big-league ballplayer, and the last thing I wanted was for magazines to run pictures of me in my underwear. To walk through the lunchroom and have people nudge each other and say, "He pitches for the Orioles," would have been very easy to live with. To walk through the lunchroom and have people nudge each other and say, "Did you see him — in little tight *underpants?*" would have been hard.

So what does a kid think today when he sees Jim Palmer of the Orioles, the three-time Cy Young Award winner, posing in magazine ads — and even on a poster — for Jockey shorts? In some ads Palmer wears matching T-shirts, but the poster shows him in nothing but Jockey's Élance briefs. The world now knows that Palmer throws right, plays tennis left (to protect his pitching arm) and dresses (an unusual case, but there it is) right down the middle.

In locker rooms over the last years, to be sure, I have noticed more and more pro athletes wearing other than run-of-the-mill underwear — some of it even briefer than Élance. Some of it apparently satin. The pioneers in this, as in so many locker-room style (and linguistic) trends, were black players, who have tended, generally, to eschew roomy attire — Muhammad Ali's and Joe Frazier's ring shorts being obvious exceptions. I can remember when a player's conversion to bikini pants might inspire his more reactionary roommate to loudly demand a chaperone. Today in clubhouses you see fewer and fewer boxer shorts or plain modest Jockey shorts like the kind Palmer's mother bought him when he was a boy.

Palmer told the "Today" show's Jane Pauley: "What I am seeing is that after 229 victories I'm going to be more famous for my underwear ads than for throwing a baseball." He didn't sound too chagrined. "Most [men's] underwear is bought by women," Palmer continued. "I guess that's why they used me in the ad." (If men bought most men's underwear, whom would they have used? Yogi Berra?)

At this point I am going to make a terrible admission, right in front of everybody: No one has *ever* bought me any fancy underwear. Are there actually, in real life, moments when the woman hands the man a little something flimsy and says, "Would you . . . try these on . . . for me?"?

According to Jockey International (a company which incidentally has its headquarters in Kenosha, Wisconsin), only 3 percent of all of Jockey's underwear sold in 1963 was "fashion underwear," but today the figure is 40 percent and as the 1980s progress it should exceed 50. During this decade, in other words, only a minority of the men's underwear in circulation will be just, you know, underwear. The rest — let's call things by their right names — is going to be men's lingerie.

"The Jockey Statement Is Bold," reads the caption of one of Palmer's ads. I don't know. Maybe it's okay for a ballplayer to make bold statements *in* his underwear, but surely not *with* it. "He's not real talkative. He leads by example in the clubhouse. He lets his underwear speak for him."

Jockey press releases also make the point that Palmer is an "All-American, All-Around Sportsman." For one thing, Palmer is married to his high-school sweetheart. "There is nothing wrong," says an ad person connected with the Jockey campaign, "with an American family man being sexy." In an earlier campaign, not only Palmer but several other athletes, including Pete Rose, Steve Carlton, Steve Garvey and Lou Brock of baseball, Jo Jo White and Jamaal Wilkes of basketball, Jim Hart, Tony Dorsett and Ken Anderson of football, and Denis Potvin of hockey, posed in their shorts. Those guys seem like All-American, All-Around Sportsmen too, but they didn't get the solo-poster treatment. Maybe Rose's being cited in a paternity suit was felt to reflect on his underwear. Maybe Brock insisted on tying in underwear with the Brock-a-brella, a combination hat and umbrella product that he has promoted. My suspicion is that Palmer just looked more like Robert Redford in underwear than any of the others.

And who am I to complain? Palmer is younger than I am, in better shape and, okay, probably better-looking. The Seattle Mariners' wives voted him the sexiest man in baseball, and they never voted me anything. Of course you might think that the Mariners' wives would have something better to do with their time, like exhorting their husbands to work on fundamentals.

Working ballplayers wear really neat underpants, which ought to be more widely available. These underpants are Bermuda-short length, more or less. Made of something like sanitary-stocking material, they are light, stretchy, and snug, but not so snug as to give either the wearer or his opponents' wives impure thoughts. If I had a few pairs of those underwear, boy, I'd have them on all the time.

How would Jimmy Cannon have handled this story? "You're Jim Palmer. You're in a magazine and your shorts are getting smaller and smaller." No. Jimmy Cannon couldn't have handled this story. He would have thrown up his hands and lapsed into a few of his "Nobody asked me, but . . ." observations, such as, "I don't like Boston because all the men look like me." If Jimmy Cannon couldn't cover it, then the hell with it.

GET OUT THERE AND
MAKE STATEMENTS!

Feature this: A pitcher dissipates only lightly, gets to the park on time, avoids fistfights with his mates, keeps his head in the game, always gives at least 110, 120 percent. Only one thing: he insists on wearing his late father's beat-up old fishing hat on the mound.

"You can't wear a *fishing hat* on the mound!" cries his owner, and the umpires, and the commissioner himself.

"Why not?" the pitcher asks quietly. "People," he adds with a smile, "wear baseball caps fishing."

"*Nobody in the entire history of organized ball has ever worn a fishing hat on the mound!*"

"Ah," says the pitcher.

Or this: A pass receiver hauls one in for a touchdown but when he enters the end zone he does not stop. He goes on to circle the entire field, holding the ball aloft, juking and springing into the air every few strides and engaging front-row fans in rudimentary dialogue, until at length a crotchety team physician fells him with a tank of oxygen.

One account begins: "Chicago edged the Lions 27–26 in Detroit Sunday to clinch the N.F.C. Central crown, as Bear wide receiver Freemason 'Sweet-Tips' Teal brought off a refreshing commentary upon the supposed finality of 'scoring.' "

Another wire service reports: " 'Wide' as applied to receivers was a cliché until Sunday, when Freemason 'Sweet-Tips' Teal opened the idea of wideness up and let it breathe, as the Bears edged. . . ."

Sound incredible? It may be the coming thing in big-time athletics.

Consider: When Dave Cowens, at the height of his trend-setting powers as an NBA center, left the Boston Celtics on an indefinite leave of absence without pay early one season, he shook everyone to the roots. Who ever heard of a man like that opting out like that? He didn't have personal problems. He wasn't holding out for anything. He's got *red hair,* for Christ's sake. It was unaccountable. Then came the follow-up quote from Pete Maravich of the New Orleans Jazz: "Dave Cowens did what I had been thinking about doing for some time now. It's funny in a way, because Dave beat me to the punch. Now I can't do what he did."

Maravich has, however, done this: he has put Cowens's step into perspective. Cowens may protest that he is "just a guy who quit his job," but a field in which things must not be repeated is not a job. It is not a trade. It is not a craft. It is an art. *Expression* is now the need of big-time athletes' souls.

Winning is no longer enough for them. (Especially in years when it looks like they might not even take the division.) Nor is money enough — now that, in these days of free agentry and renegotiation, there is so much of it. Sports stars now, it is becoming increasingly evident, want to make a *statement.*

Thus Reggie Jackson signs not with the Montreal Expos, who offer him more money, but with the New York Yankees — because, as Yankee owner George Steinbrenner puts it, "When we were walking around town last week, a couple of kids came up to him, kids who didn't have a dime. And he told me later, 'We can do something to make those kids feel better.' " (Not give them a dime, but give them a World Series winner.)

A grand and also a very allusive gesture. What is Reggie doing here but paying an *hommage* to the Babe's promise of a homer to a hospitalized kid — and also, further and more tellingly, turning Shoeless Joe on his head: the kid comes up to *this* Jackson and says, in effect, "Say you're the edge, Reg." And this Jackson does not turn away.

Let us look again at the Cowens move. Only six feet eight in a position that had seemed to require seven feet, Cowens had already proved that less can be more, had established a new style of play, just as in the late nineteenth century Toulouse-Lautrec had proved that painters needn't be tall (pace Anthony Quinn and Charlton Heston), at least in the demimonde. Cowens had done that *already*. He was repeating himself.

Then, I think, he heard about artist Robert Rauschenberg's aesthetic coup of the fifties: erasing a drawing by de Kooning. Cowens, though, had long been negating other people's work with his aggressive defense. He had even been upstaged in that department, imagistically, by a lesser player, Marvin Webster, whose flair for blocking shots had earned him the sobriquet "The Human Eraser." Cowens decided to carry this concept further, to turn it in upon itself. He would erase his own work. Suddenly, the Celtics were without Cowens. Or rather, a phantom Cowens was on the floor forty-eight minutes a game, glaring in his absence, nonperforming inimitably. Within three weeks of his departure, a headline in the *Boston Globe* referred to the UN-COWENS ERA.

Imagine Maravich's vexation: Maravich, whose passes —

bounced through his own and opponents' legs, *rolled* the length of the floor, and so on — are so creative that nobody *including the intended recipient* is ready for them. And yet it is clear when the ball bounces off the teammate's head that he *should,* ideally, have known the pass was coming, would have if his imagination had been as rich and quick as Pete's. For years, Maravich has been like Bobby Fischer trying to play team chess. It is a hell of an act, one that many critics prefer to ordinary effective basketball, but Maravich has by now rung all the changes on it. He has of late even been toying with ordinary effective basketball. The more inspired stroke, though, would have been withdrawal. Like James Agee belatedly leaving Time Inc., Maravich could have built a myth of the hoop-artist-better-than-his-context, going on to various nearly realized free-lance projects implying what might have been achieved if only the context had held up its end.

But Cowens — ironically a quintessentially functional, winning, "team" player — beat Maravich to the punch; left him holding the ball. Cowens leaving the Celtics, a class act that he had to a great extent defined, is like E. B. White in the late thirties taking off from regular employment at *The New Yorker,* which he had seemed essential to; going off into the country to do some things on his own. ("He's out right now on a tractor," Cowens's mother told a reporter, "bush-hogging, clearing some ground.")

For some time now we have been hearing athletes say things like, "I don't want to be thought of as just a goalie." (Or "just a Supersonic," or "just a person with incredible quickness," or even "just Professor Up There Novotney.") "I want to be thought of as a human being." It is not much of a jump from there to "I want to be recognized as a person of vision."

There was Ali — vaunting, rope-a-doping, making himself up as he went along. There was Wilt, missing free throws in rather the same way that Theodore Dreiser dangled modifiers. An early earth-artist was Richie Allen, writing cryptic words (*Mom, Coke, No*) in the base-path dirt with his foot. Baseball perhaps had its Duchamp in Jimmy Piersall, who circled the bases backward after hitting a home run. But Piersall was before his time. Baseball thought he was not an innovator but crazy.

Ten years ago, basketball would have thought Cowens was crazy. But today even crusty Celtics general manager Red Auerbach concedes that the eccentric, no-nonsense Cowens has his own way of doing things and that he knows what he is doing.

Never apologize, never explain. Surely it will not be long before other NBA'ers will be off on new departures. The concept of "moving without the ball" may be extended — dancing without the ball, moving without the ball *or shorts,* moving without the coliseum . . .

As usual, the owners, administrators, and legislators of sport (except for the NCAA, which has cannily suppressed spiking and dunking for years) have misperceived the threats posed by the new independence of players. The danger is not that they will sell themselves so freely and dearly to various high bidders as to destroy the respective structures of their sports, but that they will begin to express themselves so freely in what Rauschenberg has called the gap between art and life (as opposed to the gap between center and left, or the gap between tackle and end) that ball games will begin to look like halftime shows conceived and directed by John Cage.

Hockey will be staged — as wrestling already is — on gelatin. Baseball on ice. Quarterbacks will begin to experiment with form — standing behind the guard, for instance, to see what happens when the center's snap sails straight up into emptiness. Antonioni has give us tennis without the ball.

Writers of free verse, according to Robert Frost, have given us tennis without the net. Ilie Nastase may give us tennis with golf balls. Who knows?

It behooves the custodians of sport, then, to start thinking of ways to accommodate the artist in the athlete. Efforts may be made to channel the new impulses into off-the-field activity: theater groups, leather craft, bizarre private behavior.

But changes are also going to have to take place on the playing fields to allow for experimentation and the development of varying styles. Heretofore the picture of a sport has been cast almost entirely in terms of points scored — a sort of intense, or perhaps reverse, pointillism, the new sports critic might suggest. Henceforth more attention will be paid to the different *modes* of sport. An all-star game between baseball's nine best sluggers and its five or six *worst* pitchers. Surely the judging of lay-ups in terms of quality — form, brio, hang time, degree of difficulty — along the lines of Olympic gymnastics scoring is long overdue. Why should Julius Erving get no more points for a whirling triple-pumping behind-the-back two-hand slam-dunk than Phil Jackson gets for an inelegantly coordinated tip-in? Football referees might award yardage for fresh, well-articulated insights and provocations (anybody can simply call the man across from him a fag) at the line of scrimmage.

Inevitably, of course, the new wave in sport will be co-opted. Owners will see the commercial potential in expressiveness and will begin to pay players not for statistics but for magicality, for je-ne-sais-quoi quotient. A Dick Stuart, who is brilliant in the role of the terrible defensive first baseman, will be encouraged more than the solid but uncreative Gold Glover. Players who have built careers on just meeting the ball and always throwing to the right base will be asked at contract time, "So where is that at? Why couldn't you once ask for a trapeze at the plate so you could 'swing from the heels'? Why don't you ever throw to the hot-dog vendor? You're not *mercurial,* you're not *alive to the moment* out there." Coaches will begin inculcating the three I's: Inspiration, Imagination, Impishness. Clutch hitting as such will be out — Tommy Henrich was doing that in the forties. Choking and then calling for a microphone to tell the crowd about it — how it felt, what you saw your parents doing when you were six years old, which probably had a lot to do with it — will be in.

Dave Cowens, of course, terminated his leave of absence after two months. I think this was a failure of nerve. "I was taking a lot of flak from many circles," he said — he who has given and withstood so much flak around hoops. You would think he might have found some way to emulate Dante, who stayed in exile and consigned all the circles to hell. Or he might have waited until the sports pendulum had swung to the ultimate in expressionism. And then come back and kicked ass.

THE PRESIDENTIAL
SPORTS PROFILE

This piece first appeared during the 1980 presidential campaign, but since its recommendations were not widely seized upon, and since there is always the chance that someone might forget and take John Anderson seriously again, it is repeated — as you can see — here.

You always hear that the CIA has secret psychological profiles of people. If the CIA really wants to know what makes world leaders tick, it ought to commission sports profiles of them.

If, years ago, we had sent a good scout down to watch Fidel Castro play ball and to chat with his coaches and the local barber, we might have anticipated Castro's affinity for Russia. (I'll bet he liked distant, unsubtle head coaches.)

It's not just foreigners who ought to be checked out this way but also presidential candidates. I'm not saying a person should be disqualified from running for President because he or she likes the New England Patriots or says "Then again . . ." when someone is about to putt, *but the people should know these things.*

After all, every recent President can be definitively summed up in light of his sports involvement.

• *Eisenhower.* Serenely played golf rather than meddle in government and mess things up.

• *Kennedy.* Sailed — the wind made his hair look good — and played highly competitive touch football with his siblings and Arthur Schlesinger.

• *Johnson.* Didn't really care much about any sport except legislation-swinging and beagle-dangling, but occasionally went out and shot a deer, or claimed to have.

• *Nixon.* Never got over warming the bench — which was perhaps the only thing he ever warmed — at Whittier College. Chose a Vice-President who persisted in hitting people with tennis and golf balls. Tried to disarm capital-besieging war protesters in 1970 by asking them how their schools' football teams were doing.

• *Ford.* Looked back through his legs all through college. Played too much football without a helmet. Liked being leader of the Free World okay, but *really* liked skiing, in the general direction of a condo.

• *Carter.* A grim competitor at softball. Suffered a rabbit attack while canoeing. Collapsed while trying to be a regular trendy guy — that is, while running in a road race. Insisted on keeping track of White House tennis-court reservations himself. [On leaving office he wrote a major piece for *Fly Fisherman* magazine.]

I ask you. Do we really need to say anything more about any of these men? Are any of them characterized so well by their interests in, say, movies? (Nixon and *Patton,* that's about it.) Clothes? (When the chips are down, they all wear the same suit.)

No, sports is the key indicator. If you have a sense of what it would be like to get stuck watching "Monday Night Football" with someone, or pitching horseshoes with him for money, you have a sense of what it would be like to get stuck with him as your President.

Network television should jump on this. Call it trashsport if you like, but instead of debating each other the candidates could play a little televised racquetball. Not to see who wins, but so we could observe their style, which is the point of the debates.

Then, too, maybe each candidate could do a half-hour or so of color commentary on the sport of his choice. Reagan would *presumably* have the advantage there, but I don't know: When he was announcing University of Iowa football on the radio, back in the thirties, he would say, if there was a running play, "It's a hippety-hop to the left," or "It's a hippety-hop to the right." And people complain about Howard Cosell.

The Freedom of Information Act does not require a candidate to reveal whether he could ever dribble with either hand, or hit to the opposite field, or how he felt when somebody ran a sweep at him for the first time, or whether he knows who Arky Vaughan and Charlie Trippi are, or how he stands on the designated hitter.

I have been able, however, to acquire a certain amount of conceivably revealing intelligence on Jimmy Carter, Ronald Reagan and John Anderson.

• *Carter.* According to Captain Ellery Clark, Jr., Carter's plebe cross-country coach at Annapolis, plebe Carter was stubborn, sincere, dedicated and, above all, "a real loner. He was more off to himself than most. He got along with the rest of the team but didn't mix much." Yet Carter as President mixes Hooverism with spending, inflation with recession, niceness with meanness, Brzezinski with Muskie/Vance. Overcompensating for early nonmixing?

Of course, notes Clark, cross-country "attracts loners. It's a very mental, individualistic sport. You're struggling against yourself." Hmmm.

Clark always told his teams, "It's nice to be a gentleman, but it's nicer to win." In a softball game in Plains before the 1976 presidential election, Carter's press secretary Jody Powell hit a comebacker to his boss, who was pitching. Carter threw to first, but Powell was called safe. The future President descended upon the umpire with all the prestige of a presidential candidate and also with all the certitude and heat of Earl Weaver. The umpire would not budge. Carter stalked back to his position. Powell turned to a reporter and said, "You know, he really is an arrogant little son of a bitch."

Unanswered question: Carter writes in *Why Not the Best?* that when he was growing up he played baseball ten to the side. The extra player backed up the catcher. Can we really believe that anybody formed by ten-man baseball will fulfill his pledge to reduce the size of the federal bureaucracy?

• *Reagan.* He portrayed George Gipp in the movie *Knute Rockne — All American.* In that movie Pat O'Brien, as Rockne, inspired Notre Dame to win by urging them to "win one for the Gipper." Not long ago, John McHale, president of the Montreal Expos and no wild-eyed progressive, was asked whether he planned to make a Rockne-style pep talk to his players. "Those days are over," he said.

Reagan played guard at Eureka College in Illinois. "No star, just an average player," says Ralph McKinzie, who was Reagan's coach. "He was a good loser, too. Of course, he got plenty of practice at that because we lost so often."

As a radio announcer, Reagan did simulated broadcasts of Cubs games — off a ticker that brought him play-by-play in rather the way that diverse newspapers have brought him canned facts for his speeches. His shows were more popular than other announcers' on-the-scene reports.

Eureka has a new sports center called the Reagan Complex. Yet the man's critics accuse him of being simplistic.

Unanswered question: In 1931 the *Eureka Pegasus* listed Reagan as one of the men in the line up front who "afford the beef." Will anyone farther back in line be able to afford beef if Reagan gets elected?

• *Anderson.* A sports cipher. When he gets a chance, he swims. That's all. He follows no professional teams, and he played no sports in college. His congressional staff used to have a softball team, but it broke up for lack of interest.

Rick Manning of *Newsweek*'s Chicago bureau once tried to josh Anderson in a sports-related way. Manning noted that there was an opening for manager of the Chicago Cubs, and he wondered whether Anderson might be interested in the job. "Why, no," Anderson replied, with no hint of amusement. "I don't think I'd be interested at all."

Unanswered question: What if, say, Robert Mugabe of Zimbabwe visits Washington and Anderson is President, and the two are sitting around getting to know each other, and Mugabe — he's a Pat Boone fan, so he may well follow pro football, and he may have relatives in Detroit — says, "Hey, how about those Lions?"

And there is an awkward pause, and then Anderson says, "This administration punctiliously supports Zimbabwean self-determination and stands squarely in favor of cultural exchange between our two nations. But . . . I don't *recall* any lions. When did you send them?"

M.D. TO THE GREATEST

In *The Greatest,* the Muhammad Ali movie, Dr. Ferdie Pacheco is played by John Marley, but in real life he looks more like Jonathan Winters, only Latin. I can't see Pacheco doing any funny — in the sense of dubious — medicine, though. If he were ever going to do any malpractice, he would have done it years ago, when this guy named Bert wanted to be dyed green so he could wrestle.

Bert made a good living estimating the value of cars for a fee and then calling people up and telling them, for another fee, where they could buy undervalued cars. But that wasn't enough for him. Evenings he refereed wrestling. "You should have seen it last night!" he once told Dr. Pacheco. "One of the Hitler brothers threw me out of the ring and I landed on an Italian fella's lap and there was pizza all over me and his Coke flew up in the air and came down on my head and then when I started climbing back into the ring the other brother stomped my hands and —"

"Wait a minute," Dr. Pacheco said. "This was good, or bad?"

"It was great!" Bert said. "The crowd . . ."

But that wasn't enough for him either. Not when Dr. Pacheco asked him, "How would you like to be green?" Pacheco raised the question in a speculative way. A friend of his, another doctor, was present, and Pacheco likes to bring out a person's character for others to appreciate. (That's why he called in a lawyer friend when a woman brought her husband to his office and complained that a " 'plosion" in a neighboring building had caused the husband to "fracture his peanits." I wish I had room here for the fractured-peanits story, but I don't.)

"How do you mean, green?"

"Everything — your whole body. Your arms and legs, your face, your teeth, everything green."

"It would rub off."

"No, it wouldn't. There's this new dye out," said Pacheco. "They use it to test for cancer. You swallow it, it turns you all green, except the cancer. The only thing wrong with it, it's experimental. It could kill you. And also, you stay green for two weeks."

"Great!" In his natural state Bert was not physically imposing enough to be a pro wrestler, which was what he wanted to be more than anything else in life. But green he could write his own ticket. He rushed to a phone and called a promoter he knew in Texas.

"How would you like a green wrestler?"

"How do you mean, green?"

"All over. My whole body, teeth, everything. Won't rub off."

"Can you wrestle?"

"Sure. I referee. I know how they fake all the stuff."

"Well, sure. We could use something like that on the tour —"

"Great! I'll be there Monday."

"You'll be green. Right?"

"I guarantee. All I got to do is be in Miami every two weeks for a pill."

Bert dashed back to Pacheco and his colleague. "It's set! Give me the dye."

Well, the other doctor was inclined to see what could be done. But Pacheco said no. "Actually," he said, "it's too dangerous. It's a government-controlled substance. I told you, you could die."

"I don't care! I'll sign a paper, release you from all responsibility."

"I'm sorry," Pacheco said. "We took an oath."

Bert was disconsolate. But ethics are ethics. I think Hippocrates would have loved Ferdie Pacheco — even if he didn't know that Ferdie paints, writes, collects antique cars, has a beautiful flamenco-dancer wife, is a friend of Candice Bergen's and Petula Clark's and was cornerman and personal physician to the one and only Ali from 1962 to 1978. The only reason I mention malpractice is that Florida medical authorities are after Pacheco, who made some $14,000 annually from Medicare. They allege "overutilization." That means collecting from the government for seeing too many patients too often. Last year the Dade County Medical Association peer review board confronted Ferdie with such charges, and Ferdie blew them out of the water. Incensed, he pointed out that he was a ghetto doctor and as such had "no peer in my enclave."

The board wanted to know why Pacheco gave so many shots. *Because his patients couldn't afford to have prescriptions filled and couldn't read the dosage instructions anyway.*

The board wanted to know why Pacheco didn't hospitalize certain patients. *Because if they left their apartments, thieves would clean them out.*

The board wanted to know why Pacheco was himself absorbing the sixty dollars each Medicare patient is supposed to pay annually before receiving benefits. *Because his patients didn't have sixty dollars.*

An orthopedist on the board wanted to know why Pacheco treated arthritis. *Because he couldn't find any specialists who would take his patients.* "Will you see them?" he asked the orthopedist. The orthopedist said, well, if his nurse could fit them into his schedule . . .

"Don't give me the Nazi-nurse routine!" cried Pacheco.

Finally the board conceded that his practice was "unusual" and absolved him. But six months later the state-level Medicare board sent him a bill for $26,000 worth of overutilization. Pacheco vows to fight out the matter in court if necessary. "I'm tilting at windmills," he says. "I'm Don Quixote."

Pacheco grew up in Ybor City, the old Spanish section of Tampa, where he began hustling for money and amusement at an early age. By such devices as peddling at a football game peanuts approved for swine consumption only, he worked his way through premed studies at the University of Florida, then pharmacy school, and then the University of Miami Medical School. It isn't easy for a young doctor to establish a practice, but in 1959, there was one waiting in the black ghetto of northwest Miami, known to blacks as Overtown and to whites as the Swamp. The people there couldn't pay much, but they did have a lot of potentially lucrative accidents. When a lady's poorly maintained ceiling falls on her while she is taking a bath or when a defective gas heater blows up a tenement, Ferdie provides the medical testimony that helps force the insurance companies to cough up healthy compensation. This practice brings him into contact with occasional spurious claimants, such as a family known as the Falling Folsoms because of their propensity for seeking out tumbles on other people's property, and also with characters straight out of old racist jokes (he once testified for a wino who fell into an open grave late at night). But besides satisfying his sense of social justice, his court work is remunerative, as is his "white office," in Miami's prosperous Cuban community. Still, he spends 75 percent of his working hours treating whoever comes into the Overtown office. He doesn't claim nearly as much Medicare as he's entitled to, he says, and anyway he ought to get a medal rather than a hard time. In spite of the bricked-up windows, his waiting room has bullet holes in the walls.

Pacheco makes a point of keeping no money or abusable drugs around, but people still try to hold him up. Once a man came in with a sawed-off shotgun. He was wearing a yellow rainhat, a yellow suit and bright yellow shoes.

"Are you new at this?" asked Pacheco.

The gunman didn't see any humor. He wanted money. Ferdie gave him what little he had left in his wallet. "Here, this is it, take it all. But put that gun down. Next time you don't need to bring the gun. You don't even need to come in personally. Just send me a postcard marked 'Burglary' and I'll mail you what's here." At length Ferdie talked the intruder off the premises. Throughout the ordeal he comforted a terrified patient. "That gave me a reputation in the neighborhood for being heroic. Actually I was keeping her considerable bulk between me and the shotgun," he says.

After Ali visited the downtown office a few years ago, he refused to sell Ferdie his Rolls-Royce. He said nobody working in such a place could afford to spend $20,000 on a car. This from Ali, who goes through his millions so fast that he had to keep on fighting, well beyond his prime, to keep himself and his hangers-on solvent. Before the first Frazier fight, Ferdie crossed Eighth Avenue three times with Ali. In the course of those crossings Ali handed out $5,000 to strangers who claimed they needed $100 to buy a ticket.

Ali won't listen to Pacheco's financial advice, but he accepted his medical treatment consistently, even when Muslims were warning that a white doctor was liable to poison him. "Ali has a big and gentle heart," says Pacheco.

In his book *Fight Doctor,* Ferdie tells of Ali's waking up after the resetting of his jaw, broken in the first Ken Norton fight. Anyone coming out of such an operation is bound to be in considerable pain, says Pacheco, but Ali never mentioned hurting. He just reassured each person around the bed, in turn, that things weren't so bad, that he had seen worse times, that he would be back to earn big money again.

Now Pacheco is working on a book called *Ghetto Doctor,* and also on a vegetarian diet book for people who hate vegetables. This last manuscript defies succinct description. One chapter begins: "Leftenant Packer-Smythe could hear his men shoving wet asparagus into their empty rifle breeches. They made a wet sucking sound as the bolts snapped shut."

Pacheco even has stories he has no book for yet. There was the mob-backed trumpet player who wanted to do some fighting. His sponsors didn't want him to ruin his lip, tried to dissuade him, eventually arranged for him to work out but warned promoters not to let him in a ring. "When am I going to get a fight?" he kept asking. Finally they got him an opponent. They told this opponent, who knew that he was dealing with people who didn't mess around, "We want you to fight our boy. But *don't hit him.*"

The trumpeter didn't know the fix was in. He was thrilled. The night of the fight, though, as the apparent reality of the occasion came upon him, he began to grow pale and rubbery. By the time the bell rang to open the first round, all he could do was walk to the center of the ring and faint dead away.

Now the opponent was shocked. He looked at the glowering boys at ringside. "I never hit him!" he cried. "I *swear.* I never touched him!" Then *he* fainted.

"Now they're both down," says Ferdie, "and the referee is counting, 'Seven! One. Eight! Two. Nine! Three. . . .' "

Ferdie looks after all of Angelo Dundee's fighters. That's how he started seeing Ali, back when Ali was Clay. Ferdie makes his rounds at Chris Dundee's Fifth Street Gym as regularly as he does at Cedars of Lebanon Hospital. At the gym the scene is changing. "We got an upsurge of white guys, and the black guys are petering out," says Angelo.

"The Olympics on TV made boxing more glamorous for the white kids," explains Ferdie. "And the black kids have welfare." He even finds himself administering to college-educated fighters now. "Angelo has a trick in the corner. Toward the end of the fight, when his boy is slowing down, he'll pull open his trunks and pour in all the melting ice from the ice bag. The fighter goes, 'Oh! Ooo! Okay, hey!' He did that to a kid the other night, and the kid looked down — there were all these cubes and cold water running down his legs — and the kid made a face and said, 'Was that really necessary?' "

One more story. "If anything was going to get me into malpractice trouble, this was it," Pacheco says. Years ago, a person in women's clothing came into the Overtown office and said, "Doc, I'm missing my period."

The person was a man. He was so sincere, though, that Ferdie didn't have the heart to turn him away. "Well, watch your diet, and come back next month," he told him.

The patient kept coming back. Ferdie began to worry that the pregnancy was getting out of hand. But he couldn't just say, "Okay, enough's enough." He is not that kind of doctor. So, as the ninth month began, he told the patient: "There's one more thing you've got to do to keep from losing the baby. I want you to take this laxative, and then I want you to hold in for six hours. If you do that, everything will be all right." The laxative he gave the patient was extremely strong.

The next day the patient was in again, crestfallen. "Doc," he said, "I couldn't do it. I lost the baby."

Dr. Pacheco commiserated with the man in the dress, pointed out that at least he had come through with his own health intact, and wished him well.

"Now whenever he sees me on the street," Pacheco says with a sigh, "he hollers, 'Hey, Doc! I'm getting my period okay!' He beams and shouts to everyone around, 'That's my obstetrician!' "

Ferdie Pacheco is the kind of doctor who will entertain an illusion. But when I asked him how he felt about Ali's fighting on after the last Norton bout, he answered, "Horrified."

Not because Ali's body can't take another outing, but because "when this beautiful fifteen-year idyllic run among the clouds goes down to an old fighter trying to stay alive, I'm going to hate it.

"People around a champion never think that age will get to him. They think Manolete will never get old, then — bing! — the bull gets Manolete. And they go on to Domínguin."

He is confident, however, that Ali has the wit to stay busy after his fighting days. Ali is as good at finding interesting work as his doctor is. And after the idyll, Dr. Pacheco will still have the diamond ring Ali gave him, with the raised letters that say DR. PECHECCO, and also the picture Ali autographed with the same inscription he leaves with thousands of other people: "The man who have no imagination stands on the Earth. He have no wings — he cannot fly."

DEDICATED TO FAIR HOOKER

THE other night a couple of the New York press lords who try to control what I do in this space were plying me with country ham and making suggestions: "Lissen. My cousin Billy throwed in fourteen the other night against East Fork Junior. You reckon you could . . ."

I was holding out for the column I had in mind — a closely reasoned proposal for cutting down on hockey violence by converting all the ice in America into cubes — when one of the press lords said, "How about a column on names?"

"N . . . names?" I said weakly.

To suggest to a sportswriter that he write about names is like suggesting to a fat man that he eat pie. If he is a fat man without character, he will say, "Aw, I better not . . ." If he is a sportswriter without character, he will say, "Ah, I don't know, I was up all night with the ghosts of Granny Rice and W. O. McGeehan choosing an all-time all-woman baseball team — Babe Ruth, Pete Rose, Larry Sherry, Tex Shirley, Bill Lee, Carlos May, Dick Sharon, Clay Carroll, Carlos Paula, Harry Ernest Pattee, Sam Leslie, Lyle LeRoy Judy . . ."

If he is a sportswriter *with* character, however, he will take a swallow of coffee, give his head a shake, and begin:

"Frenchy Bordagaray, Roscoe Word, Earsell Mackbee, Chuck

Cherundolo, Orval Overall, Marcelino Lopez, Coy Bacon, Native Dancer, Ebba St. Claire, Eppa Rixey, Ebbie Goodfellow, Sibby Sisti, Garo Yepremian, Cornelius Warmerdam, Coco Laboy, Fair Hooker, Evonne Goolagong, Napoleon Lajoie, Larvell Blanks, Boots Poffenberger, Jethro Pugh, Gump Worsley, Beattie Feathers, Cloyce Box, Hackenschmidt and Gotch, Lavern Dilweg, Pudge Heffelfinger, Honey Mellody, Council Rudolph, Jubilee Dunbar, Cesar Geronimo, Syl Apps, Fidel LaBarba, Van Lingle Mungo, Dit Clapper, Jesus Alou, Young Stribling, The Only Nolan, Coleman Zeno, Small Montana, Clair Bee, D'Artagnan Martin, Wilmar Levels, Clyde Lovellette, Verl Lillywhite, Roxy Snipes, Burleigh Grimes, Urban 'Red' Faber, Urban Shocker, Urbane Pickering, Enos 'Country' Slaughter, Schoolboy Rowe, Preacher Roe, Perrine G. Rockafellow, ChaCha Muldowney, Harthorne Nathaniel Wingo, Steve Smear and Vida Blue."

Then, ". . . and Coot Veal and Bubba Bean."

Then, ". . . and did I say Orval Overall?"

Then he will go on to propose a few names that *would be* great sports names: Obadiah "Bad" Minton, Cesar Spang, O. L. "Oh Well" McFee, Memphis Briggs, Quick Ralph Click, Oliver "All of a" Sutton, Oliver "All Over" Musgrove, Arnold "Baby" Lonian, Chub Norsgaard, Laud Passwater, Eston Gozando (which Xaviera Hollander says is Portuguese for "I am coming"), Earl Riplet, Jr., Stash Hoist and Armstrong McKimbrow. And new nicknames for actual players: Larry "Good Old" Bowa, Roger "Pearly" Wehrli, Don "Bird Thou Never" Wert.

Then he will just wander off into *The Baseball Encyclopedia,* where he will discover, on virtually every page, one or more great names he had forgotten or had never heard of: Guy R. Sturdy, George "Yats" Wuestling, Irving Melrose "Young Cy" Young, Tony Suck, Inky Strange, John "Happy" Iott, Debs

Garms (of Bangs, Texas), LeRoy Earl "Tarzan" Parmelee, Os-
sie Bluege, Flint Rhem (of Rhems, South Carolina), Elmer
"Slim" Love (of Love, Missouri), Clarence William Pickup
(played one game, 1918 Phillies, lifetime batting average,
1,000), Homer Estell Ezzell, Clarence Waldo "Climax"
Blethen, James Harry Colliflower, Hap Collard, Clayton Maf-
fitt Touchstone and Emil "Hill Billy" Bildilli.

Yes, sports are richer in names than any other aspect of
culture except possibly literature, and in literature somebody
made them up. Many sports names seem inevitable, fated.
Imagine the future Mrs. Trucks saying to Mr. Trucks, "I don't
know if we better get married, 'cause my family don't hold
with baseball."

"What in the world does that have to do with it?"

"Well, we got to have a boy. And name him Virgil. For my
daddy. That's the main thing I want out of marriage and life,
is have a boy named Virgil for my daddy. And anybody with a
name like Virgil Trucks, why, there wouldn't be anything for
it but that he'd go to be a ballplayer."

"I guess you got something there. Probly hurl for the Tigers."

I wouldn't be any good as a coach because I would automat-
ically play anybody named John Buick Sprawls or Butterfly Link
over anybody named something flat like Joe Morgan or Bert
Jones. I wouldn't be any good as an athlete because I would
see somebody coming through the line and think, "I can't
tackle him! He's named *Roosevelt Leaks!*" Alex Karras has
pointed out that it was the *K* in his name that enabled him to
kick ass in the NFL. Considering the cases of Dick Butkus,
Ray Nitschke, Larry Csonka, Chuck Bednarik, Jim Katcavage
and Karl Kassulke, he has a point.

But I'm not here to give you just a bunch of jack-off ono-
mastics. I got name *stories.*

Everybody has heard about the confusion over whether "Dick" or "Richie" Allen is correct. But few people are aware of how that controversial first baseman's brother Hank, who also put in a few years in the big leagues, got his name. Hank himself told me the story:

My first year in the minors, the manager took me aside and said, "What's your name?"

"Allen."

"No, your first name."

"Harold."

"No, what do they call you?"

"Allen. Or Harold."

"No, what's your nickname?"

"Haven't got one."

"All ballplayers have nicknames. How about Henry?"

"Naw."

"How about Hank?"

"Naw."

And he went on with that for ten minutes! Finally he settled on Hank. He started calling me Hank and nobody else knew me, so they called me Hank. People back home would read in the papers and didn't even know it was me.

My mom came to the first game and they announced Hank Allen and she jumped up and yelled, "They changed his name!"

At least Harold's manager got his last name right. When Leo Durocher managed the Houston Astros, he called pitcher Doug Konieczy "Gomez." Then Preston Gomez took over the club. He called Konieczy "Garcia."

A sadder case was that of a placekicker once listed on the Pittsburgh Steelers' training-camp roster as Peter Jarecki. When someone called out, "Hey, Jarecki," he always responded. Then, after the departure of another kicker (named

Kambiz Behbahani), Jarecki got a chance to kick in an exhibition game. The day before that game, Peter approached Steeler publicity director Joe Gordon.

"It's Rajecki," he said.

"Huh?" said Gordon.

"My name is really Rajecki."

It was too late to make the correction in the program and on the press handouts. In his first public appearance in professional competition, Rajecki was known as Jarecki.

The case of Rabbit Wingfield was sadder than that. In 1934, after he'd spent a couple of years in the New York–Pennsylvania League, Rabbit Wingfield was invited by Connie Mack to Fort Myers, Florida, for a tryout with the Philadelphia Athletics. If Wingfield made the team, Mack told him, the Athletics would even pay his expenses.

Wingfield was a utility infielder. So was Rabbit Warstler, who came to the Athletics from the Red Sox that same spring. Once in an exhibition game Wingfield struck out trying doggedly to hit to right field. When he returned to the dugout, Mack said, "Warstler, I want to give you some advice."

"Mr. Mack," replied Wingfield, "I'm Wingfield."

Connie told him not to keep trying to hit behind the runner when the count reached 0 and 2.

Later during the exhibition season, Mack sent word for Wingfield to meet him in a drugstore. "Thanks for coming, Warstler, I want to talk with you," said Mack.

"Mr. Mack," said Wingfield, "I'm not Warstler, I'm Wingfield." Mr. Mack bought him a vanilla milk shake and offered to sign him up. Wingfield accepted.

A month into the season, the Athletics' second baseman, Dib Williams, was hurt and had to leave a game. Connie Mack surveyed his bench, looked right at Wingfield and said, "Warstler, second base." The real Warstler ran out and took the position and did a good enough job to stay on the team.

Wingfield was released. His name is not listed in *The Baseball Encyclopedia* because he never played a regular-season inning in the big leagues.

Some years later, Wingfield was in a hotel lobby when Connie Mack walked in. Wingfield went over, extended his hand and said, "Mr. Mack, my name is not Warstler."

"No, of course not," said Connie Mack. "You're Wingfield."

That is the kind of story that makes it a pleasure to recall what former Athletic pitching great Lefty Grove once said about Connie Mack (whose real name, of course, was Cornelius McGillicuddy): "I don't know what he was like. I never paid any attention to him."

Have you ever wondered whether Jo-Jo White of the Boston Celtics could possibly for some strange reason have been named after Joyner Clifford "Jo-Jo" White of Red Oak, Georgia, who toiled for the Tigers, Athletics and Reds in the thirties and forties? In case you had, I called the Celtics' publicity office. I was told that basketball's Jo-Jo got his name in high school. His coach was going over a play on the blackboard, and Joseph Henry White was dozing. "Joe," said the coach, "what do you do on this play? Joe! Joe!"

Ah, names. When Pie Traynor was a radio announcer in Pittsburgh he always referred to Yogi Berra as "Yoga Berry."

Yoga Berry would be a terrific name for a ballplayer, but not as terrific as Rowland Office. Rowland Office plays the outfield, very well, for the Atlanta Braves. If by any chance Office has a fat brother, the brother might be known as Oval Office. If Rowland has a favorite exclamation that he comes out with frequently, "Nuts!" or something, then that would be the oath of Office. Rowland is too fleet afoot for someone to take over for him when he gets on base, but if that ever did happen, the pinch runner would be running for Office. If someone trying to get into a dressing room to see Rowland Office got angry enough to draw a gun and fire it at the man blocking the door, then that man could be said to have been shot by a frustrated Office seeker. Or if the would-be visitor tried to pass himself off as Rowland's brother or uncle, he could explain when the judge asked him why he was arrested, "For impersonating an Office, sir." If a fan got into trouble with the law for trying to act out his strange compulsion to hold Rowland Office in his lap in a rocking chair, and the judge asked the arresting officer, "What's the problem with this defendant?" the cop could answer laconically, "Office rocker." Of course if Rowland Office himself went out looking for Stan Musial, it would be a case not of The Man seeking Office, but of Office seeking The Man.

And then too if a club owner tried to trade Cirilio Cruz, of the Cruz brothers, for a veteran on another club who had the right to refuse a trade, and the veteran did refuse, then the owner who wanted to make the deal might call the veteran directly and ask, plaintively, "Won't you let me take you for a C. Cruz?"

The only other thing I have to say about sports names, for now (a whole subcategory awaits another column), is that my favorite sports name of all time is not that of a famous sports participant. It is that of a lady who once wrote *Sports Illustrated* to advance the theory that swimming went without any black stars for so long because black people used to avoid frequent immersion in water because it messed up processed hair. Her name was Mrs. Le Sans La Rue Robinson.

WIRED INTO NOW

Nothing surprises me anymore. Nothing.
— Ann Landers

WIRED INTO NOW

Want the Real Answers? Write Wired Into Now, 33231 Sepulveda, Beverly Hills, Calif.

Q. *Isn't it a fact that all those magazine editors who claimed God was dead a few years back have mighty red faces now? Or is it? How old is God?* — Vaughn G., Salt Lake City, Utah.

A. If anyone knew how old God was, He would not be God. It takes more than a too-hasty interment of the Deity, however, to make most editors blush.

Q. *If I knew famous people, would they like me?* — C.T., Rolla, Mo.

A. Tastes of the famous vary, but you may be sure they would like you well enough if there were something in it for them. It was the conclusion of Dr. Ray Wade Beamer of Cornell, who studied over 3,000 famous people, that they would have responded to his questionnaires if he had provided some not inconsiderable inducement.

Q. *All those people on "Love Boat"* — *do they actually, you know, do it?* — Jana Coaple, Scale, Ark.

A. Yes.

Q. *Is it true that Swiss chocolatiers are seeking to buy up the Ronald Reagan family? Isn't that why an exotic Kuwaiti-Swiss*

*operator named Achmed Arnaud or Antonin Kif is converting his
gigantic oil holdings into cocoadollars? — Jerlyn Wheat, College
Station, Pa.*

A. You probably mean Habib Aucune, who heads an Iraqi-
Haitian digital-terror group. No one can plumb the true moti-
vations of such a man, when he is not dancing away the night
with exiled Princess Uami of Imau and their photographer-
swain Hsiu, at La Lude.

Q. *They do? All of them? On "Love Boat"? — Riley Coaple,
Scale, Ark.*

A. Yes.

Q. *Now that Britain's Queen Elizabeth II has given lover-boy
Warren Beatty the air, who is he living it up with now? — Joe
O., Duxbury, Mass.*

A. Beatty, 44, has been seen most often in the company of
President Ferdinand Marcos of the Philippines.

Q. *Why aren't I a supernova? — Mrs. H.I., Okla, Okla.*

A. Probably due to a combination of factors. You prefer to
be identified solely by your husband's initials, you live in Okla,
Okla., and you are the kind of person who has to ask the question above. And yet, you may have a certain spark.

Q. *The Emperor Caligula. Was he what I think he was? —
O.R., Bevel, Ind.*

A. Gaius Caesar Germanicus, or Caligula, emperor of Rome
during some of its most sensational years (37–41 A.D.), de-
lighted in torture and made his horse a consul, but he was not
bisexual. That was Tyrone Power.

Q. *Tel Polymer, who burst onto the TV dramatic scene as Ra-
mirez in "Tampa!" and founded a secret sect, has three 30-year-old*

sons, Ham, Juan and Uwe. Why won't he marry their mother, songstress Ina Bord? — *Lula W. Vickers, Lula, W.V.*

A. Polymer, 56, is director of FIOD (Freedom Is Our Deal), no sect but an affinity group devoted to the problems of single parents who are being traced by other single parents. In 1963, Polymer was briefly jailed for contemptibility, but charges were waived following a public spectacle by his aunt and uncle, wealthy philanthropists Nana and Trimble Leouvis, who reared him first as a Libertarian and then as a Sikh. Polymer, five foot eleven, is no newcomer to drama.

Q. *Why does no one in my entire tri-county area ever say "divine"?* — *Mrs. Dom N., Glen Falls, Wis.*

A. It would seem forced.

Q. *My husband R. worries that I am involved with a man named Rod who operates the All-U-Can-Crunch Perpetual Salad Bar near our home, but I'm not, but I did go in there for lunch Thursday and, you know, they have the dollar plate and the two-dollar plate and I always try to pile two dollars' worth on the dollar plate because we are frugal and it was raining out Thursday and I had my husband's umbrella hooked over my arm as I went down the line, and the big serving I had of Rod's famous grape-and-carrot congealed salad that he is known for, that nobody else can make, so you know it had to come from Rod's, slid off into my husband's umbrella. Have you ever tried to get congealed salad out of the inside of an umbrella? But that is not my question. I got it all out, I thought, but then Saturday it rained again and my husband used the umbrella to go check the car windows and when he opened it a big dob of Rod's famous salad fell out on his Windbreaker. And even though nothing whatever wrong had gone on, I lied. I said I lent the umbrella to our next-door neighbor Mrs. Showalter, who nobody would dream would be involved with Rod, poor thing. I wouldn't have brought Mrs. Showalter into it if I'd thought that if it got back to Mr. Showalter he would worry, because he has his own problems. He is our mail carrier and yesterday he came putt-putting by in his cart with another cart following right alongside him with his supervisor in it, monitoring him all day, with a clip-board. The supervisor is a black man half Mr. Showalter's age. But anyway my husband R. believed me and we are more caught up in each other than ever. Would that be a good story for "Love Boat"? If it took place on a boat? — J.C., Scale, Ark.*

A. Well . . . A luxury cruise ship would not have a . . . Can you actually get lunch where you live for a dollar?

Q. Do world-renowned people ever, like, smell funny or anything? You don't have to answer. — Mrs. Julio Nugent, Overlook, Ariz.

A. Yes. Sure. Sometimes. It doesn't matter.

THE IN-HOUSE EFFECT

Twenty years ago we could have run articles on anything from toy rail-roads to wild boars to American politics. Now every one of these subjects has a magazine of its own.

— *Harper's* editor Lewis H. Lapham,
quoted in *Time*

We had just finished packaging *Knock and Twinge: The Magazine for People with Psychosomatic Car Trouble,* and Hepworth could have been forgiven a few moments, even a whole afternoon, of complacency. But that wasn't Hepworth. Hepworth was looking off into space. He was *glaring* off into space.

"It's out there," he was saying. "There's something else out there. I can *feel* it. I can almost *read* it. *Fever!: The Newsletter for People Running More than 101° Temperature* — no, too ephemeral. *Deep End: The Depressive's Campanion.* No . . ."

"Hepworth! Let up!" I expostulated. "You have tested the very limits of the special-audience concept with *Illiterate Quarterly. Protective Coating Annual* is a hot book, as is *Chain Saw Times.* Not to mention *The Earthworm Breeder,* which thrives despite a slump in the earthworm industry itself. Why can't you take a week or so and just lay back —"

"*Layback: A Guide to Unobsessive Living.* Unh-uh, Doane, unh-uh."

"Hepworth!" I cried. "Listen to me just once as a friend."

"Feed me, Doane!" he snapped. "I don't employ you for personal counseling, I employ you for *concepts.* Military wives! What was that one you had for *military wives?*"

"Hepworth, I . . . was just jacking around with that one."

"*What was it?*"

"*All Turn Out: For Those Who're There When Johnny Comes Marching Ho—*"

"So. 'Jacking around.' You were jacking . . . around. Doane . . . Wait a minute. *Jacking Around: The Magazine of Idle Raillery.* Now at last a regular publication for the man willing to risk his very career for a few easy laughs. Hm . . . It won't go."

Hepworth fell silent. He sifted distractedly through the *Knock and Twinge* dummy layouts. "Doane, we need *something else*. Readership does not stand still. No target audience is a sitting duck. Today the need for maximization of advertising efficiency is greater than ever. We want to produce magazines whose ads in the business section of the *Times* can state proudly, 'Continuous tracking of both *anticipated* and *actual* purchases has demonstrated that the *Blacktopper's Journal* reader, alone in the splendid isolation of his own consumer-mind, *buys* as *planned*.' There are widgets out there, Doane. And people who want to sell those widgets. And people who want to read about those widgets. Out there. And we have to put them together."

I knew. Something hit me. "Hepworth. Widgets?"

"It's a term, Doane, a figure of speech. I'm just —"

"I know, I know. But just a minute now. What *are* widgets?"

"Doane, that's not the point. I'm just . . . What *are* widgets?"

"Right back to you." I moved to the unabridged, flipped right to the *w*'s, read: " 'A usu. small device, contrivance, or mechanical part (as a fitting or attachment) . . . ; *specif*: a small cylindrical container for carrying messages . . . through pneumatic tubes.' "

It was a definition, at first glance anyway, that didn't exactly blow horns and whistles. But Hepworth seemed to be off in a pneumatic tube of his own.

"Well . . . ," I said. "*Widgetry, the Bible of Cylindrical* . . . Actually, I don't think there's much upscale there, Hepworth. Hepworth?"

" 'Usu.'?" he mused.

"It's short for *usually*."

"I didn't think . . . anything was short for *usually*."

I had never seen him quite like this. "Well, just in dictionaries," I said.

"*Dictionaries! Widgets!*" Hepworth suddenly erupted. "Doane! You've got me sidetracking! Off-targeting! I don't have time to brainstorm about dictionaries and widgets! Nobody has that kind of time today! What people have is leisure time for focusing on how they're going to cope with spending their money. *Quality* time . . ."

I don't mind admitting it, I was chastened. My mind dug in. "Time. That's something . . ."

"*Doane, we can't call a magazine* Time!"

"No. No. I know. I was just thinking, the whole digest field. How about *Digestive Juice: The Essences of the Month's Digest Magazines!*"

"No, Doane. That's too general-audience. What kind of subculture is that? People who want a diet of boiled-down digests."

"Well, people on shuttle flights."

"But what do people on shuttle flights want to *buy?*"

"A good short martini," I said, but we both knew I was spinning wheels. We had been through the whole alcohol thing before, getting nowhere with *Sloshed: The Magazine of Serious Drinking.* At the bar, it had seemed like a zinger. There'd be a guest column headed "The Drunkest I've Been," a regular feature written while blitzed, great drunks in history, hangover remedies, an AA column . . . Then we realized why nobody had done it before: nobody would run any liquor ads in it. So we changed it to *Mellow: The Magazine of a Recreational Pop or Two,* and boom, it went. However, the staff never seemed able to get it out on time. In the end, we had to let liquor flow back into the mainstream.

Past history; I couldn't dwell on that. Hepworth was aching to have something good bounced off him. I scanned the room. Drapes: no. Awards and citations: no. My eyes came to rest on Hepworth himself.

"How about . . . you, Hepworth? What are *you* interested in? What would *you* want to read a magazine of?"

"Me?" His tone was gruff.

"Sure. Who better? What would make *you* respond to a mailer? What would *you* find *yourself* picking up on the stand?"

Hepworth all but smiled. "I . . . ," he said. "Demographics. Magazine packaging. I would read . . . a magazine of magazine packaging."

Hepworth rose, walked to the window, looked out at the Newsweek Building. "And what is more, I would write a one-sentence description of that magazine and sell forty points of it at five thousand dollars a point. I would pull together a year's worth of tables of contents (with bylines), a logo, an art director, eight contributing editors, and a complete dummy including an emotional service piece, a rate-the-packagers feature, a buzz-of-the-industry items column, a personality profile, and a letter from the publisher. And I would go to direct mail on that sonofagun and it would test out at ten, twelve, fifteen percent: phenomenal. And —"

"I've got a title for it!" I cried.

"I don't want to hear it," said Hepworth, each word bitten

off. I was brought up short. "And I'm going to tell you why," he went on. "Because we would put that magazine out, Doane, and two hundred thousand people from coast to coast would read it and start packaging magazines. That's right. *Hundreds of thousands* of magazines, Doane: teeming, piling up, renewing, scattering blow-in subscription cards, feeding on one another. Have you ever heard, Doane, of the In-House Effect?"

I, of course, had. In a general way. An implosion, I supposed — or an explosion, or both — of the organs of communication. A chain reaction so pervasive, so metastatic, that no lane or avenue in America, business or residential, would be without a floating ad conference. And every chat, set-to, birthday or tender moment along those lanes and avenues would be photographed, laid out, angled and written up, in thumbthrough-speed prose, quite specifically for all those people who wanted, and could afford, such products as might be germane to it; and all the staffs of all the publications involved would publish smaller inside publications for and about themselves. *There would be no* Life *magazine,* as we knew it or even as we know it, *and yet also no form of non-magazine-related life.*

"There *is,* to be sure, a magazine-packaging boom," I heard Hepworth saying. "But that is one boom that must not have its own magazine. Because there is something else, Doane — there may not be a boom in it, but it's called professional responsibility."

Hepworth, of course, was right. There are stories that cannot be written. Confidences that cannot be shared. Bombs that cannot be dropped. Markets that cannot be zeroed in on. I would go through fire for that man.

THE TEETH FESTIVAL

SOMETIMES we fail to appreciate certain hard, basic factors enough, I told my lady friend Felice, as I brought her to the Teeth Festival. I doubted she shared my *sense* of teeth, though hers are glossy from regular brushing with a sweet, white paste she first heard of through a television ad, in which a young couple sang.

As we entered, we saw display cases highlighting various kinds of teeth:

BUCK

CARIOUS

GAT

Teeth through the Ages was an eight-minute film. Early teeth, it is felt, were crudely designed, even soft. They could themselves have been chewed up by a set of modern home-fried potatoes. It was amazing, the progress across the years.

CHIPPED

GNASHING

MISSING

Over next to the refreshment booth, maintained throughout the festival by the floss industry, a shapely couple in flesh-colored body stockings took turns reciting.

"Why must *you always be uptight?"*
Said Eve to Adam. "Take a bite."
Fair as she was, however, fairer
Is mouth-ease to a denture-wearer.
The male was toothless in those days —
"Scarce as men's teeth" was the phrase.
It may be Eve was made of those
And not of rib, as most suppose.

If Adam had 'em, they were false.
Eve prepared some applesauce.
"Still al dente," did he mutter.
Eve prepared some apple butter.
And then they had some. "Oh wow, we've
Been going naked," *fluted Eve.*

"I guess we are . . . ," said Adam, "nude."
You know, for all these weeks and months
I only told the difference
Between us by the way we chewed."

The Tooth Fairy passed among us, mincing, winking, in costume, leaving to each visitor a facsimile quarter. Look at your teeth, said an old Army latrine notice, in the nostalgia section. Everybody else does.

FALSE

EYE

CANINE

We heard a song sung in country fashion, with guitar:

When you
Said you
Were on my side,
You lied.

When you
Said your
Love would abide,
You lied.
When you
Said I'd
Be satisfied,
You lied.

But when you said
You'd hit me and knock out my tooth,
You told the truth.

Musing, I held Felice. Nibbled mentally three, four, five of her vertebrae. Sweetflesh-muffled. Six.

HORSE
JAW
DEAD

Ruminant is how she seemed. I told her of a man I met in my travels, near Tigerdale, Florida, in a trash-and-treasures shop, who had had all his teeth removed, who said: "I keep 'um on the shelf in a little plastic dilly and after supper in the ebenin' or after breffust in the mawnin' or after lunch in the affnoon or after cheese 'n crackers fore bedtime, I get 'um down and take 'um out and count 'um and spread 'um out on the breffust-room table and arrange 'um like they was in my mouth. And then diffunt ways, the back ones front . . ."

CROOKED

WISDOM

BABY

I led Felice to where a dental-hygiene jingle was being sung, by the Cuspid Singers, in another part of the hall:

> *Don't call it incidental —*
> *It may be sentimental*
> *But teeth are quite important in romance.*
> *Whether owned or rental,*
> *Teeth to some extent'll*
> *Sway the course of love as much as pants.*
> *So keep your dentifrice*
> *Close by you, Bro or Sis,*
> *When going out to dinner or to dance.*
> *If bad teeth make you hiss*
> *While framing that first kiss,*
> *It may be you won't have a second chance.*
> *Oh, whether owned or rental,*
> *Teeth to some extent'll*
> *Sway the course of love as much as pants.*

"There should be a crockery/mockery rhyme in there," I chuckled to Felice. "Listen," I added — for we were not the only enthusiasts present, and the air was filled with snappy talk:

"Molars are like nothing so much as the stumps of trees. What if the rest of the strange white trees were there: trunks, branches, leaves, burls, crotches, twigs, bark, moonlight through the branches, and acorns or whatever."

"We cherish teeth. Vide savage tribes. And chain saws."

"Teeth are the only bones we have that show. If we were arrows, they would be our heads."

PERMANENT
GRINDING
NICE

We heard readings from that great symbolic naturalistic dental work *McTeague,* by Frank Norris — whose dentist hero, upon unwrapping the lustrous, four-rooted sign his betrothed has bought him, is beside himself: "It was the Tooth — the famous golden molar with its huge prongs — his sign, his ambition, the one unrealized dream of his life. . . . No danger of that tooth turning black with the weather . . ." Later, the dentist finally gains the upper hand over his wife, on the way toward utter ruin, when he develops the practice of biting the tips of her fingers till *they* turn black.

Erich von Stroheim, I told Felice, made of that great story an epic lost movie, *Greed,* whose original version ran longer and far more compellingly than a working day; and the studio — MGM, the one with the growling lion — chopped and ground that gargantuan, unprotected film down to a venal two and a half hours, for shopgirls to enjoy.

BAD
LIED-THROUGH
LOOSE

" 'The fathers have eaten a sour grape,' " I quoted to Felice, " 'and the children's teeth are set on edge.' " We were passing a breathtaking exhibit: long, long ranks of teeth set just so; so delicately balanced, one upon the other, that it seemed a breath of wind would send them pittering to the floor like sleet; set just perilously shy of meshing; not short of, but just finely higher than, meshing; we do not appreciate enough teeth's flinty interaction.

GRITTED

JEWELED

ACHING

"Ah, but 'the Lord who made thy teeth,'" I continued, "'shall give thee bread.' And you are toothsome, Sweet. And all of mine are sweet for you. But will you still esteem me," I said to her lightly, "when my teeth are gone?"

"No," she said.

She bared hers for me.

Mine fell in my lap.

All around was a sound like castanets, only harder, whiter.

THINKING BLACK HOLES THROUGH

Just by thinking on such a grand scale, humanity not only enlarges its universe but expands and ennobles itself. Perhaps the ideal metaphor is not Piglet's Heffalump but Browning's famous declamation: "Ah, but a man's reach should exceed his grasp, / Or what's a heaven for?" To the growing fraternity of black-hole theorists, that cosmic vision is the ultimate lodestar.

— "Those Baffling Black Holes," *Time*

"You can call them Great Big Old Nothings all you want," says Mrs. Vern Wike of Baruma, Michigan, "but when that thing came along and seized me up by the clavicles and turned me into a grain of dust five or six times and set me down fourteen miles from my home, it did me a world of good. I feel like a new old lady."

"Idea I got, it was trying to tell me something, trying to, you know, to *communicate*," says Roster Toombs of Fillings, Maryland, who maintains that a black hole reached him in his garage apartment, transferred him to at least two other universes and left him with "kind of more perspective on life than I can use."

Ex-President Jimmy Carter is interested in black holes.

Sings Benno Zane II in his black hole–inspired pop hit "So-uh Dark":

> *You-uh so profound,*
> *Grand Canyon like a levee.*
> *Billion tons-uh like a pound,*

You-uh so heavy.
Yeah so-uh dark in there
You got Noah's ark in there?

But the hole is greater than some of its poets. From Slippery Key, Florida, to Bosco, Washington, from England's Cambridge University to cooperative observatories on mainland China, mankind is going further than it ever imagined possible with thoughts of black holes, those mysterious antiwombs of collapsed stars in which time and space are so warped that they gasp, enclose themselves and become nothing; the speed of light is just nothing, flat; and as for matter, it is spaghettied-out, shamed and compressed into a nothingness billions and billions of times smaller — and more potent — than it was when it was something.

To some theorists, a black hole admits no escape. Under special circumstances, others argue, it may transpose things into another universe or back in time as far as, for instance, the Hoover administration, via passages dubbed "wormholes." One school of thought posits phenomena dubbed "white holes" (which *spew out* nothing instead of ingesting it), but these — as anyone can understand who has watched both "American Bandstand" and "Soul Train" — have laid a lesser claim on the imagination. The possibility of a "yellow hole," in which everything is sunny and visitors find themselves robed in buttercups, is generally dismissed as wishful thinking.

So what kind of thinking is right? Even the savants wonder. When Sir Waring Tifit created the first mathemo-mechanical model of a black hole in 1964, famed Astrophysicist Vivien Soule took one look and exclaimed, "This is so dense that thought must become like Thousand Island dressing, or petroleum jelly or something, and time become u.s. news and world report."

The distinguished Pure Mathematician Seiji Kamara took one look and observed, "This is so dense that the birds must leave off their singing and crawl like little bugs upon the ground. It's not the blackness so much, it's the *density*."

Little Joey Fulks, the brilliant if ill-focused graduate student who later withdrew into market research, took one look and said, "This is so dense it makes me want to *shriek*."

The great Rabinrasha Charawansary took two looks and said, "I don't think it is so dense." But that was just Charawansary. He also didn't think Kamara's mathematics were so pure. Later that same evening, at a faculty cookout in his back yard, Charawansary reasoned aloud about black holes so deeply that his mind evidently passed into one. Because of relativistic effects, he appeared to observers to be forever nearly coming to a point but always more and more slowly and never quite. To Charawansary himself, he seemed to have summed up magnificently, in one great flash while bunning a wiener, and everyone else was just sitting there like sacks of wheat. In fact, the phenomenon Charawansary presented was so extremely trying a thing to observe that all of his colleagues had murmured months ago that they had better be getting along, leaving him with Mrs. Charawansary, who was disconsolate until a troupe of quantum mechanics came through town and showed her some models of what goes on inside the atom that made her laugh and laugh.

Can a person *become* a black hole? Not likely, believe most theorists. But just say someone were to. What if? His knees would in effect become his respiration . . . his past, future and sense of smell would be telescoped into an infinitesimal pelletlike item . . . and he would literally be worn by his own shoes. In earthly geographical terms, an area the size of Maine, Asia and the city of Detroit and environs would be squeezed into a single copy of the *New York Post*.

All airy speculation? Not so, insist some of today's brightest young stars of physics and math. "Oh, the holes are there, for sure," says Caltech's Flip Kensil. "It ain't no big thing. Could be there's one of infinitesimal magnitude coursing within a hair's breadth of your face right now powerful enough to swallow human life and the federal bureaucracy. But hey, that's the universe all over."

A "singularity" is what scientists tend to dub a black hole in the scientific papers that they read to each other. A "singularity." These scientists! They don't give much away, do they?

The state of the art of black-hole thought is enough, in short, to tempt the layman to throw up his or her hands. But that would be defeatism — and in fact many laymen are doing anything but.

Fulpus Wsky and Livianne Wills of the Yale-Rockefeller Institute for Astrophysics believe that public enthusiasm for black holes is such that the holes may well be in our own homes, in some form, before the turn of the century. "When we happen to mention at a cocktail party that at any moment we might receive in the pit of our stomach a golf ball the 'size' of a million suns," note Wsky-Wills, "people's heads turn our way instantly."

All very well, humanity's ever practical side will counter, but what is in the hole for us? The answers to that question are by no means clear. A black hole, if harnessed, would be of undeniable value in trash removal and national defense. But so far the principal benefit derived is a sense of elation, of expansion, even of pride, gained by those hardy reflectives, in science and out, who make a level effort to comprehend the concept. Black Hole Clubs, NOTHING IS BEAUTIFUL buttons and "singularity bars" are springing up. In many parts of the country, black-hole mental-picturing sessions are replacing wet-T-shirt contests in popularity.

Not all of these "holeys," as the trendier enthusiasts dub themselves, rise to the gravity of the phenomenon. Misfits, many of them, acting out compulsions that are psychological at bottom and may have little or nothing to do with nothingness itself. These people, it may be, tend to cheapen the hole thing — but under our laws they have the right to think about what they please, as they please; and that includes the laws of nature.

And in the end, who can readily say which response to black holes is authentic and which is not? Who can say that the Toombses and the Mrs. Wikes of this world are real zeros? Who can say — although we may know what a black hole *is* — what a black hole is *like*? Not the experts.

" *'Like.'* Oh, it can't be *likened* to anything," says Rocky Top Observatory's Bern Rogovin. "It's . . . different from any-thing. It's — I wouldn't say *opposite* — it's . . . Oh, what's the word?"

Antimatter?

"No, not that. Yet definitely not *matter*. I would say, per-haps . . . amatter."

What's amatter?

"Oh, nothing."

WEEKLY NEWS QUIZ

Questions are based on what you should have learned from the New York Times *by the end of any given week in 1979, if you were paying that newspaper the attention it expects. Answers appear on pages 260–262.*

1. A member of Israel's negotiating team raised new hopes for the Mideast peace talks in the face of growing tensions. What is his name, what names was he called in the Knesset, and what new tensions caused him to withdraw, the following day, his growing hopes?

2. The mystery of plant life's interaction with animal life has been deepened by researchers at Fordham University. What is the mystery? Name five plants and four animals.

3. The man pictured on page 258 seems to have everybody in America (except, of course, anyone in a position of real authority at the *Times*) buffaloed. Who is he and what is his charm?

4. The mood in Sri Lanka is more pensive now. Explain.

5. "We have flatly denied that we plan to take over Holland and I can confirm that," says a high-ranking official of a major nation. What kind of shoes do they wear in Holland?

6. The State Comptroller's office in Albany has revealed that the disbursing procedures of 71 departments of the New York City government are being placed under tighter scrutiny. Who is the State Comptroller? Where *is* Albany? Is it up around Lake George somewhere? Up around Cornell? Where *is* Cornell?

UPI

7. There is a worldwide shortage of (breath/gasoline/people/time).

8. In a midyear economic review, the Carter administration forecast that over the next six months the price of gas could go as high as $4.97 a gallon, unemployment could rise to 38 million and inflation could climb to 42.3 percent without its being whose fault?

9. The Pffowles-Sargeaunt system of orthography, according to which Iranian names have been converted to English spelling since 1934, is being replaced by a more accurate system, whereby "Ayatollah Ruhollah Khomeini" will be rendered as "I.O. Tolaruhola O. Maney," Prime Minister "Mehdi Bazargan" as "Idhem Nagrazab," and Brig. Gen. "Saif Amir Rahimi" as "Bear Man Jackson." Where did they ever dig up Pffowles and Sargeaunt?

10. Among the various consultants in different fields sum-

moned by President Carter to Camp David for his latest sum-
mit session on the energy problem was (Ralph Bellamy/Joseph
Gargan/Bernard L. Barker/Norman Vincent Peale).

11. According to (C. L. Sulzberger/William Safire/Arthur
Daley/Mimi Sheraton), the inane hypocrisy of the Department
of Health, Education and Welfare's antismoking campaign is
revealed by its peculiar refusal to follow the tangent of "the
smoking Lancegate pistols packed by Puffabilly the Kid Brother
and the Loan Arranger." Can you spot and name all the rhe-
torical devices employed?

12. An increasingly popular means of enhancing the fun of
camping out is Portacoals, a carry-along low campfire (can be
set to glow or smolder) in an eye-pleasing off-red Bakelite case.
It is $69.50 at what East Side shop?

13. The man below has been sliding in the polls. Who is he,
what is his job and whose idea was he in the first place? Name

UPI

three good places within the bounds of New York City where the increasingly popular pastime of sliding in the polls may be enjoyed.

14. John Leonard was bemused in his garden, "growing tensions," when he and Dmitri got each other in a sort of mutual hammerlock and had to be prized apart by a vaguely, multiply allusive remark. What was the remark? How would you have answered it? Would it have prized you and either Leonard or Dmitri apart?

15. President Carter said he plans to whip a portion of Sen. Edward Kennedy's anatomy. Do you know what portion? If you do, if in fact you are aware that any hint of anatomy was involved, then you have been reading some other newspaper. Why? Don't you like the new Science section? There was something fascinating in there about anatomy just last Tuesday. How did you like that? Didn't you see it? Didn't you even look at the graphs?

16. As a matter of fact, your name was on page A4, column 3, last week. We haven't heard anything from you about it. Did you miss it? Why? Don't you read the first section of the paper? That's where the hard news is. Don't you enjoy hard news? The *Times* has to have some hard news. Why do you read this quiz and don't read the news? Do you read this quiz? Does anybody? Anybody who is upscale? Should we offer prizes?

Answers to Weekly News Quiz

Questions appear on pages 257–260.

1. The entire Asian landmass.
2. Coriander, minced.
3. A human heart. The transplant, made possible through

the use of deductible corporate jets, two bright red fire engines and the combined efforts of Rhodesian and South Carolinian surgical and negotiating teams, did little to alleviate growing tensions.

4. Matisse.

5. Twice. Smallpox. A panel on coal.

6. Franz Josef Strauss was chosen as the opposition's candidate for chancellor in the 1980 elections. The day before, he had been ejected for punching a referee during his team's victory over the Virgin Islands. The referee had made a slighting reference to "The Blue Danube Waltz," by Strauss.

7. Mr. Pol Pot.

8. In the first two cases the Court brought in decisions of *ejectamus manus nostra,* or "we throw up our hands." In the third ruling, the Court upheld sweeping federal procedures for disclosure of news photographers' wisecracks.

9. "The wartime equivalent of morals."

10. Misses Capelius and Puhl.

11. Soft leathers, patent leathers, suede, snakeskin, and metallic vinyl, with covered buckles, and buckleless versions of stretchy elasticized fabrics. Reds, purples, hot pinks, and yellows.

12. Loss of U.S. aid over car fumes.

13. Near Kalgoorlie, Australia, because of cracks in the Backfire bomber's underwing engine mounts, or pylons, which an emerging congressional consensus proposes to remedy by attachment of clarifying riders or "understandings" which could seriously increase U.S.-Soviet tensions in light of the 78-degree cooling limit in public buildings this summer.

14. If Mr. Brown is the engineer, and the engineer's son is wearing yellow trousers, and the brakeman is *not* named Mr. White, then the fourth passenger from the left must be the

one with the sandy beard, which makes Mr. Black the son of the uncle's wife.

15. The rebel junta will not be recognized as such until it withdraws its demands.

16. Feet.

THAT DOG ISN'T FIFTEEN

KEEP the TV in its place in the home. We don't *watch* the
TV constantly — we leave it *on;* you know how you'll do.
But you have to live your life."

"That's been our feeling."

"Able to hold a conversation. You know."

"You can't just be rapt."

"No. But Jim's Mama —"

"That's a new TV, Irene? Is the hue just right? What happened to your *old* TV?"

"This is what I'm telling you. Jim's Mama —"

"With the walnut grain."

"Had it four years. Never the first sign of trouble. Until
Jim's Mama —"

"Your hue is off, Irene. See, Orson Welles's white wine is
off."

"Well . . ."

"Was it the old TV you said started having the little funny
smell?"

"But that was later. See, Jim's Mama would come over, and
she'd watch the TV, and — like when that man comes home,
in the artificial-cream commercial? The grown son, visiting his
mother? He gets up so *perky* in the morning, Jim's Mama would

say. *He* acts so *sweet* — about his Mama fixing him a big old-fashioned breakfast just like he remembers but with artificial cream. All *we* do, Jim's Mama would say, when she makes *us* breakfast, is sip a little coffee and act sour."

"It's a little *fuzzy,* too, isn't it, Irene?"

"We'd say, Mama, that son on television — that's television, that's not life. We said, Mama, what they're trying to do is sell you something. That's all. And —"

"Trying to sell you that artificial cream."

"Uh-huh. We'd say, Mama, in real life that man has probably been up for *hours.*"

"Maybe — I think I'd try the brightness knob, too, Irene."

"And, but Jim's Mama, another thing she'd say was, there was never a night around here when anybody would announce, 'Tonight is kinda special.' We'd say, Why, Mama, how about the other night when we had you and the Willetses over, wasn't that kinda special? No, she'd say. She'd say, Our friends didn't ever tell us, 'You're beautiful.' Now, Mama, we'd say, Life just isn't *like* that."

"And the TV had the smell then?"

"That was later. We'd say, Mama, they're just trying to sell you something. She'd say fine. Said she wanted to buy whatever it was. Said she liked buying things. Said that's what America was built on."

"It *is* hue, Irene. See her leg?"

"Yes, we'd say, Mama, but don't you want to have a little something left to leave behind? She'd say no, she wanted to give us a big old-fashioned breakfast like we remembered it and see us acting perky. Wanted to get up and make us breakfast even with all the arthritis in her feet, like the grandmother in the what is it — the arthritis commercial, you know?"

"Pain commercial."

"And when she did have us over and cooked, she'd serve

something and we'd just barely bite into it — just get it hardly in our mouth good — and she'd say, You don't like it? We'd say, Mama, we haven't *tasted* it yet. She'd say, On TV they taste things *immediately*. And they *light up*, and say . . . We'd say, Mama, you don't give us *time*."

"See now, Robert Young is *tanner* than that."

"Well, maybe he's —"

"At her house would she watch much TV?"

"No. Really, you know, I think that was the trouble. She didn't *have* her own TV. Maybe Robert Young is just getting old."

"No, Irene, at our house he's real tan."

"We'd say, Mama, if you watched it all the time you'd realize. But she'd say no, no, she never had a TV when Jim's Dad was alive. And she had her little motor scooter she'd scoot around on, and all her fish."

"I believe you said she had beautiful fish."

"She'd say people on TV look you right in the eye and smile. Said we were her closest family and we wouldn't look her right in the eye and smile. We said, '*Mama!*' She said we wouldn't even look her right in the eye and *frown*. We said, '*Mama!*' "

"No, see that rabbit. You *know* that rabbit is off."

"People on TV are s' bright-eyed, she'd say. Always s' helpful-looking, s' friendly. She'd say people on TV have a little chuckle that goes with things they say. A little 'huh' laugh before words, to show they're thinking about how you'll react. And . . . Well, we'd just look at her and look at each other and shake our heads. But then it started happening."

"The little smell?"

"That, and —"

"Was it a bad smell?"

"No. No. It —"

"Did it smell like it was burning?"

"No, it wasn't a *mechanical* smell. . . . More like an aroma. Not an aroma. What's the word I mean?"

"Bouquet?"

"No."

"You know, Irene, too . . . your vertical hold. That black band on the bottom? You know how it'll get? When it just eddddges up. And eddddges up?"

"But we'd look over, and Jim's Mama would be on one side of the room, and the TV'd be turned that way. It'd — We'd look over, and the back of it would be to us. We didn't move it. Jim's Mama didn't move it. It'd even — it was almost like it was pulling away from us, just singling out Jim's Mama. On its *own.*"

"You didn't get up and move it?"

"No."

"Jim's Mama didn't get up and move it?"

"No. She'd just be sitting there. Chuckling at it."

"At — just whatever was on?"

"Jim's Mama didn't care. She wouldn't switch or tune it. She didn't even know how to work it. Jim's Mama couldn't turn a TV on or off, to save her. But it seemed like it give her a better *picture,* too."

"Irene, see, there's more of that black at the bottom."

"Course, the children complained. You know Dawn and little Jim. They'll sit there glued to that TV and yell at it, *'That's stupid!'* Listen to a commercial about how some product's so wonderful for you and yell, *'Yeah, it probly poisons you!'* Lorne Greene'll come on with his fifteen-year-old dog, you know, and they'll yell, *'That dog isn't fifteen!'* "

"Children get so critical."

"But they do want to *watch.* *'The TV just likes Nannaw! We want another TV! We want a TV with Remotronic control!'* Said they couldn't concentrate on their homework without it."

"And . . . it was an *odor,* though?"

"Yes. And anyway, last . . . a week ago Friday night, Jim's Mama was sleeping over — she had baby-sat, you know, while we were at Jim's Elks installation — and when we got home she and the kids were all gone to bed, and in the night we heard a clattery noise. But we didn't think about it, at the time. . . . There *is* a lot of black down there."

"It's edging up, Irene. You can almost see the color again below it. And, Irene, the hue is still not —"

"We got up the next morning and Jim's Mama? Was *gone.* And the TV? Was gone."

"Gone?"

"No note. No trace. No explanation."

"Why, I-*rene.*"

"We haven't seen that TV. Or Jim's Mama. Since."

"Can you *imagine?*"

"Uh-huh. We don't . . . *Look!*"

"Irene! Is that —?"

"Look! *Jim!* Turn it up! *Jim, c'mere! Your Mama's on 'Real People'!*"

"And she's — Irene! *Isn't that your old TV?*"

NOTES FROM THE
EDGE CONFERENCE

LeFebvre, opening remarks:
Don't know all there is to know about edge. Do know: Misconceptions abound. Fixed? No. Plottable? No. Like line on map, where important things lie on either side? No.

"Sometimes my edge is a round edge." Now tongue, now groove.

Edge, as in: Lip. Verge. Pungency. To sidle. Advantage. "Near bound of nerves' end, inside of out."

(*Mutterings.*)

Registration packets: Should have been plenty. Ppl. who took more than one should return same.

Armentout, "Edges and Hedges: Things that Get in the Way":

Ppl. say, "I want to live out there close to the edge. But I don't want to look funny."

Cf. Gary Busey. Look at him first time: "Damn, no *way* that man can be a star." But: "Sure, the man looks funny at first — anybody they thought of to play Buddy Holly had to look a little funny right off. But next thing you know, hey, he's *out* there." *Beyond* a star. Where it is. Raising hell in the social notes. "Jumping into people's sets, man."

Hully, Perl, Tibbett panel, "Getting Words in Edgewise":

"Outfit" self for E.? (Figurative goose-down, asbestos.) Whole industry growing up. But is to gear for it to be not out close to it? Or to . . . temper it? Perhaps.

Out on E. for its own sake, or should we wait until propelled there by just cause? Hard question. Finally unanswerable.

Diff. ppl. higher/lower threshold of E.?

"I mean, I'll start a sentence sometimes and halfway have to stop — *skreek!* — not on the edge anymore. But the first half . . ."

"Would you be interested in approaching the edge again, possibly in a more definitive manner?"

"Well . . ."

"Or a less definitive one?"

"Ah!"

Diff. cultures, diff. E's. Navaho: Whole notion of edge as maze. (Maize?)

"Out on E.," as compared to "hip":

Rohle: "Yeah, but whoever heard of *The Razor's Hip?*"

Many ppl. hip. Well, to be fair, not *many* — not untold numbers. More aren't.

Basic point of hip: Certain people know you know what. "You know, it's a *social* thing."

Hip: Pick up on yet unassimilated Black English. "Come on over to the crib and we'll . . ." "This johnson." Call everything a "johnson."

For some ppl., hip not enough.

Van Roud II, on Loss of E.:

"Suddenly this sinking sensation. Put a foot out one way, and . . . solid ground.

"Put it out the other way, and . . . solid ground.

"I was in some kind of Kansas of the mind — Sunday afternoon of the soul. I said, 'Whoa, get back.' I was *upset*."

Stapenink, "Lines: Toward a Definition":

Where does closeness to E. begin? Is there fine line separating area within which one may be said to be out close to E. from area within which one may be said to be cut off from E.? In that case: Does E. have an e.?

That line past which being close to E. begins. Greater value in being on that line? On edge of that line?

E. an absolute, or gradations? Sort of close to E. Really really close to E. Marginally barely close to E. Nearly close to E.

(*Grumblings.*)

During mixer, overheard:

"My friend and I were talking. I'm saying like who is your best rock star and who is your best this star and that star and it hits us, all our best ones like live out near the edge. And we're talking you know and I go, 'That's why you like me. I'm out near the edge.'

"And he goes like he's not believing me, he goes, 'Yeah?'

"I go, 'Yeah.'

" 'So what's it look like over there?' he goes.

"I go, 'You put your toes out over it and look out and down and you feel something pressing up evenly on each one of your toes, toe toe toe toe toe, and you see somebody looking out and up at you.' Because —

"And I don't know what hit him, he goes like, '*Yeah!* Oh, *yeah!* Oh *yeah*, Lori! Sure, Lori!' and goes out and rents this motel room somewhere and tears it up."

"Seeing the Humor of It" — Dr. Ardis Wickwire:

"How you like yr. edge?" "Which first, chicken or edge?" "Big butter and edge man."

Ha.

Grosjean, Three types *not* near edge:

(1) Don't know where edge is, never will. Don't even know what direction it's in. (Voice: "That's cool.")

(2) Grew up along the edge, or had one or more parents who were out close to it or named them something like Guava, and now want to spend their adult lives getting far from edges as possible. Beer on table, some art on walls that don't mess over their relaxation, nobody after them with knife. (Voice: "That's cool.")

(3) Don't believe there even *is* an edge. So-called "Round-Earthers." (Voice: "Yeah!")

Overheard conversation of electricians outside conf. rm.:

"Christ, my mom is dying and getting this SSI. Supplemental Security Income. You can only have fifteen hundred in the bank, so we took the rest of it out for her, put it in the house, and Christ the money come pouring in. For my mom, fine, but Christ how about all these guys who *won't* work. There's a limit. There's a limit. It's the middle-income guy — fifteen, eighteen, twenty thou, and you and me are paying for it. Christ my mom is dying and getting this SSI. . . ."

(Poss. paper for next year: "Middle-Edge Spread"?)

Crits. of conf.:

(1) Missed most fundamental point.

(2) What those splotches up on Vu-Graph?

    a. Finger smudges

    b. Insect matter
    c. Eyesight
    d. Weren't any
(3) Same old crowd running.
(4) Ppl. screaming in ppl.'s ears.
(5) Should have been more registration packets. And more in them.
(6) Not out close to E.

LeFebvre, closing:

Always "same old crowd running things," because when something has to be done you find out pretty quickly there are only a few people you can call on.

Cutting/leading E. dichotomy? "So fine, can only be palped by surprise."

(*Boos.*)

Banquet, installation new officers 8:30 in Ballroom C. (Thing of throwing food: "Just obnoxious.")

Proposals for new award categories *must* be in Sept. 1.

FACING ISMISM

PEOPLE say to me, "Why don't you go on the lecture circuit, like so many others do, and rake in so many dollars a night while stirring vocal, even bodily, enthusiasm in auditors numbering into the hundreds and thousands right there physically in front of you, instead of sitting all alone like you do going ticky ticky ticky on an empty piece of paper rolled into a lonesome machine?"

I say, "Well I tried that."

Sure. I used to go out there on the hustings, which is what those of us who were in that profession called them, in honor of Colonel Reece Hustings, who, in 1907, took his oration about galvanism and microdots (which he thought he had made up out of thin air; he didn't live to see microdots become a reality, but then I don't know anybody who has *seen* any microdots, you have to take them on faith) around to 117 different American cities and towns in 129 days.

I never threatened the colonel's record, and I never developed the eloquence it would take to convince crowd after crowd, as the colonel did, that microdots were scattered like silica gel (something else he thought he'd made up, he just liked the sound) over every American's skin and hair and could tune in the infinite. He never even had to move into galvanism many

a night, he could go on about microdots alone to the great majority of hearts' content.

What I did do, though, was get into Creationism very early
on. I went from community college to community college at
$200 a pop, telling groups of the credulous (and I don't put
credulousness down) that what we needed was not just Creationist Science but Creationist Football and Creationist Journalism as well. And Scientific Religion.

Sure, religion can be scientific, I made clear. Back with the
ancient Greeks, religion was empirical. If you propitiated the
gods, there wouldn't be any of them swooping down and
mounting you in the guise of a swan. And it worked. You could
test it out. And by the same token today, if you believe that
there is a Creator behind every snowflake, every war and decent TV show, it makes you feel better. Don't it? It works.

But where I ran into trouble, I had a backup group, the
Roylettes, behind me going, "So fine, so fine, so fine." Three
black women back there, gitting it.

And I had people come up to me after the show and say,
"That's racist."

And I had to stop and think. Well, I guessed it was. I guessed
I was implying, unthinkingly, that black people could git it
better than white. So I engaged three white women. To tell
the truth, they didn't git it quite as well, but they got it pretty
well.

And I had people come up to me after the show and say,
"That's sexist." And I had to stop and think. Well, I guessed
it was true, I was implying that women could git it better than
men. So I got me three backup men. Called them the Roysters.
They didn't git it quite as well as the women, for my taste,
but they got it all right. But then they'd get to fighting so bad.
And then, too, some people came up and said, "Are your men
all straight?"

And I said, "Well, I think so," and I went off to the side and made them "Dress right, dress" and they looked pretty straight to me, but "No," the people said, "we're talking about you being heterosexist." And I had to admit that I was implying, without meaning to, that straight men got it better than gay, so I made some changes and next time I was all ready to say, "The one in the middle is gay and the other two don't mind at all," but this time the people said, "You're being ageist."

And I had to admit that I had been unconsciously implying that young people git it better than old, so I got three old men, one of whom was straight and one of whom was gay and one of whom was so old it didn't make any difference to him, and they didn't really git it as well as the young ones but they still added something, and the next show some animal rights people came up and said, "That's speciesist."

And I had to admit that I was suggesting that people git it better than other species, so I tried pigs. Well, first I tried dogs, but they got to fighting worse than the Roysters used to. I'd be pounding home a point and the Royotes, I called them, would be back there going, "Yark, yike, aroo, grrngrrIKE!" and chewing on each other. Then cats, but they were too independent, and threw up.

So, pigs. Pigs are smart. But they aren't meant for a chorus. You're on tour and your bus is getting lower and lower on the shocks and you come to realize it's them pigs, the chorus, getting heavier and heavier. But I stuck with them and then one evening I was waxing up a pretty high sheen on Creationism and the pigs were back there gitting it, not too well but pretty well (you notice I don't say "for pigs"), and somebody came up right in the middle of my talk and said, "That's elitist."

So, I put the pigs out front. Went along that way for a while — tried it with them gitting it out front while I tried to make the talk, and with me gitting it in back while they tried to make the talk. And one night a committee came up to the stage and said, "Is your man back there a secular humanist?"

And tell you the truth, I just tiptoed away and let the pigs deal with it. I decided if people couldn't tell where I stood with the minority community, on the one hand, and with the Divine Presence, on the other, just from the text of my remarks, they weren't ever going to be placated in my presence.

So now I do text exclusively. And I know in my soul, there are people out there finding me wanting on all kinds of ismic and istic grounds, but I can't hear them doing it. I do miss having somebody going "so fine, so fine" behind me, but let me tell you one thing. Black, white, men, women, straight, gay, old, young, human, canine, feline, pork: they will all eat and drink up 4½ cents of every nickel you clear, and there's not a blessed one of them that you can be safe in assuming is not hopped up on some kind of drug.

FOR THE RECORD

"I was asked to demonstrate the step," said England's Wayne Sleep, 25, a soloist with the Royal Ballet and specialist in the entrechat. . . . "Then the producer said how about breaking the record? So I did." . . . Sleep's acrobatics on a London TV program stunned balletomanes all over the world; he became the first person in recorded history to cross and uncross his legs five times in a single leap. The feat is known as an entrechat douze for its twelve movements: the leap, five crossings, five uncrossings and the landing. Not only was Sleep's feat unprecedented, but only Russia's late, great Vaslav Nijinsky had ever been credited with an entrechat dix.

— Newsweek

A dreamlike leap
By England's Sleep!
He didn't doze,
He did a douze.
His legs arose
In curlicues.

He shrugged, "Okay, I'll make a run,"
And then went heavenward (that's one),
And five times crossed, and uncrossed five,
And then returned to earth alive.

And on TV, no less. Voilà!
Sleep's the king of entrechat.

Nijinsky, may he rest in peace —
Would that he were above the ground!
Nijinsky settled for but dix

Movements in a single bound.

A joy forever. He will last.
And yet . . . his mark has been surpassed.
Will Chaplin, too, be cast in doubt?
Will someone edge Caruso out?

But look! As consternation reigns
Among the world's balletomanes,
We see Nijinsky rise again.
His spirit jumps into our ken:

He climbs, descends, meanwhile with ease
Weaving patterns with his knees,
And stops just off the ground, and says,
To open with some humor, "Treize."

And now he's serious; now he soars
Sufficiently to cry "Quatorze!"
And now, although he starts to pant,
Up he goes — he's done a vingt!

And now he's really going good.
Nijinsky, folks, has just vingt-deux'd.
We sense he could go on to cent-deux
But evidently doesn't want to.

For now, with one great closing spring,
He goes through untold scissoring
And disappears — a quantum leap —
And leaves the blinking world to Sleep.